"I made you u~~ncomfortable~~

Charity's heart lurched.

"Because I asked you out," Wayne said. "You're sitting there trying to make casual conversation with someone you have nothing in common with except work."

He'd nailed it. A little while ago she'd felt giddy about meeting him. Now she was uncomfortable and floundering.

"It's okay," he said. "I know you're leaving. This is what you want to make it, nothing more. I like you. You're very attractive. But maybe mixing business and pleasure was a stupid idea."

"No. I was glad you asked me out. Truly. I like you, too. It's just that..." Charity hesitated.

"We have an advantage here," Wayne continued.

"We do?"

"Sure. When you go back to Atlanta, you never have to see me again. That ought to be freeing, not inhibiting."

"Sort of like Las Vegas?"

"Yup. Or not. But I guess what I'm saying is, relax. Be yourself. I won't hold it against you."

He made sense, she realized. There were advantages.

"Ah, you're smiling again," he observed. "Good. This was supposed to be fun, not trial by fire."

***

Be sure to check out the next books in Conard County series!

NEWHAM LIBRARIES

90800100241082

PLAYING WITH FIRE

BY
RACHEL LEE

All rights reserved including the right of reproduction in whole or in part in any form. This edition is published by arrangement with Harlequin Books S.A.

This is a work of fiction. Names, characters, places, locations and incidents are purely fictional and bear no relationship to any real life individuals, living or dead, or to any actual places, business establishments, locations, events or incidents. Any resemblance is entirely coincidental.

This book is sold subject to the condition that it shall not, by way of trade or otherwise, be lent, resold, hired out or otherwise circulated without the prior consent of the publisher in any form of binding or cover other than that in which it is published and without a similar condition including this condition being imposed on the subsequent purchaser.

® and ™ are trademarks owned and used by the trademark owner and/or its licensee. Trademarks marked with ® are registered with the United Kingdom Patent Office and/or the Office for Harmonisation in the Internal Market and in other countries.

Published in Great Britain 2015
by Mills & Boon, an imprint of Harlequin (UK) Limited,
Eton House, 18-24 Paradise Road, Richmond, Surrey, TW9 1SR

© 2015 Susan Civil Brown

ISBN: 978-0-263-91560-0

18-0815

Harlequin (UK) Limited's policy is to use papers that are natural, renewable and recyclable products and made from wood grown in sustainable forests. The logging and manufacturing processes conform to the legal environmental regulations of the country of origin.

Printed and bound in Spain
by CPI, Barcelona

Rachel Lee was hooked on writing by the age of twelve and practiced her craft as she moved from place to place all over the United States. This *New York Times* bestselling author now resides in Florida and has the joy of writing full-time.

To the brave men and women of fire departments everywhere. You tread where angels fear to go.

Chapter 1

Charity Atkins drove into the outskirts of Conard City and suddenly felt sickeningly out of her depth. It was a grandiose name for a small town, she realized, and although she was a good arson investigator, she'd only worked in industrial areas and other businesses in large cities, not on ranches out in the boondocks.

It didn't help to remind herself that location didn't matter, that figuring out whether the arson was attempted fraud remained the same no matter where it occurred. For the first time, though, she knew why Todd had claimed he couldn't handle this job and had recommended Charity take his place. All the stuff he'd said about how she was such a great investigator? She'd thought it was exaggerated at the time, but now she knew why. Separating Todd from his metropolitan comforts might have been too much to ask. She snorted.

Two minutes later she realized she couldn't have been

more inappropriately dressed. The casual clothes of people she passed were mostly well-worn versions of Western style. Wearing a gray business suit and high heels was going to make her stick out like a sore thumb. Of course, given the size of this place she'd probably stick out anyway.

She felt like an alien, but that was something she was fairly used to. Always being on the road kind of created that feeling.

She reminded herself that arson was arson no matter where it occurred. Still, when she'd been told to come to Conard City, she'd envisioned a much larger place. Flying in on a four-seater Cessna hadn't concerned her, and she hadn't really thought about it when she climbed into a rental car that wasn't new enough to have a GPS mapping console.

Only now, driving down Front Street toward what she hoped would be the fire station, did she get a clear picture. The houses were all older Victorian and Craftsman styles commingling contentedly. The leafy trees looked as old as the houses, and for a main street this one struck her as awfully narrow, narrow enough that parking was allowed on only one side. She'd been in some older neighborhoods in Atlanta like this, but if this was the whole town…oh, boy.

She was a city girl in rural territory, and immediately she began imagining all kinds of problems with the locals who'd probably resent the heck out of her. She had traveled the world throughout her entire life and knew that outsiders were rarely welcomed. Looking into a big industrial fire often only drew flak from the owners. In a place this small she might draw flak from the entire community. But she always drew flak, some of it potentially dangerous. She'd been threatened more than once.

She shook herself and continued the slow drive. She'd manage. She wasn't here to be liked, merely to protect her insurance company against fraud.

The firehouse was near the town square, she'd been told at the airport. Couldn't miss it. Well, she hadn't passed anything resembling a town square yet so...

Just then sirens penetrated her thoughts. She pulled over immediately to the curb, and soon a fire engine came racing by. Behind it was a red SUV with flashing white-and-red lights. She hesitated, then figured that in a burg this size it was unlikely the chief would still be at the station. He'd probably be out helping.

So she pulled an illegal U-turn and followed the truck. Might as well see how this department operated in action. That could sometimes be useful to her investigation. An ambulance, horn blaring, raced past her, forcing her to the curb again.

She kept to the speed limit, unlike the trucks, but soon reached them. They had pulled over on a side street, already being blocked by police to traffic. Two men in yellow firefighting gear were heading indoors as flames leaped out one lower story window. There must be a potential victim inside, as they didn't wait for the hoses. Others were hooking up hoses to the truck and a nearby hydrant. Not bad yet. It was clear where the fire was, and apparently the window had been open. She studied it with a practiced eye.

One guy stood out, mainly because of his white helmet, the word *Chief* stenciled in black on it. He was clearly directing operations, his arms and hands moving as he pointed where he wanted things.

She stopped against the curb outside the cordon. After a minute, she climbed out and joined concerned neighbors across the street who had either been ordered out of nearby houses or were gathering out of interest. "She's got a baby!" one of the onlookers shouted, trying to be heard over the racket of the pump truck, other vehicles and raised voices. "Upstairs, bedroom on the right."

The chief turned, gesturing that he'd heard. He pulled up his flash hood, donned his face mask and, moments later, he ran into the house, to rooms that had to be right above where flames spewed out the open ground floor window. He went alone, seeming to ignore the two-in, two-out rule. Another firefighter saw and raced after him.

Yet another two stood near the truck, ready to run in if any firefighter ran into trouble. The two out.

Charity felt her heart speed up. She didn't know these people, but she hated fires, hated what they did, and was intimately acquainted with the dangers for those who fought them. Her career of investigating arson wasn't just a job, it was a mission. Preventing fraud was one thing. Stopping people who killed and hurt others was even more important to her, though it wasn't often she had an opportunity to do that.

"Who are you?" one of the onlookers asked her. She glanced over and saw a man of about seventy, thin and a bit bent.

"I'm here to see the chief," she answered quietly. "Business."

"Oh, no!" someone cried.

Charity looked at the house again and saw flames had reached the second story. The beehive of firefighters began to swarm even more rapidly. A hose doused the outside wall of the house. One was aimed right inside the lower floor window. The roof, too, was getting its share of water. Another truck pulled up and in seconds was fanning water over the neighboring roof and side wall to prevent the fire from spreading. That must be a constant danger with the houses so close.

She knew all the dangers. Fire spread fast enough, but when combined with the gases it created, it could turn into an instant conflagration at the point of flashover. That was why windows were giving way to axes even though the fresh air would fuel the fire. It would also dilute the explosive gases and flammable black smoke that was roiling out the front door.

She'd lost track of how many firefighters were now in the house. Her heart was slamming like a trip-hammer.

Then one came out of the house carrying a woman. His buddy followed close on his heels. Others immediately went to help him, quickly putting her on a stretcher and turning her over to EMTs. Two more firefighters ran in to battle the blaze, but already the flames were shrinking from the side window. The smoke coming out the front door was turning gray. The water was doing its work.

Where was the chief?

Almost in answer to her silent question, he burst out through the front door, carrying a tightly wrapped bundle. Ignoring everyone else, he threw off his respirator mask and helmet, then knelt on the grass, unwrapping a baby.

Charity's heart nearly stopped. The infant looked pale, almost blue. She raised her fingers to her lips, trying to hold in the anxiety. Not a baby. Please, not a baby.

"Oxygen," the chief shouted. He bent close to the child, listening for breath, then feeling for a pulse. An EMT rushed over and joined him. The infant's color improved within seconds after the oxygen mask was placed over its face. The child was swiftly moved to the ambulance.

Relief nearly caused Charity to sag. Leaving the spectators, she returned to her car, watching the scene unfold. She'd seen this many times. Too many times. She'd even trained with firefighters and had volunteered so she could understand.

Now she understood too much.

An hour later, the scene had quieted. While firemen, including the chief, moved through the house, axing open walls to make sure they concealed no fire, others rolled up the hoses. The house still stood, but it was a mess. The outside wall was covered with soot, two window frames charred black. Inside, everything would be ruined by smoke, ash and water. She wondered how much these poor people would be able to salvage.

Pulling out her cell phone, she went to her company's site, logged in and tapped in the address. Her company covered that house. She scanned the firefighters and realized the chief was once again outside, occasionally speaking to his crew. The small crowd of onlookers still lingered, talking to each other. Already she heard plans to help the family. Good people.

No one hindered her passage, and she reached the chief's side. He was preoccupied and didn't immediately notice her. He was still talking to the other firefighters, making sure everything had been taken care of. She was certain he had a running head count going in his mind. She didn't want to interrupt it.

His face was smudged with soot. Apparently he had wiped it a few times, probably to get rid of sweat. The gear he wore was heavy and hot, at least fifty pounds as he was dressed now, more in full paraphernalia. She had worn it and hated it even though her life depended on it.

At last a firefighter came out of the house. "Clear,"

he called. The second truck, which had been hosing the adjacent structure, was already pulling away. The fire rescue ambulance had departed a while ago.

It was then the chief noticed her. His gray eyes slid over her from top to toe. "Who are you?" he asked bluntly.

"Charity Atkins, Chief. We had a meeting."

He shook his head a little. "Wayne Camden, and the meeting has to wait a little while."

"Of course." She didn't even try for a smile. She held out a card. He looked at it, pulling off one of his huge gloves to take it.

"What am I supposed to do with this?"

"Be sure the family gets it. My company insures this property, too. What happened?"

He had fully placed her now, his mind leaping from the all-important mess in front of him to her purpose in being here. "You're the arson investigator about the Buell fire."

"Yes."

"Well, this wasn't arson. Looks as if a grease fire started on the stove and was mishandled. The woman's burned. Her husband's out of town. You'll have to wait to get your answers."

"I don't want answers. I just want them to know I'll have an adjuster out here tomorrow if possible. We'll cover alternate accommodations."

He nodded. "Fair enough. I need to finish up here. You can wait for me at the station, unless there's something else you want to do."

"I'll see you there." She returned to her car and called her company to give the family a head start on their coverage.

* * *

Randy Dinkum loved fires. He always had, even though it was a relief to open that damned turnout coat and feel cool air on his skin again. As he closed the last panel on the fire truck and got ready to board for the ride back to the station, he looked one more time at the house. Tragic now, but no one had died. Poor woman was a mess, though. He might love fire, but he hated it, too.

He wanted to pat his own back for how well they'd handled the whole thing. It hadn't spread to neighboring houses, although that was always a huge risk in town, what with all these old buildings so close together. Dried out by the years, their frames and siding were practically tinder.

Kind of surprising they hadn't lost the whole house. The interior was wasted, but a contractor should be able to fix that.

"Great job," said the chief, clapping his shoulder briefly before moving on to the next fireman.

Randy beamed, then pulled himself up onto the truck. A few seconds later, Jeff Corner hopped up beside him. "That was a beaut," Jeff said.

"It sure was," Randy agreed. As the truck started moving, he saw the stranger in the business suit drive away. "Who was that woman talking to the chief?"

"Dunno. Heard him tell her to meet him at the station."

"Girlfriend?" Randy suggested. They both laughed. "That'll drive Donna crazy."

"You think he moves in those kinds of circles? That was a fancy suit."

"Wish we saw more of that around here. Damn, I want a cigarette."

Jeff laughed again. "You know what the chief thinks of smoking in public."

"Considering the amount of smoke we breathe on the job, why should he care?"

"Public image," Jeff said knowingly. "Haven't you heard? Gotta be a good example for kids."

The familiar jolting began as they rolled down the street. They weren't a big fire department and didn't have the fanciest equipment, so they hung on to the rear of the truck since they all couldn't fit inside.

Eventually, Jeff and Randy would graduate to inside seats and younger men would stand here. But even hanging on here was better than being a volunteer, those who responded only when needed.

Soon the summer would dry out the grasslands and firefighting would sometimes become a full-time job for them all. Randy liked those times best, not only working to beat back the flames but because firefighters came from everywhere to help out. When they weren't actually facing the flames it was like a big party. A tired party, but still.

And those were the times he felt best about himself. People treated them all like heroes. He guessed they were, actually. Today they'd saved a woman and a baby.

He hadn't known about the baby. No one had. "Say, Jeff?"

"Yeah?"

"Why do you think no one knew there was a baby in there until Old Man Kroner shouted it out? Was it, like, a secret, or something?"

"I dunno," Jeff answered, leaning as the truck turned into the station. "I thought everyone around here knew everything about everyone."

"Yeah. Kinda weird."

"Well, it looked like it was just born. Maybe the grapevine didn't reach us yet."

"Maybe." Randy pondered that as the truck slowed to a halt. One of the advantages of being in such a small town was you knew who might be in a dwelling when you responded. People didn't get easily overlooked. Which made the Buell arson even weirder. Someone who'd burn a house full of people was scary.

It was troubling, something Randy hoped would be solved—and soon.

Charity walked into the firehouse through a side door just as the final truck rolled up and joined two others in the bay. A young woman with red hair, wearing a comfortable dark blue station uniform, sat at the desk. Those uniforms were designed not to impede movement, as they were worn under the turnout suits, and designed not to ignite easily. Over her breast, a shield was embroidered, her last name below it.

The woman sat facing a wide plate-glass window that looked into the truck bay, surrounded by consoles and equipment. Her eyes widened as she took in Charity's apparel.

Definitely going to have to change into native garb, Charity decided. Soon. "Hi, I'm Charity Atkins, arson investigator for the Buell fire. The chief has an appointment with me and he told me to wait here for him." She wondered if she imagined the flash of instant dislike on the woman's face, then brushed it aside. A lot of people, including officials, didn't like arson investigators. Or maybe it was the suit.

The woman stood and offered her hand. "Donna Willem, fire inspector and admin, former smoke eater. Have a seat. Help yourself to coffee."

Charity looked at the dregs in the pot and decided to do without. She took the simple metal chair and summoned a smile for Donna. "Thanks. Why former?"

Donna patted her hip. "I took a fall during a barn fire. Can't climb ladders anymore, and frankly carrying the equipment got painful, too." She sat. "We're not so busy that I don't get bored." She held up an e-reader. "But I do read lots of good books."

Charity laughed. "There are advantages to most things. I volunteered with a fire department for a while."

"Yeah?" Interest sparked in Donna's gaze. "Why'd you quit?"

"It was a temporary thing from the start. Sort of job training so I'd be a better arson investigator."

"Ah." Donna studied her as if she didn't much care for Charity. It had to be the expensive suit. "Arson infuriates me."

"Me, too. Do you see much of it?"

"Kids sometimes get careless. But in the past year or so…" She shrugged. "Sometimes things come in bunches. Chief says three fires have been arson, including the last one at the Buell Ranch. Say, can you tell me something?"

Charity tensed. Her investigations had to remain private. "If I can."

"Edna Buell's a friend of mine. I'm worried about her and her family. Does your insurance cover arson? I've always wondered."

Well, that was easy. "Unless the arsonist is the owner of the property or his agent, yes."

"Good." Donna swiveled her chair a bit as if trying to loosen up some back muscles. "Must be difficult to figure out sometimes."

"It's always difficult." Even more difficult when you

had some guy with loads of money breathing down your neck and you suspected he'd gotten tired of owning that building. Or couldn't pay the taxes or upkeep. Some guy who could afford to pay some slime to start the fire. But you had to prove it.

"You gonna be here long?"

Charity shrugged. "Only as long as it takes me to clear the Buells. A few days, I hope."

"Bet you work with cops, too?" Donna asked.

"When it's needed."

"Must be an interesting job."

Charity nodded, watching through the plate-glass window as the next important tasks were carried out. No rest for the weary. Equipment had to be cleaned, checked out and stowed. Then the truck would get babied. No relaxation for these men for hours yet to come. By the time they hit the showers, they'd be dead on their feet, probably.

Fighting a fire took a lot out of person, she'd learned. Not just the weight of all their equipment, but the heat inside the protective gear, the inevitable adrenaline rush, a lot of hard labor... Fatiguing. This hadn't been a terrible fire—they'd only battled it for an hour or so—but they were guzzling water from bottles as if they'd spent a week in the Sahara.

A door to one side of Donna opened and Chief Wayne Camden stepped in. He was swigging from a water bottle, too, and his hair was damp. He must have just showered, because the soot was gone.

He wore the simple blue uniform of this department, with black work boots on his feet. Apparently he didn't always follow the custom of white shirt for higher-ranking members. For the first time she noted that he was tall, lean and muscular. Staying in shape was important in this job for a variety of reasons, and he apparently knew it. His hair looked almost black, maybe because it was still wet, but his eyes were a silvery gray that reflected some of the blue in his uniform.

"Ms. Atkins," he said. "Sorry to keep you waiting."

Charity rose, smiling. "For good reason, I think. You took quite a risk going for that baby."

He shrugged it off. Of course he'd taken a risk. That was what firefighters did. She felt almost stupid for even saying it. "Come into my office. It's not the neatest place in the world, but it works."

She saw what he meant as he ushered her through the narrow door. Files were stacked everywhere, as if the filing cabinets had run out of space. They were neat stacks, but still stacks.

"It's all on the computer," he said, gesturing to the machine on his desk. "Eventually the paper goes to the archives."

"How many years does that take?"

He glanced at her as he motioned her to take a seat, then sank into his own chair on the other side of the desk. Battered leather, it had clearly seen better days, and it creaked beneath his weight. "Seven years," he answered, then laughed. "You'd be surprised how often the paper is needed."

"Probably not," she said, returning his smile. "Bureaucracies."

"At every level." He leaned back and the chair creaked some more. "So you want to examine the Buell place."

She nodded, wishing his gaze was less steady. Something about it made her aware that he was a man. She didn't want it, didn't need it, and she wouldn't be here long anyway. The sting of her last breakup was still fresh. She needed to focus on the task at hand, not this man. "You said it was arson."

"It most definitely was. You ever walk into a building a day after a fire?"

"Quite often."

"Then, you know. You can sometimes smell the accelerant. I always thought that was odd, that it can leave behind an odor when it should all burn up. The aromatics should be gone."

"Aren't they usually?"

"True. But the stench of kerosene and gasoline cling for a long time. If you use too much and some of it doesn't burn…" He shrugged one broad shoulder. "Of course there are some you can't smell."

She wondered why he was schooling her. *She* was the arson specialist. She might have gotten annoyed at being patronized, but somehow he didn't give her that feeling. It was more as though he was trying to shift mental gears and get into the groove on the Buell fire. He drank more water and offered her a bottle from the small fridge beside his desk. She accepted it gratefully. Flying always left her parched.

Suddenly he zoomed in on her and on the subject at hand. He leaned forward, as if he had finally fully switched mental zones. "It was arson, all right. I don't think the Buells did it, and you can't smell accelerant in the house—just in the barn. More important, it went up too hot and fast. Who the hell around here would know a different way to start a fire?"

He had her full attention now, too. And now she understood why he'd mentioned aromatics, the things you could smell. He hadn't been schooling her. He'd been working up to something.

"Do you think the Buells did it?" he asked her.

"I haven't seen the site."

He shook his head almost irritably. "Don't fence with me. You're the insurance carrier, you know their coverage. Do they stand to gain from this?"

"It's always possible," she said truthfully. "Even the minimally insured have been known to set fires in order to get aid. But really, I have to see the extent of the damage and evaluate some other things before I can say." And if that made him feel protective of people he knew, too bad.

"Black bones pointing to the sky and some dead livestock," he said shortly. "There isn't a whole lot left except the herds out in pasture. Amazingly, we didn't get a grass fire. It was hot, it was too fast and the Buells were damned smart to have alarms. Now Fred Buell is out there every day trying to tend his cattle from the back of a truck with the help of neighbors. He didn't gain a thing that I can see except a whole pack of new problems."

She nodded, willing to accept his judgment for now. Her own would come later.

He stood up and went to stare out his own plate-glass window at the men who were finishing the cleanup. "We got us a firebug, Ms. Atkins. Bad and mean. I want him."

"Your inspector mentioned this was the third arson in a year."

"Close to. Less than a year, to be specific. The first two were definitely gasoline, but this one is different. If they're the same perp, then we have a huge problem. He's getting smarter." He turned and looked at her. "And more dangerous. The first two didn't go up like a bomb. We had time to get out there, and the ranchers are pretty good with a hose themselves. This time…" He shook his head, a dark frown on his face. "Are you gonna help me?"

She started. She hadn't expected this. She had come to assess one situation, not hunt for an arsonist. But something in her quickened, and she felt a touch of his fury.

"I hate arsonists," she said finally. "Passionately. I'll do what I can, what my job allows."

After a moment he said, "Fair enough. You're an expert. I'm not really. I can recognize arson, can usually tell where the fire started and what caused it. But this is different. I need some expertise around here. I sent for a state investigator, but they're shorthanded. I've covered the points of ignition I could find, but with every passing minute, evidence is disappearing."

She completely understood and shared his concern. While she had no stake in any of this, she did indeed want to help figure out what had happened and who had done it before this creep managed to kill someone. Still, given her job, there were definite limits on what she could do. She also liked that Wayne Camden cared this much. She'd known some who didn't.

"All right," he said. "We'll go out first thing in the morning. Where are you staying?"

"There's a motel…"

He shook his head sharply. "You won't catch any diseases there, but you'll be right across the street from the truck stop. It'll be noisy and it's probably not what you're used to."

"I'll survive," she answered, but just from the way he'd objected to the idea, she already felt her skin starting to crawl.

He returned to his desk and picked up his phone, dialing a number from memory. "Hank? Wayne. Listen, I got an arson investigator in town for a few days. You wanna do me a favor? She needs a place to stay, and I don't mean the La-Z-Rest. Yeah, okay."

When he hung up he said. "Solved. A friend of mine has a furnished house for rent. You can use it, no charge."

Astonishment filled her. "Why would he do that?"

"Because he used to be a fireman, too. Come on, I'll show you where it is."

She followed his red SUV down narrow tree-lined streets for a few blocks until he pulled up in front of a small house. A man was waiting for them outside, the perfect image of a cowboy except he canted a little, suggesting he had some kind of back trouble.

He smiled and held out his hand. "Hank Jackson."

"Charity Atkins. It's so kind of you to do this."

He shook his head. "Teeny little thing. The place is empty. Empty houses aren't happy houses. It's fully furnished, though. Some groceries and you'll be all set. Let me show you."

"Tell her about Maude's," Wayne Camden said. "I need to get back to the station. Paperwork awaits." He paused and looked at Charity. "I live just one street over, not that I get home often. Hank here can help you with just about anything, okay?"

"Thanks so much."

"No problem. Not for me anyway. Should I pick you up around eight in the morning?"

Converted to Eastern Time, she realized, that would be her equivalent of ten. "Or I can come by the station after I get some breakfast."

"Okay, I'll see you there."

He strode to his car, leaving her with Hank Jackson, a man with a weathered face and eyes that crinkled when he smiled.

"So you were a firefighter, too?" she asked.

"A long time ago. Now I'm just a cowboy. Come on in. Make yourself at home."

Elsewhere, an arsonist pondered the arrival of the insurance investigator. How much did she know? How much could she figure out? Was she like the state investigator?

That was worrisome. The delay in getting the state guy down here created time between the fire and the investigation, and time made evidence go away, killing it with sun, wind and rain. Longer was better.

If the woman was a threat, the arsonist needed to know. Certainly, the fires had to stop for now. Frustrating, but necessary. There was no way to explain that the fires were meant to be helpful. Watching the investigator became paramount. If she became a threat, she would have to be removed somehow.

But that Buell fire had been something else, far more than the arsonist had expected. So fast, so all-consuming, way beyond the plan. Watching it erupt had been a thing of pure beauty and pure terror. The arsonist had been afraid of it, even at a distance. Way beyond control, not supposed to happen that way. The kind of fire that would draw major attention from every direction. A mistake.

Looking through binoculars, the arsonist had made sure the family escaped, and only then could enjoy the show. Sheets of flame reaching heavenward, whirling in fiery tornadoes, the sparks creating fireworks as the house and barn had collapsed. The biggest fire, short of a wildfire, ever. Two buildings, barn and house. That hadn't been intentional, but the show… Well, maybe that made it worth it.

A perfectly created work of art. And all of it for a good cause.

But that arson investigator could prove to be a huge headache. Something drastic might need to be done.

With memories of that gorgeous fire still dancing, the arsonist decided the investigator needed to be driven away. Somehow. With any luck, it wouldn't take much.

But if she nosed around too much, killing her was a possibility.

Chapter 2

By morning, Charity felt she had begun to land. Yesterday had been long, with a red-eye flight out of Atlanta to Denver so she could catch the puddle jumper to Conard City in time for her meeting with the chief.

She was used to it, did it often enough, but by the time she could finally hold still, she was ready to crash. She hadn't even considered getting dinner. A shower and a comfy bed met her needs.

It was dark when she awoke, still on Atlanta time. She turned on all the lamps and light poured through the house, revealing it to be pleasant, and dashed with color here and there as if someone had tried to brighten it. Better than most motel rooms any day, and Charity felt grateful to Wayne and Hank. She'd only be here a short while, but she'd at least be comfortable when she wasn't working.

Today, however, looked like the day to start wearing

her real work clothes: jeans, shirt, boots and jacket. No place for the fancy suits while wandering around the fire scene.

She found coffee of an indeterminate age and a coffeepot. She made some and tasted the staleness, the oils just on the brink of going bad. She guzzled half the pot anyway, then realized that morning was beginning to arrive. Already she felt halfway into her workday. Funny how much difference a two-hour clock change could make.

Now that she felt fully rested and awake from the caffeine, Wayne Camden popped into her thoughts. Attractive man. Very. Then she struck that off her mental list. No time, no desire. One-night stands weren't her thing, and these days she was burned out on relationships. It amazed her how often men could become controlling, resenting her work hours, her frequent trips out of town. Her job was part of the package and she was up-front about it. Yet still, sooner or later, the guy would get unhappy. Danged if she could figure it out.

She rubbed the last of the sleep from her eyes and headed to the bathroom. To makeup or not to makeup, she thought humorously. The familiar face that stared back at her from the mirror showed few remaining signs of fatigue, so she went for a very light touch. Then she clipped her long auburn hair firmly out of the way and hunted up her ball cap and hard hat. She was ready, from the top of her head to the tips of her toes.

And she figured that she needed to get some things straight with Wayne today. He'd asked for her help in finding this guy, and she shouldn't have left the possibility open. She was an insurance investigator, not a criminalist or a cop. She'd gone to the arson academy, but her job most often involved checking out the evidence provided by forensics, and then looking for motivations and links. Yes, she was good at what she did, but she needed to make her limitations clear.

He really *did* need a fire marshal from the state.

She found the diner Wayne had mentioned without any trouble. Shortly after seven, local time, it was pretty well packed, although most of the patrons appeared to be older men who might be retired. A grumpy woman whose name tag announced she was Maude took her order with all the grace of an angry rhino, but the coffee came fast, and the eggs were perfectly cooked. Charity noticed the grumpiness extended to everyone else and no one seemed to mind it, so it must be par. She could ignore it.

Through the window she caught sight of the sheriff's office up the street on the corner across from the square she had seen for the first time this morning. Maybe she could find some assistance there. They were surely going to need it.

She ate quickly with her laptop open, scanning the fire reports that had brought her out here. No mistaking the all-caps word *ARSON* typed into the blank for the probable cause. The rest offered little enough information except that both house and barn had been destroyed, horses and calves in the barn had died, but no other injuries.

Really. No other injuries. From the way Wayne had described it, she was kind of amazed. Fast and hot, almost like a bomb. Achieving that was no simple task. Most arsonists fell down in that area. Partial damage, a fire that ran out of fuel too soon, an accelerant that wasn't as good as they thought, not enough ignition points…

She closed the laptop, the limited facts fresh in her mind. As soon as she paid the bill, she hotfooted over to the sheriff's office, only peripherally noting that men were playing chess and checkers at stone tables and benches scattered in the gardens of the square.

The wizened woman at the dispatch desk was smoking a cigarette right below a no-smoking sign. Charity almost laughed when she realized that none of the deputies in the room seemed disturbed by this fact. An ashtray of butts nearby seemed to indicate this wasn't a onetime infraction.

The woman eyed her from rheumy eyes. "Need something?"

Charity offered her card and the woman took it. "I'm Charity Atkins, an arson investigator. I'm here about the Buell fire. I was wondering if I might get some information here."

Thin eyebrows reached for an equally thin graying hairline. "You need the sheriff. Straight back that hall on the left. Can't miss it."

She found the door labeled Sheriff Gage Dalton and had just raised her hand to knock when the door flew open. The man who faced her appeared to be about fifty, one side of his face marred by a shiny burn scar.

"Whoa," he said. "Sorry if I startled you." He held out his hand. "Gage Dalton."

"Charity Atkins, arson investigator." She pulled out a card for him. "If you have a minute, I'd like to ask about the Buell fire."

"Sure." He stepped back in. "Wayne's the guy you need, though."

"I'm meeting him in twenty minutes at the firehouse."

Dalton's eyes crinkled with a crooked smile. "Not much time, then. Take a seat."

But before he joined her, he called down the hall, "Velma! We got a statey on the way over. Get rid of your butts. And while we're at it, why don't you take up electronic cigarettes?"

He didn't wait for an answer but limped around the desk to sit facing her. Files teetered on one corner. A computer occupied the other. He sat with a grimace of pain, then smiled again. "Velma's too old to change. But she's not too old to get me into trouble."

"I hear you." Charity wanted to laugh. "I know you're probably busy, but I was wondering what, if anything, you might know about this situation. The fire chief is hoping I can help him solve this somehow, but honestly, I'm an arson investigator who is primarily concerned with fraud. Fire and law enforcement are the people who do the real work. I just put it together."

He nodded, drumming his fingers. "I don't know much. I know Wayne is worried. Third arson in less than a year, but this was the worst by far. As for the Buells... Hardworking family. They've treasured that place for generations and never caused a lick of trouble. I wish everyone was like them."

"But ranching is a hard life," she said quietly.

"Not hard enough to give up everything he's worked for. Not the kind of man who'd kill his own livestock, either. And you should talk to his wife and kids. They got out by the skin of their teeth. Fred Buell is now one very angry man, and I can't say I blame him. If you're still in town and want to get a measure of the regard folks around here feel for that family, come to the barn raising on Saturday."

She blinked. "People still do that?"

"Don't have to do it often, but yeah, they still do. Give the man a barn, he can take care of his business and his family will have a roof until they can put up another house."

Charity tried to imagine it. "Living with the animals?"

"People used to do it all the time. Anyway, I got nothing on the Buell family. He's not exactly in high clover, but he pays his debts and takes good care of his family. I can't imagine him doing this to himself."

She glanced at her watch. "Thank you, Sheriff. Guess I'd better run over to the fire station."

"If you need anything else, let me know. It's not like we're not trying to look into this. I've battered the phone lines with demands for an investigator, and I know Wayne has sent samples to the forensics lab. But right now, we're pretty much stalled without a trained arson investigator."

She shook his hand again, then paused in the doorway. "Are the property appraiser's records online?"

"More than mine," he chuckled. "Yeah, they kept up with the times. Around here, we're still catching up with the twenty-first century."

Her car was still parked in front of the diner. She hurried back to it, then set out for the fire station. One thing to say for small towns, it was easy to find most places.

The only guys she saw as she walked up to the station, carrying her hard hat and laptop, were two men in the bay busy running on treadmills. She wondered if they had a weight room. Probably. There was even a basketball hoop hanging above the bay doors. That had been a favorite pastime when she'd volunteered.

Donna was still at the desk and simply waved her on through. "Chief's waiting for you."

Wayne rose the moment she opened his door. This morning he looked rested and his smile came easily. She found herself wishing he lived in Atlanta. She'd gladly get herself into some trouble with this guy.

"Ms. Atkins."

"Charity, please."

His smile widened a shade. "Wayne. Ready to head out?"

"Actually, do you have any internet Wi-Fi hotspots around here?"

"Not many," he answered. "We've got Wi-Fi for law enforcement, the schools, the library, and us, but you need a password. I can get you one if you want."

Oh, boy, she'd come back to the Stone Age. She quashed the thought immediately, as being rude. This area was extremely rural, and she was simply spoiled to think she could find a hot spot behind every storefront. "Thanks. I need to look at the property appraiser's records on the Buell place."

"Before we go?"

"It would help me understand what I'm seeing."

Without another word, he turned his monitor so they both could see it. "Take a look," he said as he began to type. A minute later, she saw the appraiser's page for the Buell homestead. At once she started taking notes, tapping quickly on her own keyboard.

"Let me print it out." As soon as the printer started humming, he rose and opened his office door. "Donna, can you fix it so Ms. Atkins can access our Wi-Fi while she's here?"

"It'll take me a few to set up a new account."

"Later will be fine," Charity said as she scanned the page. Big house, big barn, big appraisal. Her stomach sank as she read. Fred Buell had been underinsured, probably painfully so when you added in the livestock. No way would he gain from this fire. How had her company let this happen? When including reconstruction costs, they usually went overboard.

"This afternoon," Donna said. "The darn thing always argues with me. I swear these machines have their own minds. Of course, if I wait for county IT to do it, it might take a week."

Charity closed her laptop and reached for the sheet from the printer. As she did so, she saw a framed five-by-six photo on his desk. A young woman with long dark hair smiled back at her. Was he a cradle robber?

"She's lovely," she said to Wayne, indicating the photo.

"That's Linda, my daughter. Seventeen and getting ready to leave me for college."

Charity smiled. "You started young."

He chuckled. "Older than I look. I guess I should take it as a compliment."

"By all means." She started to open her mouth and ask about his wife but realized it would be rude. Not everyone with a child had a spouse. She didn't want to risk opening an old wound, if one existed.

"My wife left us about five years ago." A shadow passed briefly across his face.

She guessed she'd given herself away somehow. "I'm sorry."

"This town doesn't suit everyone," he said, closing the subject. "All set?"

"All done. Thanks."

"Ride with me. Better for the roads than your rental."

Wayne noted Charity's change of garb and approved. She'd been pretty in that suit yesterday, but *city* had been written all over her. He could be excused for wondering how she could do a job like this. How could anyone do it in a business suit, male or female?

Now he saw the signs of a woman who'd be capable

of climbing through the ruins with him and across the rough, open spaces. Even her boots were sensible and looked as though they had steel toes.

But she was still a pretty package. When he'd stared at her in surprise yesterday, all duded up in city clothes, the first thing he had noticed were her gentle curves. Just gentle ones, reminding him overall of a thoroughbred, perfectly shaped and in shape. Those curves hadn't vanished in jeans and a long-sleeved button-down shirt. If anything, they stood out more. Her hazel eyes were probably a little more expressive than she realized. The rest of her face revealed little, if anything, and he suspected she had schooled herself to keep her secrets.

Regardless, she was still a lovely package.

Food for fantasy, he told himself, and nothing more.

He stared down the roads, amused by himself. Why even waste the time noticing her appeal? She'd be out of here the instant she could shake the dust from her heels. Same as a lot of women. Same as his woman. She'd grown a taste for flashier towns, and coming back here had about killed her. At the end of a year she swore she was losing her mind.

Finally, feeling he was being too silent and far from friendly, he asked, "What did you find out from the appraisal?"

"Plenty. Mr. Buell was underinsured. That shouldn't have happened. Somebody was asleep at the wheel."

"Meaning?"

"We generally look at appraiser's records and adjust values accordingly. We don't want our clients getting caught short like this."

"You mean you can charge more."

She didn't answer for a few seconds and he wondered if she was hanging on to her temper. Her face told him nothing. Too bad, but he didn't believe insurance companies were in the charity business.

"Yes, that, too. Although it doesn't affect our bottom line any if we pay out less."

"But how often do you have to pay for a total property?"

He glanced at her and at last saw a faint frown on her pretty face. "Sorry," he said. "It's reality. Everyone needs to make a living." Even if some of them made more than a decent living. Way more. But this time he guarded his tongue.

"Look," she said finally, "I don't want to argue with you. Believe it or not, I'm not here to cheat our client. My job is to prove that he isn't trying to defraud us, then we'll pay. From the look of it, fraud's out of the question for now."

He didn't miss the qualifier. He wanted to respond, but decided against it. Her job was to be distrustful. He let the conversation drop.

"I'll need to see the files from the other two arsons," she said finally. "They're not my clients, obviously, but there might be links."

"The biggest link is three arsons in such a short time. That's not a routine problem around here. And ranchers are especially good about avoiding fires. It takes too long to get help."

"I know."

He glanced over and saw her staring out the window at the sage and fresh green grasses of spring. If the Buell place had gone up in a few months, they might have been fighting one hell of a brush fire. As it was, it was bad enough.

"Our usual rule," she said, "is not to insure a dwelling or business more than eight minutes from a fire station. We make exceptions for ranches and farms because, you're right, they avoid fire. We get the fewest claims from that segment. As you noted, most of these folks are equipped to deal with a small fire on the spot. My company even gives a discount if they have a high capacity water pump and fire hose. You know, like we do for households with fire extinguishers and security systems."

"That's good to know. I can tell you one thing for sure, these ranchers out here regard fire as their worst nightmare. They worry about it all the time, especially when we dry out in the late summer. Fighting brush fires and wildfires is a lot of my job. These guys are all over it. I've arrived at more range fires than I can count to find every rancher and hired hand in the area already trenching a fire line."

"I can believe it," she answered. "I was impressed with the way you handled that fire yesterday, by the way. Good work."

He didn't know how to evaluate that. "Thanks." Then, "Do you watch many fires? I wouldn't have thought so."

She made a small sound. A laugh? "Before I got into this business I was a volunteer firefighter."

Okay, then. He wasn't dealing with a bean counter who knew next to nothing. That settled him a bit. The woman in the suit had transformed from a threat into a potential ally. She knew both sides of the problem.

A few minutes later she spoke again. "The sheriff said you sent samples to the forensics lab already?"

"I did. I'm sure I didn't get everything. I need to look some more. It's only been five days, and there's a lot I still need to look at. I'm not even sure yet that I've found all the ignition points."

"It's harder when there isn't much left."

"No kidding." He turned onto the Buell's road. In the distance he could just make out the black smudge of what was left, an ugly hulk against a beautiful blue sky. Fred Buell was probably out there somewhere taking care of his herd as best he could. There were a lot of young calves at this time of year, still frail enough to develop problems. They probably needed all kinds of care, too, and Fred might even be sorting out the ones he'd sell. Wayne had never run a ranch, though, so he didn't claim to know much about it. As a kid he'd lived in town, his dad a lineman for the electric co-op. Adulthood had taken him through some college and into working for a fire department in Glenwood Springs. Then he'd come home to be chief here.

"How big is your department?" Charity asked.

"Full-time? Part-time? Volunteers?"

Her laugh surprised him. "That kind of headache, huh? And only three trucks?"

"Only three plus two fire rescue ambulances. We have other heavy equipment garaged on the end of town. Never needed more yet."

"But what about wildfires?"

He shrugged. "Then we get help from everywhere, up to and including heavy equipment lent to us by ranchers and the state. I've got twenty career firefighters. Sixteen part-timers. And a whole boatload of volunteers."

"Twenty full-timers doesn't seem like a whole lot."

"There are smaller volunteer departments. But the full-timers make the core, and usually between them and the part-timers, we can handle the average incident. We spend an awful lot of time on training, though, especially with the volunteers."

She nodded as if she was familiar with that. "I was

impressed yesterday, so don't take my questions as criticism. I'm just curious."

"Well, if it'll settle your mind any…" He paused as they went over a bump in the road and he had to steady the wheel. "There are a few very small outlying towns in the county. I'm talking around a hundred people per. They have their own volunteers. And of course the ranchers stand ready to jump in at a moment's notice. It's not as if we have to cover thousands of square miles with just three trucks. But we train everyone."

"A lot of open land," she remarked.

"A lot," he agreed. He supposed it could be startling to someone from back East. Out here you could drive dozens of miles, sometimes hundreds of miles, and see nothing but fences and a ranch road from time to time. And the mountains. They could be seen from everywhere.

At last they jolted to a stop in front of the burned-out lumps of the barn and the house that used to be the Buells'. He hoped that, underinsured or not, Fred and his family could come back from this.

Charity didn't immediately climb out of the car. She sat staring at the blackened ribs of what had once been structures. "My God," she said finally.

He didn't answer. The scene spoke for itself. Without a raging wildfire, you didn't usually see this kind of destruction. Blackened areas surrounded the remains, but the fire hadn't spread. Green grasses still waved in the breeze. It almost looked as if the house and barn had been blasted from above.

"How many ignition points did you find?" she asked.

"So far eight."

She shook her head. "There must be more."

"Seems like it. Short of a bunker-buster bomb, this shouldn't have happened."

She turned her head, looking at him straight on. "You have more than a firebug. Did the Buells have enemies? Because whoever did this was awfully determined. It wasn't about thrills."

His chest felt heavy. "No," he agreed quietly. "It may have been about murder."

Then he climbed out of the vehicle, unable to say any more. Blue tarps rippled everywhere he'd managed to find ignition sources, protecting them from the elements. But time was short. Even without rain, each passing day destroyed more evidence. Although at this point he couldn't imagine what evidence was going to get them any closer to the sick mind that had done this.

"No pyromaniac," she said when she stood by the car.

"No," he agreed. "Too organized. But angrier than all get-out about something. Or making some kind of point." He paused and looked at her. "I know my department is under suspicion, too."

Something flickered across her face but he couldn't read it. "I didn't say that."

He shook his head. "I'm well aware that a small but significant number of arsonists are firemen. So don't count us out. I'm not."

Then he went to the back of his vehicle to pull out his evidence gathering equipment, a handled rack of glass bottles, a large metal equipment case and protective gloves. "Let's see what we can find."

Charity hung back as he walked toward the blackened ruins. Lifting her laptop, she began to take photos of the scene, and his silhouette provided a good perspective point. It also reminded her how solidly and well he was built, but she brushed the thought away like an annoying gnat. No time to be experiencing her own brush fire. Time to get to work.

When she was satisfied with her photos, she tossed her ball cap on the seat and replaced it with her yellow hard hat. Computer in hand, she followed Wayne toward the mess.

While the scene looked as if a huge gasoline bomb had demolished it, some items survived. After a fire there were always surprises that left her wondering how they hadn't burned or melted. There wasn't much this time, though, and that disturbed her. Wayne was right—this had been hot and fast.

Few arsonists achieved so much destruction. Most acted on impulse with little knowledge of how a fire burned, and they weren't necessarily interested in burning up an entire property. Most often they wanted the excitement of the fire, and the excitement of watching the firefighters. Except for firefighter arsonists, who often were just bored young men, most especially in rural departments, and who wanted some action. She knew that as well as the chief, but she wasn't going to say it to him. His department was under suspicion, all right. Especially the younger firefighters.

But this fire hadn't been set for entertainment. That many ignition sources, and perhaps more, meant that this had been carefully planned. Whether the Buells were chosen at random or with reason, she could only guess. One thing for sure, this hadn't been prepared all in one night.

When she turned around and surveyed the remains of the house and barn, she judged it unlikely that one fire had set off the other. Oh, it was possible, but if the barn had blazed first, the family would have had some notice. What was more, it was doubtful that sparks hitting the house could have caused this kind of destruction so fast. If the house had gone up first, upon escaping the family would have attempted to remove livestock from the barn. Two buildings burned to the ground in one night. An amazing haul for an arsonist.

Crunching her way across charcoal, avoiding a steel-framed chair that still had its cushioning and a stove that looked as if it would still work once the soot was removed, she joined Wayne at the far side of the black.

"You can judge the heat of the fire by the standby propane tank," he said as she came up beside him. "It used to sit here on a rack a good ten feet from the house. You can see the legs here on the ground and the crumpled drum over there. No black leading toward the house, and the drum was blown twenty-five feet."

She snapped another photo. "Not buried?"

"Fred has a much bigger underground storage tank. This fifty-gallon job was used only if they were close to running out, like during a bad winter storm. Probably didn't even have much in it this time of year."

She took some more pictures. It didn't seem to have abutted the house, which would have been really unsafe, but right now it was a display piece for the power of the house's collapse. It could have been sucked in by the fire, but had been blown that whole distance. She made a mental note to think about that some more. "LPG is tremendously volatile once it mixes with air."

"Yeah." He squatted down, surveying the surrounding area. "But he could have left the barrel open and the gas could have run toward the house before evaporating if it was pouring fast enough." He shook his head. "I don't see any sign of that. And it still wouldn't have been enough to make the house go up that fast."

She agreed wholeheartedly. Now, if the house had

been *full* of gas vapors… Her mind was fully engaged, trying to imagine the ways enough ignition points could have been placed to create this kind of mess. "It looks to me like his fire starters would have needed to be inside."

"Or they sprayed accelerant everywhere just before ignition. Come look at this."

He led her to another point, just outside what had once been a wall of the house, and pointed at a strongly burned area along the remaining concrete foundation and the black burst that spread out from it across the ground as if soot had exploded outward.

She saw it immediately. "It looks like a backdraft, as if the fire was in the walls and was trying to breathe. But how could that be? You'd need heat without fire because of the lack of oxygen, and surely they would have noticed the walls getting hot, or paint bubbling. Unless that happened awfully fast, too."

"Yeah. Some headache." He waved to the barn. "That's easier to grasp. He picked a few good points in there. There's always plenty of hay in a barn, and quite a few other things to help. Dust, for example. Acetylene. Paint thinners, maybe, although Fred doesn't remember having any. The barn was old, too, probably tinder looking for a match, at least inside. Easy enough to burn the barn hot and fast. It's the house that's the problem."

"Did you run across anything resembling ignition devices? Because from what you say, everything went up at the same time."

"Seems like it, but who can be sure? It was three in the morning. You'd think they'd have wakened if the barn went first, given the racket the animals would have made, but no one did. They woke up to the sound of shrieking smoke detectors."

She knelt down again and looked at the clear sign at

the obvious burst of soot just outside the wall. Whatever was left of the foundation had charred. Pulling on a glove, she reached out and touched the wall. So severely burned it nearly crumbled at her touch. Gently she brushed a finger over it, her mind sorting through possibilities and discarding many of them. This was looking like an impossible fire. "Did Mr. Buell go for a hose when he got out?"

"Yeah. But according to him, he couldn't make a dent. The house was burning everywhere, and he couldn't seem to get anything to cool down. He said by then the barn was already clearly lost."

"So the house was a little slower, if not by much. That makes sense to me." A house had lots of things to stall a burn, not the least of them gypsum wallboard or plaster. She'd have to find out what his interior walls had been made of.

Then she saw it.

"Wayne? Look at this."

There was a small, unmistakable hole at the base of the remaining wall. Without a word, he pulled out a swab and ran it around inside the hole and dropped it in a screw-cap jar. Then, and only then, did he cuss.

It was midafternoon by the time they headed back to town. Charity had dozens of photos, and spent the ride tapping away at her laptop, recording impressions and ideas for her next move. When she saw the outskirts of the town approaching, she spoke for the first time. "I need to talk to Fred Buell. And you and I need to talk with some privacy."

He turned a corner onto Front Street. They soon passed the street where they'd had the grease fire yesterday. "My office is far from a sanctuary. Let me check in there, get your internet log-in info, then run to the diner for takeout. I'll meet you at your house."

"I can't make you coffee."

"I'll pick up a couple at the diner. I can run out for more later if we need it. Anything you don't like, food-wise?"

"I'd love a latte, but that's probably out of the question."

He chuckled. "We're not entirely in the backwoods. I'll get you a latte. Anything else?"

"I'm okay with anything except wilted salads." She closed up her computer. "Chief?"

"Yeah?"

"Those holes make an argument unfavorable to Fred Buell."

She noticed that he didn't answer immediately. In the end, all he said was "We'll talk to him."

So he was wondering now, too. She let it lie for the moment. At the station, she climbed into her own car. One of the guys in the engine bay cheerfully gave her directions to the grocery and assured her it wasn't far.

She headed down the narrow streets, noting how gracious some neighborhoods appeared while others looked so worn. She got the impression of a town that was barely hanging on, and it didn't surprise her. Small towns everywhere had troubles these days. A paid-off ranch might even be a liability. She wondered what other debts Fred Buell owed, because running a cattle opera-tion had plenty of costs attached that accrued year by year. It wasn't always possible to keep ahead of them and support a family.

At the grocery she bought fresh coffee and some cream and sugar just in case. She also grabbed a fruit tray that looked reasonably fresh, then hurried back to her house.

Wayne was just pulling up out front. She turned into the driveway and climbed out with her laptop, then went around to the trunk to get her grocery bags.

"I see you sidestepped me," he said jokingly as he approached with his own bags and his clipboard.

"I'm hard to corral," she said lightly. "Actually, I decided I'm not starting another day without decent coffee."

He laughed and grabbed her bags by their handles so she only had to juggle her computer as she unlocked the front door. Boy, he was attractive when he smiled. She doubted that he'd be smiling for long.

Inside, while she unpacked her few groceries, he hunted through the cupboards and set the kitchen table for them. She noticed he wasn't saying anything, not even casual conversation, and while she wasn't the type herself to make unnecessary talk, she began to get uneasy. Was he as disturbed as she? Or was something else going on?

Finally they sat at the table facing one another, foam containers beside each plate, and tall lattes in heavy paper cups in front of them. A pile of napkins sat in the middle.

"I got us steak sandwiches," he said, "Maude's specialty."

"That sounds good. Is she always such a bear?"

Again that devastating smile. "Always. Ignore it. Everyone else does."

"I kind of got that impression but I thought I'd make sure." She opened her container and found a sandwich big enough and thick enough for two, along with a mountain of fries. She moved some of the food to her plate, then took a bite of sandwich. Her eyes widened at the flavor explosion. Then she sent him off into another laugh by saying, "I didn't know beef could taste this good!"

"When you buy locally, someone's reputation is on the line. This is always prime grade."

"I couldn't afford it in Atlanta."

"Most likely not. So you were a volunteer firefighter?"

She nodded and grabbed a napkin from the stack to wipe a dribble of juice from her chin. "For over a year. My company encouraged it when I expressed an interest in arson investigation. They thought it would be good training."

"Was it?"

She regarded him across the table. His gray eyes returned her look. "Very," she said. "It's amazing how common small arson fires are. Just small ones, though. Nothing like what we saw today. Most are kids fooling around, looking for excitement, and most aren't very big. It's hard to make a big fire."

He nodded and swallowed. "Did you ever see a big one?"

"Abandoned industrial building. Smart arsonist. There was enough trash in that basement to cause a huge conflagration. Three departments had to respond."

"Did you catch the guy?"

"Actually, they did. He bragged about it." She sighed. "Sixty percent of arsonists never get caught. The ones who do most often have big mouths."

"Which makes figuring out the psychology of an arsonist fairly difficult." He took another bite of his sandwich, clearly a hungry man.

"What about you? Do you ever want the excitement of being with a bigger department?" She took another bite, watching his eyes narrow in response.

He raised one brow. "Frankly? No. Turns out I wasn't

built to be an adrenaline junkie. And I don't enjoy some of the memories I carry with me."

She looked down, wondering if he had thought that question critical of him. Then she linked it back to their earlier remarks about arsonists. "I wasn't implying anything," she said carefully. "Sometimes I miss firefighting myself, parts of it anyway. I just wondered if the slower pace here was a good fit for you."

"A much better fit in some ways." He smiled as if to let her know he hadn't taken it wrong. "We don't have as many fires, not nearly, but that means I don't have to worry about my men as much. I guess it depends on your motivation in joining a department. If you want to save lives, we get plenty of opportunity to do that, especially in the winter when auto accidents are common enough. We're often the first responders for injuries and heart attacks, too. But if you join mostly to fight fires, you might be bored."

And boredom, she thought, was one of the leading causes of arson among firefighters. In bigger towns and cities, a fire team got plenty of action. Not so much in rural towns. Although that could probably change drastically during wildfire season.

"I know what you're dancing around here," he said. She glanced at him again, felt that instant of sexual attraction, then shoved it aside. To her surprise, he'd already eaten most of his sandwich. She looked down again at her own and figured she had dinner and maybe breakfast staring back at her.

"You don't have to answer," he continued after a few beats. "I brought it up myself earlier. It's been gnawing at me since the first fire."

At that she looked up. "Slow down. Because you said something when we were out at the Buell place that disturbed me. You said that fire was attempted murder. That doesn't fit the fireman-as-arsonist profile."

"No?"

She shook her head, feeling a little more energized as the calories began to hit her system. She guessed she must have still been worn out from yesterday. "The fireman who sets a fire almost always picks a building that's unoccupied. Arson conflicts with his desire to save lives."

He leaned back, fries totally untouched, and watched her as she began to put her food back in the foam container. "That assumes the perp ever gave a damn about that to begin with."

"Well, that's a problem, isn't it? How little we really know about arsonists."

"Exactly. The profile is next to useless. Saying that most are below average in intelligence only speaks to those who've been caught. Among the other sixty percent, you could have a lot of really smart guys with all kinds of motives."

"Yes," she agreed emphatically as she closed her box. She rose to carry it to the fridge. When she turned around to come back to the table, she saw frank male appreciation on his face. She smiled inwardly. The two of them might strike a match themselves at any minute.

The momentary amusement acted to clear her head almost the same way the food had. Feeling more comfortable with him now—silly when the sexual tension *should* have been a concern—she returned to her seat and reached for the latte.

"Great coffee," she said, unable to contain her surprise.

The smile danced across his face again. "Maude finally bowed to reality when she bought that espresso machine, and when she bowed she did it right." He pushed his plate to the side. "You ready to talk about the incident site?"

She nodded. "Let me get my computer. We can use the photos, and I have some notes. You brought yours, right?"

"Always." He pointed to the clipboard on the table. "Which reminds me." He pulled a piece of paper off the top and handed it to her. "Your log-in for the Wi-Fi. It's pretty good here in town."

"Fire and police are separate?"

"Different codes, so while you'll be able to access all public records, you won't wander into any files you shouldn't see."

"Great. I was wondering how you worked it."

"*How* it works is beyond my scope. I'm not an IT guy. It's enough that it does."

His tone held self-deprecating humor and she liked it. She felt herself smiling faintly as she went to get her laptop from the table by the front door.

When she returned, he had cleared the table except for the coffee, and was rifling through his notes. It was a thick stack, probably begun from the moment he'd first seen the Buell place in flames five days ago.

He folded some pages back, then pulled a cell phone off its belt clip. He punched in a number, reading from the sheet, and waited. Finally he put the phone down. "Fred must be out on the range. Cell connections can be questionable there."

"Will we get him later?"

"No problem. He and his family are staying in town with his wife's sister."

She opened her laptop, skipped through photos to one

of the tiny holes in the charred wood. "We have a scenario now. Impossible, but valid."

"I know." He stared at the photo. "It's not impossible, but it's disturbing. Sickening even."

She nodded her agreement. It appeared that someone had drilled small holes and filled the walls of the house with a volatile accelerant. It would sit in those walls, little of it escaping because the place had probably been fairly well sealed up for the frigid winters. Seeping throughout the building until the walls had become a bomb ready for one spark. Until it built up in the attic.

Devious. Diabolical. A fire in the walls would have plenty of fuel from the timber framing. It would probably spread quite a way before it did enough damage for smoke to seep out and set off the alarms. In such an old house, it was doubtful the walls were filled with a nonflammable insulation, but even if they were, the frame could have provided enough chinks for the fire to spread once it got hot enough. And some of the hottest, fastest fires were those that smoked for a long time because they didn't get enough oxygen, releasing even more volatile vapors until flashover was possible the instant oxygen poured in.

She flipped back to the assessor's record and saw the house was a century old. In those days insulation often consisted of newspapers, if any was used at all. Plaster walls, like gypsum board, were fairly noncombustible, but between the house siding and the interior walls, a whole world of possibilities lay. "Do you have any idea if the wiring was inside the walls?"

He looked up from his notes. "No. The house was built before we had electricity out here." He paused. "You're thinking an accelerant could have spent a lot of time inside those walls without escaping. No socket holes."

She nodded, making a note. "I'm not a criminalist," she said. "You really need your state arson investigator. I need to be clear on that, because most of what I know involves detecting fraud, not solving fires."

"I understand. But you've already helped, just by noticing that hole. I can't believe I kept missing them."

"I can. I never would have found that one if I hadn't been brushing charred wood away. Too small. It would pass for a nail hole, and I'm sure I don't have to tell you how often nails pop out in fires because of expansion differences. It hit me only because it was right above one of your ignition points."

"As hot as that fire was, they might still be nail holes."

She pushed the computer back and rested her cheeks in her palms, her brain spinning around with ideas, most of which she discarded. "It's the only explanation for the way you described it."

"So far." He turned some more pages on his clipboard. "By the time we arrived, the barn had collapsed, the house was fully engulfed and only minutes from collapsing. Most of our job seemed to be cooling things down. An accelerant filling the walls, maybe suffusing the attic, would explain it all perfectly. Nothing else I can think of does."

She lifted her head, folding her arms on the table. "This guy scares me, Wayne. He terrifies me."

This arsonist was indeed the stuff of nightmares.

Chapter 3

Wayne left a short while later, after making sure she could access the Wi-Fi and reach the records of the earlier arsons. By comparison, those seemed trivial, and she was inclined to think they weren't the work of the person who'd torched the Buell place. Then she warned herself not to leap to conclusions, a dangerous place to go on any investigation.

She also reminded herself that she wasn't here to solve the crime, merely to clear the most obvious suspect, Fred Buell. But after seeing that homestead, she had a hunger to do a lot more than that.

She called a fire department arson investigator she knew in Atlanta and discussed her suspicions with him. For long moments the phone line was silent after she finished explaining. Then Mark Vincent swore explosively. "That's a whole new level."

"But it would work?"

"It sure could. And if you're looking for perps, you should be on the lookout for abandoned places, out of the way. I don't know what it's like out there, but he had to have tested this somewhere unless he was just damn lucky."

She sat bolt upright. "I didn't think of that."

"Why would you? It's not your job." He paused. "What are you doing out there?"

"My job. But curiosity is killing me."

He laughed. "Go for it. Just don't lose your job over it. And keep me posted. Damn! Now I've got something new to worry about. Keep this under your hat."

"Trust me, I'm not planning to hand out ideas."

"Good. Charity, I know you've already figured out this had to be well planned. This guy had to drill all those holes beforehand. He couldn't have put any accelerant in the walls until he had his access points. Too much danger of throwing off a spark. Then after he inserts the accelerant, he's got to wait for the vapors to work their way through the house. A day, maybe two. And he has to do all this without being seen. Check into when everyone would have been away from the house."

"Will do."

"And he had to have used some kind of timed ignition device. He sure as hell didn't run around throwing matches in all those holes. Although it's possible that once the accelerant spread around, one ignition would have set off the whole shebang. Have they found anything?"

"Not yet, as far as I know."

He swore again. "I want to hear all about this. Really."

"For you and you alone." She certainly wasn't going to write it into her report to the insurance company. She doubted Wayne wanted it in his files, either. Need-to-know on this one, unless they caught the guy.

The prospect of an arrest and a trial appealed to her, but it always did. Unfortunately, she knew how rare and unlikely that was.

Deciding it was time to quit for the day, unless Wayne called to tell her they had a meeting with Fred Buell, she carried her phone into the living room and settled comfortably on the couch. Evening was beginning to arrive, judging by the deepening shadows outside. She'd sure picked a weird business to get into, considering that she hated problems she couldn't solve quickly. These investigations could run into days and weeks, or even months, depending. Once she cleared the property owner, her part would be done.

But instead of thinking that she might be able to go home in a few days, she wondered instead if she might be able to hang around longer and take some vacation time. Wayne wanted help, and he wasn't dismissing her puny efforts.

That brought her full circle to the gnat that she'd been batting away all day: her strong attraction to Wayne Camden. While she wasn't into short flings, wanting something a little more durable and solid, she began to wonder if she might be able to manage it just once.

She'd felt attractions many times in her life, and most of them evaporated the minute she walked away from the guy. Wayne was different somehow. He was creeping into her thoughts even when he wasn't around. She kept seeing him in various mental snapshots—out at the Buell ranch, in his office, in the kitchen here. His smile. His body.

She wondered what it would feel like to have his arms around her. His lips on hers. Her head on his shoulder. To explore him with her hands and discover his shape and texture in the most basic of ways. In short, she felt like a schoolgirl with her first crush. She had to look back to her teens to remember feeling like this.

A quiver of yearning settled between her legs, the first she had felt in a while. It made her feel heavy with expectancy, anticipation. Longing.

Oh, boy. She snapped her eyes open and forced herself to sit up. Running in mental circles about the arson would be more productive than this. Especially when she was beginning to realize that as long as she held this job, any man she invited into her life was going to get fed up, eventually. Two had already ditched her for that reason. She spent entirely too much time on the road or involved in investigations. She definitely didn't work on a clock. No guarantee she'd be there for a dinner, or a weekend or a movie. Her company's interests were far-flung, and when a fire was questionable, answers needed to be provided fast. The insured deserved that speed, and the company's reputation demanded it.

She knew some in her position who worked entirely from a home base, sorting through information that was turned in to them by fire investigators and the police. Researching the credit reports on the insured, learning whether other insurance was also involved. Her company preferred to have one of their own investigators go on scene, feeling they might be able to learn things that wouldn't be reported, and also feeling they could get quicker resolutions.

As she'd found over the past five years, they were right. Just hanging around and talking to people sometimes brought useful information to light that wasn't in any report anywhere. And in this case, she'd already learned something very important that wasn't in any of the fire department's paperwork.

Someone had a serious grudge with the Buell family. Serious enough to go to this much effort to wipe them out. Either that, or Buell had done this himself, because it was hard to imagine who else would have that kind of access to his property. Which was something else she needed to discuss with the man. Hired hands? Contractors?

Then there was the question of how fortunate he'd been to get his family out of that place. Looking at it, she imagined they had had to move awfully fast. Either that or they hadn't been in the house when it had gone up. Which meant she needed to talk to the wife, as well. They probably wouldn't let anyone near the kids, but it was worth a try.

None of these questions would have arisen if she'd worked from the fire department's assessment, Buell's credit report and a few phone interviews.

Her phone rang. Her caller ID announced it was the entire state of Wyoming. She always found that ID amusing and was smiling when she answered, sure it was Wayne to tell her they had an appointment this evening with Fred Buell.

It was Wayne, all right.

"Hi, Charity. Wayne. We can't see the Buells tonight because their church is holding a fund-raising potluck for them and they have to be there. He said he could be in my office at eight in the morning, though. Okay with you?"

"Definitely okay. That's nice of their church."

"We're mostly nice people around here, even if it doesn't look like it right now."

Her smile widened a shade and she was sure he could hear it in her voice. As it was, she loved his smooth baritone pouring into her ear. "Most people are nice when you get to meet them."

There was a pause. Then he said, "My daughter has abandoned me for her boyfriend tonight. Can you imagine it?"

That elicited a laugh from Charity. "Naw. Really?" she teased.

"I know. Something about true love and hormones. Anyway…"

He hesitated and her heart quickened. She closed her eyes and nearly crossed her fingers. She didn't care how stupid she was being because nobody else knew it.

"So…wanna hit the diner with me for some coffee or dessert? I promise I won't mention arson."

Her heart lifted as if it suddenly filled with helium. This man was trouble on the hoof, but right now she didn't care. She just wanted to sit across a table from him and actually talk with him, instead of imagining that he was with her.

"Sure," she answered. "Sounds good to me."

"Want me to pick you up?"

"That would be super. Give me a few?"

"Twenty minutes?"

"Plenty." When she disconnected, she looked at her phone as if it had developed a life of its own. She had just made a date with the chief. Really.

Feeling a bit giddy, she jumped up and went to get into some clean jeans and a light sweater and brush out her hair. Some things were worth risking, even if you were miserable later.

A half hour later, they sat in a corner booth at the diner with tall lattes and slices of rich cherry pie in front of them.

"So is Linda abandoning you a lot these days?" she asked.

"She's seventeen. What can a father expect? She has an actual life now, which she's told me more than once."

Charity stifled a laugh. "I can almost hear it. I think I used to say the same thing."

"I think all of us did in one way or another." He raised his fork with a mouthful of pie on it then paused. "What about you? Any kids?"

"If I had kids I wouldn't be here. At present, I'd need someone to give me a photo to remind me what my own apartment looks like."

He nodded. "Traveling all the time?"

"A lot of it." Might as well have that clear, although it hadn't saved her in the past. The fact that she was leaving soon might be her only salvation.

"That makes it hard." He chewed and swallowed his pie. "Any future plans?"

"For kids you mean? Not exactly. I'm not married but I *am* thirty-two. What I'm noticing is that babies are getting cuter with every passing year."

He laughed, a rich sound of enjoyment. "Funny how they do that. People keep asking if I'm glad to be almost done with child raising. First off, I'm not sure you ever stop being a parent, but second, I've been noticing how babies are getting cuter, too."

She joined his laughter. "The old biological urges are pretty strong."

A flame ignited briefly in his eyes. "Yeah, they sure are. There are times since Linda became a teenager that I've been glad I didn't have any more in the pipeline. But now that she's getting ready to leave…" He shrugged. "I'm going to miss it. And don't tell her I said that."

Everything inside her softened for some reason. "I suspect she knows that, but mum's the word."

"Oh, she knows she has me wrapped around her finger. I haven't driven my own car since she got her license."

Charity laughed again. "I bet you stay wrapped because she doesn't abuse it."

"No, she doesn't. She's a really good young woman. But it's time for her to fly." He looked down and ate some more pie, letting her choose where to go or to fall silent.

She drank some of the latte to wash down the pie. It was tart, not unbearably sweet like many cherry pies. "I was noticing your firefighters."

He looked up. "Why?"

"Because they're in remarkably good shape for a rural department."

"Ah." His eyes crinkled at the corners. "I'm a slave driver about that. To keep the job, you have to keep in shape. It's a regular lecture. Otherwise they endanger everyone, including themselves."

"I've visited some departments where they don't seem to understand that."

"So have I. But we're lucky enough to have weight-training equipment and treadmills. They get used, not dusty. It's probably a lot harder for an all-volunteer department."

She realized she had brought the conversation back around to business. It might not be arson, but it was still about work. His work. When he had called he had sounded like he wanted a break. She ate some more pie as she considered a different direction to take. Problem was, she didn't know him well enough to guess what might interest him.

She watched as he finished his dessert and pushed

the plate aside. After he'd wiped his mouth, he regarded her across the booth with a faint smile. "I made you uncomfortable."

Her heart lurched. "Why do you think that?"

"Because I asked you out for what's essentially a date, you're not really interested because you'll be leaving soon and now you're sitting there trying to make casual conversation with someone you have nothing in common with except work."

He'd nailed it. She returned his look, feeling strangely miserable. Just a little while ago she'd felt giddy about meeting him, and now she was uncomfortable and floundering. What was wrong with her?

"It's okay," he said. "I know you're leaving. This is what you want to make it and nothing more. I like you, and you're an attractive woman. But maybe mixing business and pleasure was a stupid idea on my part."

"No," she said impulsively. He arched a brow, waiting. "I was glad that you asked me out. Truly. I like you, too. It's just that..." She hesitated. How truthful should she be? She'd barely met the guy. Not a time for heart-to-hearts about problems that wouldn't matter in the long run.

His gaze wandered away for a few seconds then snapped back to her. "I shouldn't have taken the fire off the table. That kind of leaves us with no other connection under the circumstance. So it's back on the table if you want. As for other subjects...well, we have an advantage here."

She blinked, surprised. "We do?"

He smiled. "Sure. When you go back to Atlanta, you never have to see me again, and you can banish me to the past. That ought to be freeing, not inhibiting."

"Sort of like that TV commercial for Las Vegas?"

He laughed again. "Yup. Or not. But I guess what I'm saying is, relax. Be yourself. I won't hold it against you."

He made sense, she realized. Two strangers meeting in the middle of nowhere, essentially, who'd never see each other again. There were advantages.

"Ah, you're smiling again," he observed. "Good. This was supposed to be fun, not a trial by fire."

She relaxed and just laid it out there. "You're right. A casual outing for coffee and dessert is hardly the place to get caught in webs of the past and future."

"Meaning?"

"I'm still singed. I think it's thrown my reactions off."

His smile faded into a kind expression. "Singed how?"

"I went through a breakup a couple of months ago. The second one where my job seems to be the main problem. Or it could be me and the job was just an excuse. Anyway, I think I'm developing a bunker mentality."

He nodded. "I can identify with that. After Linda's mom left me, I figured I was done. She couldn't stand life here anymore, and I've seen plenty of other folks leave because this place is too small for them. I mean, our theater is a community group that stages plays at the local movie house. We have dancing at the roadhouses. Occasionally the community college entices us with lecturers or exhibits of some kind, but around here if you can't make your own entertainment with friends, you're pretty much stuck with the TV or a trip to a larger town."

"So you're still feeling scorched?"

He nodded. "Still. Five years."

She was surprised to feel a sinking in the pit of her stomach. To his eyes, she must be wearing danger signs plastered all over her. The woman from the big city. The gallivanting traveler. Why the hell had he asked her out? Because it was safely impossible. The very reason she ought to be enjoying this herself. Instead, she seemed to be regretting things that weren't even in the cards to begin with.

Kinda early for a midlife crisis, she told herself sourly.

The slices of pie were too generous by half, she thought, pushing her plate aside.

"Maude's going to want to know what's wrong," he warned her, eyes twinkling.

"Nothing's wrong except I'm full. Maybe she'll feel better when I tell her that it's the best cherry pie I've ever eaten." She reached for her latte. "The sheriff tells me there's going to be a barn raising this weekend for the Buells. And you said the church is holding a potluck for them tonight. Whatever downside this place may have, it seems like an awfully caring community."

"While I'm not as widely traveled as you, I tend to think most people are pretty caring if they just know what they can do to help. Did Gage also tell you that the local lumberyard is providing most of the supplies?"

She put her chin in her hand and gazed at him. Looking was okay, she supposed, and looking at him was pure pleasure. "That's awfully generous."

"I suspect some others chipped in, too, but did it anonymously."

"Are you going to help out?"

"We're going to have fire rescue out there in case of injuries, but we still need to maintain our readiness in town. Which brings me back to the fire. I've got to make sure I've collected every bit of evidence I can from the barn before they bulldoze it."

"I'll help," she said. It wasn't part of her job, but once upon a time she'd helped with collecting information from incidents. She figured she could still remember some of it. Then it struck her that Donna ought to help, if she was his fire inspector. Was she that badly injured? "Donna said she was injured on the job. Was it too bad to help you with this?"

"Bad enough. She broke her hip and hurt her back when part of a building collapsed on her. Not too steady on uneven ground. She's been a good egg about it, though."

"Seems to be. She was joking about all the books she gets to read."

He smiled. "That's Donna, all right. She was a good firefighter. Now she's the best inspector."

"What exactly do inspectors here do? Terminology can vary so much department to department. Does she investigate arson?" Which might explain Donna's initial antipathy.

He shook his head. "She inspects buildings and new construction. Fire code enforcement."

"I'm glad you were able to keep her on."

"So am I."

And Donna would be a far better fit for him than she would. Really, she shouldn't even let such thoughts cross her mind. But there was an emptiness inside her, a great big hole that her job couldn't fill, and her awareness of it had mushroomed after her breakup with Ted. She was living a distinctly lopsided life, but it was her own fault. She'd chosen to do this, and she wasn't ready to quit.

Arson. It drove her like a goad. It was the enemy that haunted her and wouldn't let her walk away. Like now. She was actually thinking about taking vacation time to do what she could to solve this one, even though she knew the odds were against it.

"I can't tell you how much I hate arson," she said. "Every single fire creates a possibility that someone will get hurt. Especially firefighters. So I'm wedded to my job. Uncovering fraud can make arson less attractive to one type anyway."

"I agree." He paused. "I didn't mean to sound critical this morning. Well, yes I did. But not about you. You're the third insurance company I've dealt with about arson in the past eleven months. I was spitting nails before you arrived. In fact, you were the only arson investigator to come out here. The rest sat at their desks in Delaware or New York and caused their clients a whole lot of grief over the fraud issue, all the while questioning my judgments. And they weren't terrible fires, not like Buell's. It makes me really reluctant to put arson as the cause."

She nodded, feeling sympathetic. "It's okay. I know the types you're talking about. They send out an adjuster, rate the probable cost of repairs and then go to work trying to save the insurance from paying."

He tilted his head a little. "Does that make a difference for your job?"

"We look better when we save the company money. But I won't play that game and I haven't been asked to. I'm lucky. My company cares about its reputation, and causing unnecessary grief for clients doesn't help. Anyway, don't worry about your reaction. I'm used to it. There are a fair share of officials who look on me as an interloper."

The evening wound down quickly after that. A nice interlude, but pointless to push it any further. Understanding weighed heavily on her as Wayne took her home. Unless she made changes she wasn't ready to make, emptiness would remain part of her life. Time to resign herself.

They were walking up to her front door when she smelled it.

"Gasoline," he said at the same instant she caught a whiff of the distinctive odor.

Immediately he went from relaxed to intent. Darting back to his truck, he pulled out a couple flashlights. "You walk around the house from that side. I'll take the other."

She nodded, her heart galloping. There was no reason to be smelling gas around here, not this late at night. Turning on the flashlight, she began her walk around, following the distinctive scent. It grew stronger as she approached the back, and her insides fluttered with apprehension.

When she rounded the back corner, she saw Wayne already there, his flashlight pointed at something. She hurried over, the gasoline odor growing distinctly stronger. She followed the beam of the light and saw a pile of rags, dead leaves, pine needles and paper. She didn't need to squat to know they were gasoline soaked.

An arsonist had been here. But why?

A million questions swarmed in her brain like angry bees. Wayne had called out his department and was using a chemical sniffer device to check around the entire house, inside and out. The police were there, hunting for any kind of evidence they might be able to use. Hank Jackson, her landlord, stood beside her.

"I was a firefighter in Denver," he remarked. "I saw plenty of crap like this."

"I bet you did."

"Of course I want to know why. And I know we'll probably never find out. Question is, was it just a prank or did someone scare this cretin off?"

She had no answers. The night had grown chilly, and she folded her arms, trying to keep warm. A shiver passed through her occasionally.

"I need to get back to my wife," Hank said finally. "We had a baby this past winter, and her days are long enough without me leaving her alone in the evenings."

Charity managed a smile for him. "We both know how little we can do right now."

"Yeah, but I'm going to be keeping a sharper eye on the place here on out. If Wayne or Gage need me, I'll be at home with Kelly. You take care, hear?"

"Thanks, I will." But another of the questions uppermost in her mind was whether she was the intended target. How many people in this town knew she was staying here? It hadn't been that long, but it was a small town.

Once everyone was satisfied with their evidence collection, the fire company hosed down the back wall of the house and the ground pretty thoroughly. They left a mire behind, every footstep raising mud up through the grass.

"It's okay to go inside now," Wayne said from behind her. "You must be cold. I'll be along shortly."

She nodded and walked back around front, wiping her boots on the drier grasses out there before she stepped inside. The heat was on, not too high, but a warm contrast to the air outside. Unable to sit still, she made a pot of coffee, then paced the house, watching through windows as the operation rolled up. At last the fire truck roared away, and silence once again blanketed the neighborhood. Curious neighbors returned to their homes now that the action was over.

Charity felt as isolated and alone as she had ever felt in her entire life. Joke? Intention? Directed at Hank Jackson? Directed at her? Or simply an opportune targeting of a house the arsonist thought was unoccupied?

There was a knock on the door then Wayne stepped

in before she answered. "Coffee?" she asked without preamble. "I just made some."

"Sure. I couldn't possibly get any more wired that I am right now."

"It wouldn't have been much of a fire," she said. "It would have been found fast. Not everyone is asleep yet."

"Doesn't matter. Property destruction. A big headache for Hank. What if you'd been sleeping in the bedroom? It was right against that wall. What if it had reached the roof before it was found? You know, that's the thing that really bugs me about this. Maybe it wasn't meant to create a huge fire, but it still could. That's the thing. *Nobody* can guarantee what a fire's going to do. Too many variables."

He came to light at last on one end of the sofa. "It's like water. Finding a leak is hard because it runs everywhere. A fire has its own behavior, like a living beast. It follows the oxygen and the fuel and it could run anywhere, and the speed is variable depending on what it runs into. It's like a living beast on the hunt for food, and it kills far too often. What if it had risen up to the eaves and got into the roof or attic? What if it had filled this place with fumes?" He patted the cushion on which he sat. "Plenty right here to gas a flashover. I realize smoke detectors would probably have alerted you in time, but then my team would have had to deal with it. You ever been in a flashover?"

She joined him, sitting at the other end of the couch. "Yes," she said quietly. "And I've seen the results of them afterward." She could read the fury all over him.

"So I'm out there wondering. Some kid sees a house has been empty for a few months and thinks, why not? Someone is pissed at Hank Jackson, although I couldn't

begin to imagine why. Or someone knows an arson investigator is staying here and is worried about it."

Her heart lurched as he echoed her own question.
"If so, they just want me to move on. This was nothing
like Buell."

"Of course it wasn't. That would take too long. But
it's a message."

She bit her lip, fighting her own fears, and worried
about him. He cared. He was a fireman. This kind of behavior was anathema to him. "Or just a dumb kid who
heard about the other fires."

"Yeah, maybe." He drummed his fingers on the arm
of the couch.

"Let me get the coffee," she said. "I'll be right back."

She returned with two mugs and again sat at the other
end of the couch. Every single question he was asking was valid, every one of them needing an answer. If
the arson was directed at her, it wasn't going to work,
though. She felt stubbornness stiffening her.

Suddenly he leaned forward and put his mug on the
coffee table. "Someone is doing this for a reason. Too
many fires and too scattered to all just be thrill-seeking
kids. They've got to be linked, as different as they are.
Somebody's driving an awful lot of miles to do this. You
know what kind of arson we usually see around here?
Some kid playing with matches who didn't mean to cause
a fire at all. Deliberately set fires are rare, at least here."

"So where does this take us?" He knew the area, she
didn't, so all she could offer was her ears.

"I don't know. It's really not your problem, though.
Maybe you should go back to Atlanta after you talk to
Fred Buell, and I'll send along whatever I get."

So he was worried about her safety after tonight. The
thing was, she'd been threatened before, in more obvi-

ous ways. And every time someone tried to push her off a case, she just dug in her heels.

"I'm a mule," she told him. "Cussedly stubborn. If you think someone wants me to go home, then I'm staying right here."

He looked at her. "Charity…"

She shook her head. "I've been threatened before and it hasn't stopped me yet. You know what strikes me about this?"

He shook his head and waited attentively.

"What strikes me is that someone is scared my being here is going to lead you to them. Or someone wants me out of the way for another reason. Considering I've been here just a little over a day, I don't think I've stepped on any toes yet. So it has to be about my being an investigator, and maybe somebody doesn't understand what my role really is. Maybe they think I'm like that TV show about crime scene investigation. A modern-day Sherlock Holmes. Somebody who can track them down. I'm far from that, but how would they know? So let's keep them scared. They'll slip up."

"Or hurt you," he pointed out grimly.

"Believe it or not, that's a possibility every time I'm on a case. People know my decision is hugely important. And to some of them, my life isn't."

He peered at her, a strange expression on his face. "I never thought about that."

"I try not to. Usually it's just background noise. If it gets threatening enough, I tell the police. They make quiet little visits then."

"Saying what?"

She smiled without humor. "That they'd better hope I don't get so much as a sprained ankle because they'll be at the top of the suspect list. It works."

"If you know who threatened you."

Her bravado slipped away, because he was right. But the stubbornness remained, pulsing through her, goading her. It was at once one of her strengths and her greatest weakness, and she knew it.

"Maybe some of those boyfriends left because they couldn't take worrying about you anymore."

She shook her head. "I didn't bring that home with me."

"Then, why did you tell me?"

"Because you're already aware of the possibility." She met his gaze straight on. "And if someone is worried about what I might find, then maybe you need to consider you're in as much danger as I am."

He levitated from the couch as if a spring had ejected him. "I need to go check on my place. Linda. Will you be okay for a while?"

"I'll be okay, period. Whoever it was won't be back tonight. Get going."

Jeff and Randy and two others were playing cards in the break room, finished with the attempted arson call and feeling pretty good about themselves. Other firefighters were bunked out upstairs. The break room was on the small side, with a long bench table where firefighters could eat. Painted white, with a black tile floor, it was cozy only in size. Nearby was a small kitchen where they took turns cooking.

Cans of pop sat on the table along with a bag of chips. The cards were well used, and there was a lot of joking about whether they were marked.

"Did you see that woman in the suit?" Randy asked one of the other firefighters, a solid wall of a man named Ken Banister, who was assistant to the chief.

"Yeah, when she came in yesterday. Think the chief's got a thing going?"

Donna walked in. While her job usually required her to work daytime hours, she often dropped by during slow times to hang with the team, all of whom were friends. "What makes you think he's got a thing? She said she was only going to be here a few days. After this arson attempt where she's staying, she'll probably be on the next plane out."

Randy hooted. "We all know you make eyes at the chief."

Donna reddened angrily. "I do not! Besides, the man doesn't date. Not once since his wife left."

Jeff shook his head. "He dated tonight."

"Coffee at Maude's is hardly a date," Donna pointed out.

Ken laughed. "Got anything better to offer a woman around here? Maude's, the movies, Mahoney's bar. The Three *M*s."

"Makes it hard," Randy agreed. "My current girl is always complaining. I tell her we could go camping."

That set off another round of laughter.

Donna watched them, a faint smile on her lips. "If I were you, I'd be more concerned about the upcoming budget cuts. You might be looking for work."

Groans answered her. They were having fun and didn't want to get serious. Only Randy looked disturbed by what she said.

"This happens every couple of years," Ken remarked, eyeing Randy. "We never get anything essential cut and you know it, Donna."

"They sound a whole lot more serious this time." Donna sauntered over to the table. "Deal me in, guys. I'll show you what a *real* woman can do."

Chapter 4

Morning brought gray skies, and the weather forecast tiptoed around the possibility of rain later in the afternoon.

Wayne had found no sign of trouble around his house, but as Linda was leaving for school he warned her to be careful.

She looked at him oddly, with her mother's dark eyes. She was a lovely young woman, starting to lose the youthful roundness to a clearer bone structure in her face. With each change, Wayne felt the impending loss. Someday she'd be leaving for good to start her own home.

"What's going on, Dad?"

"Maybe nothing. You've heard about the fires? That's all. Some lunatic on the loose, so just be careful."

"I always am."

He watched her drive away in his car, then set out

in his official vehicle. For the first time since Lisa left, he had a woman other than his daughter on his mind. Charity Atkins danced around the edges of nearly every thought he had.

He blamed the fascination on her being new around here. Well, that and the fact that she was built to catch a man's eye. But someone fresh always caught attention. All the faces in town were familiar to him, most of them married and all of them friends.

So a new woman, totally new, comes along, and of course he felt a fascination. He knew it could never be more than that, but he didn't mind fantasizing about it. Her leaving was a guaranteed exit point before things got too mixed up.

The most it could ever be was a couple of rolls in the hay, and her own clear reasons for distrusting men only made it better. No strings, no mess, no stupid decisions to be regretted later.

He knew she was attracted to him. Her face revealed very little, but failed to conceal everything. He caught a look in her eyes, and knew. But each time she felt it, he watched her pull back. Good. He got the ego boost without the trouble.

He tried not to think about his ex-wife, told himself the scars were all patched, but sometimes he wondered. They'd been married for thirteen years before she bailed. Thirteen good years, he had thought. Then she'd escaped because life in the boonies was driving her insane?

He still had trouble believing that was the only reason. Glenwood Springs wasn't much bigger, but apparently it had spoiled her for life here, maybe because it catered to tourists. On the surface it had seemed brighter and fresher, unlike Conard City, which was clearly a work-ing town barely hanging on, at least until the ski resort opened this fall. So while she'd never said one bad word about him, except for the hours he worked, he often wondered what else had been going on. She'd left here for Denver, had remarried and took Linda most summers.

He still shook his head over the whole thing. He could empathize with what Charity had said about her job ruining relationships. His job may have been the biggest factor for Lisa. In a big-city department, the chief could often work regular hours behind a desk. Here he was just another firefighter with added duties that ate up time.

But he hadn't been willing to quit. Nor had Lisa asked him to. He gave her credit for that. She had some inkling of the nightmares he lived with, and why he had wanted to work a quieter town.

Not that he wasn't building a whole new set of nightmares, especially lately.

He pulled up to the station and around the outside drive to park in the bay behind the trucks. Everything gleamed from the constant attention. When firefighters weren't at fires or accident scenes, they worked on equipment and their station. Just last spring they'd painted the whole place inside and out.

There had to be some outlet for all that energy.

Which brought him back to the firefighter hypothesis for arson. He hadn't noticed the kind of discontent that would lead any of his team to do something like the Buell place, but he didn't know everything.

The idea that someone who worked for him might be behind this made him feel sick. Really sick.

But that attempted arson at Charity's house bothered him just as much. Sure, it could have been a copycat, a kid who wanted a thrill. Maybe it was a message, never intended to be lit. The message idea nagged at him. What if Charity was right, that someone thought she was a threat?

Scary thought, but it hardly made him feel any better to think bored kids could be getting ideas from the rash of arsons.

He felt pretty grim by the time he'd greeted everyone and entered his office. He glanced at his watch and saw he had twenty minutes before Fred and Charity would arrive. He reached in his bottom drawer and added some more notes to a private file he was keeping on the Buell case. Later, when they'd cleared up the facts as much as they could, he'd enter the salient points to the regular file. But for right now, he didn't want anyone to know their suspicions about how this fire had been set.

It felt odd to be keeping secrets. He never did that. But this time he didn't know whom he could trust, even here at the firehouse. He supposed some of this needed to be shared with the sheriff, but not just yet. First a conversation with Fred Buell.

Donna entered and he flipped the file closed. She put a cup of coffee on his desk. She did that every morning, even though he'd never asked her to. Once he'd even tried to tease her out of it, telling her that she was still a member of the department and he could get his own coffee like everyone else. It was the unspoken sexism that got to him, but he didn't know how to stop her.

"How's the investigation going, Chief?"

"Like every other arson investigation. Nowhere."

She nodded and leaned a shoulder against the wall, folding her arms. "They're tough, all right. You don't think Fred Buell did it, though?"

"Not likely. Unless they were all lying, that family barely made it out. Fred loves his kids."

"That he does." She hesitated. "I saw you having coffee with that arson investigator. I was hoping she could come up with something."

His alert bell started ringing, even though it was a perfectly normal question. Any fireman might have asked it. But after last night, he was worried about Charity, despite her idea that being perceived as a threat could bait the arsonist into making a mistake. He didn't like that plan at all. Maybe if he made her role appear simpler and less threatening word would get around, and she wouldn't get any more messages.

"It was just coffee. Seemed like the neighborly thing to do, seeing as how she doesn't know anyone here. But she's not that kind of investigator anyway."

Donna looked surprised. "What kind is she?"

"The paperwork kind. Not like when we get the state down here. If we ever do. She doesn't solve arsons, she just determines whether the owner or his agent might have been involved."

"Oh." Donna hesitated. "Too bad. I thought you were getting a lot of help finally."

"Not yet."

God, he hated deception. Charity had already helped him immensely, perhaps because she'd seen the investigations of so many fires, maybe because she'd fought them once herself. If she never offered another lick of an idea, she'd offered enough already. Enough to seriously worry him.

"So what's the story on the attempted arson at Hank Jackson's rental?" Donna asked.

"I was just writing it up," he lied with too much ease. "Looks as though some kid got an idea that shouldn't be going around."

She nodded and straightened, evidently getting ready to go back to work. "That's what I heard from the guys.

Just wondered if you thought something different. Need anything, just holler."

"I will," he promised. He wondered if Donna hated being stuck at a desk away from the action, then shrugged the thought away. If she did, she could find other employment, he was sure.

Two minutes later, just as he tucked his secret file away and locked the drawer and was about to start his incident report from last night, Donna entered again. "Insurance adjuster here for the fire the other day."

He stifled a sigh and sat back. "Send him in."

A portly man of about fifty or so shuffled in, his suit looking rumpled. "You need a better motel" were his first words as he stuck out his hand. "Larry Grimes."

Wayne shook his hand and offered him a seat, then accepted the guy's business card. "You're just here for the Mackey fire? Or are you doing Buell, as well?"

"From your report, there's nothing left to assess at the Buell place."

"Nothing."

Grimes shrugged. "Then, I just need to talk to the Mackeys and look at the damage." He pulled out a cell phone and tapped. "Grease fire, right?"

"No question. Hot oil on the stove, and apparently Mrs. Mackey got distracted for a moment. The point of ignition was obvious. They're definitely going to need some help as soon as possible. Mrs. Mackey's in the hospital with third-degree burns. You can probably find her husband there."

Grimes tapped industriously. "What about the infant?"

"Fine, I guess. It was Mrs. Mackey's sister's baby. You'll have to ask them. I don't ride herd on all that. Just fires."

Grimes rose. "Thanks for your time, Chief. If I need any more...?"

"I'm usually here unless there's a fire."

Grimes managed a faint smile. "We both need a life." Then he walked out.

Cold fish, Wayne thought as he pulled the computer keyboard closer. Last night's incident was going straight into the computer files. No need to open a paper one for that. But it was going to stay in his personal memory banks, along with a whole lot of other things.

Charity showed up a couple of minutes early, armed with her laptop. Today she wore a suit again, possibly to appear professional to Fred Buell. He rose and greeted her warmly, shaking her hand, aware that there were eyes everywhere. His secret longings could remain secret, especially from his team. Their coffee date had attracted enough attention. For the first time he felt a pang of sympathy for his ex. Sometimes Conard County felt like an awfully small fishbowl.

She crossed her legs with the sexiest sound of swishing nylon, or whatever they made hose out of these days. He didn't often see them anymore.

Donna immediately popped in with coffee for her. Charity smiled warmly. "Thank you, but you didn't have to."

Donna shrugged. "I'm keeper of the coffee. What can I say? You need more, Chief?"

"I'm fine, Donna. Thanks." When she closed the door behind her, he said, sotto voce, "I've tried to convince her not to bring me coffee."

Charity smiled broadly. "Maybe it makes her feel useful."

"She's already useful. Fred should be here any minute."

"I hope the fund-raiser went well. He's going to need it." She frowned faintly. "I need to talk to you again."

"Away from all this?"

"Let's just say I don't want it getting around. I meant to tell you last night, but then we were avoiding the topic."

"True." He'd been at work for twenty-five minutes and already he was beginning to feel irritated. That wasn't like him. Too much worry? Maybe. "Your adjuster just left a few minutes ago to look at the Mackey place."

"The fire from the other day? Good. No point in keeping people waiting."

"He's not going to look at the Buell fire."

She shook her head a little. "No point in it. I told the company it's a total loss."

"Just as well. I hope he's gentle with the Mackeys."

She regarded him with concern. "Did he say something?"

"I just don't like him. I got the feeling he'd rather be anyplace else on the planet."

"He works out of Casper. This shouldn't be the ends of the earth for him."

"For some it is," he admitted. "Anyway…"

"I'll tell you 'anyway.' If this guy gives the Mackeys any trouble, let me know. Their plates are full enough right now."

He really did like her. He liked her instant concern for people she didn't even know. Too bad she was flitting through like a lovely butterfly. "I also let it be known what your job really is. That you're not here to solve the arson."

She blinked. "I thought we talked about scaring the guy. Why did you find that necessary?"

"Because of a heap of fire-starting materials last night and a question I got this morning."

A slow, warm smile dawned on her face. "You do like to take care of people, Chief. You're a protective man."

He hadn't blushed since high school, but his cheeks warmed a little. He hoped it wasn't visible. "That's the only reason I stay in this job. Helping people. Few enough other benefits."

"And plenty of PTSD," she said, her smile fading and her voice quieting. "Fires, auto accidents… I had enough in little more than a year. I honestly don't know how you guys keep coming to work every day."

He couldn't answer that. Sometimes you just had to do it because it needed doing. Because you could, and a lot of other people couldn't.

A sharp rap on the door and Fred Buell walked in. A man in his midthirties, today he looked a lot older. In less than a week he'd lost enough weight that his jeans bunched under his belt. Wayne rose and made the introductions, then pulled a chair in from the outer office so that Buell could sit. Fred's face seemed frozen somehow, as if it would crack if he tried to smile. A man barely holding it together.

"I ain't got much time," he said. He looked at Charity. "I know it's important, but I have to take care of my herd. If I lose too many of them, I won't be able to feed my babies."

"I'm trying to help with that," Charity said gently. "Really. This isn't a trial and I'm not making any accusations, okay? I just need some help here."

Buell nodded, turning his battered, stained cowboy hat in his hands. "Ain't never seen a fire like that. Heard them damn smoke detectors screaming like mad, me and the wife jumped up and there's fire some places on the ceilings. On the ceilings, by God! Grabbed the kids, ran down the stairs and got the hell out the back door. Couldn't get out the front."

"Why not?"

"Porch was a wall of fire. Lucky we could get out the back." He shook his head. "It's a hard time to give thanks, but I'm giving thanks for my family. A minute or two more and we'd be dead."

Charity's expression had grown grim. "I am so, so sorry."

Buell looked at her. "Got outside and grabbed the hose, but it was too late. Couldn't cool any of it. Didn't even try to save the barn. I could hear them animals screaming..." He looked down.

Both Charity and Wayne remained silent, giving the man some time. Finally he swallowed hard and raised his head again. "What do you need?"

"What kind of smoke detectors did you have?"

"Battery ones. Put 'em in just a month ago. Never thought I'd be so glad."

Wayne's interest perked. So did Charity's, he could see. She spoke. "Any particular reason you put them in?"

"Been meaning to, but you know how that is. Edna started badgering me after them arsons, and I decided to do it. Stopped by here to ask where to put 'em. Donna out front told me every bedroom and downstairs in the kitchen, and at the top of the stairs. She even came out to make sure I done it right. That lady knows her stuff."

"Yes, she does," Wayne said. "It's her job and she does it well. And everyone should have smoke detectors."

"Reckon I know that now." He sighed. "What else?"

"Did you fire anybody in the past year?" Charity asked.

"Nope. Hands come and go. Most rarely stay long enough to screw up."

"Any work contracted out recently?"

"Hailstorm last fall dinged up the siding pretty bad. I hate that metal stuff. Roof was fine, but not the walls. So yeah, we hired someone to do it." He looked at Charity. "You all paid for most of it."

"So lots of strangers on the place?"

"A few. Good workers, though. Had to send them home at dusk to get some peace so the babies could settle."

"No other strangers?"

He shook his head.

Charity smiled gently at him. "Just one more question. How often are you and the entire family gone from the ranch?"

"Every Sunday morning. That's it. Sometimes I'm out on the range, and once in a while the missus will take the kids into town. Can't say it's regular or nothing. She usually does the shopping on Saturdays because she can get me to watch the kids. Or Sunday after church we all go." He shook his head again. "You can't leave a ranch alone for long."

"I don't suppose so. I think that's it," Charity said. "I appreciate your time."

Buell looked straight at her. "You don't think I done it, do you?"

She shook her head. "No, sir, I don't. But I need just a little more for my report. How can I contact you?"

"Chief here knows the Lockes, my wife's sister. Me and the family are staying with them. I won't be around except in the evenings."

"Do you mind if I talk with your wife?"

"She's not talking much right now, but sure, give it a try. I gotta get back out there."

A man on a miserable mission, he rose, nodded and left.

Silence hung heavy on the air for a couple of long minutes. Finally Wayne broke it. "You didn't ask him who the contractor was."

"I didn't need to. If my company wrote a check, we'll have the records."

He nodded. "What else?"

"A private conversation."

"How about a walk?"

She shook her head and astonished him by raising one leg and waving her high-heeled pump at him. "Not in these. I'm not crazy."

After all that misery, he was surprised to hear a laugh escape him. "Go home. Change. I'll catch up."

And now a lovely length of leg was branded on his memory, too. Sometimes a guy just couldn't win.

Donna looked up as Charity walked out. "Did you get what you needed?" she asked.

"Most of it. A few more things to look into."

Donna bit her lip. "Fred didn't do it," she said firmly.

Charity paused, her hand on the knob of the door that led outside to the street. "Donna, I'm sorry. I can't discuss cases openly."

Donna frowned. "I'm with the department."

"I know, but unless I need to question you about something, I'm limited to talking to the chief, the sheriff and my clients." Charity softened it with a smile. "We all have rules to deal with."

She was glad to see Donna smile faintly. "Guess so."

Charity climbed into her car and drove home. She

could understand Donna's curiosity. The whole town
was probably waiting to hear what happened to Fred
Buell and whether an unlikable insurance company paid
what it owed. Plus Donna had said Edna Buell was a
lifelong friend.

She was used to it. Most people resented paying for
insurance until they needed it. Year after year those
premium notices would roll in, and then large sums
of money would roll out. And everyone, it sometimes
seemed, had a horror story to tell about an insurance
company.

At home, she powered up her computer and checked
out who had been paid for the Buell siding work. Then
she changed into jeans and a sweater, and pulled out a
light jacket. It was cooler here than Atlanta, and if they
were going to walk, she needed to deal with her thin
Southern blood.

The interview with Fred Buell had really troubled her
that morning. She felt true sympathy for the man and all
the problems he was facing. At least the barn raising Saturday might help him get going again. She wondered just
how fast that might happen. A single weekend? Longer?

She shook her head a little at herself. She had a lot of
experience, but it was of a different kind. Even though
he'd grown up here, Wayne Camden admitted he didn't
know a whole lot about ranching. Separate worlds.

And she needed to remember she came from a very
separate world and had to go back. What had possessed
her to raise her leg that way at Wayne? That went a bit
beyond mere flirtatiousness, and she'd seen the heat in
his gaze. Was she angling for a fling? Thank goodness
she'd glanced out into the bay to be sure no one could
see before she did it.

Why not a fling? she thought. If they went in with

clear ground rules, nobody should get hurt…unless this whole town heard about it. There was that to consider, because Wayne had to live here and had a daughter to think about. Also, she'd never been the type before to want a fling. How would she feel about herself if she did it this once?

Probably pretty good. She giggled to herself. The temptation was huge. The downside minimal, as long as she got through it with some self-respect.

A knock on the door startled her. She hadn't heard a car pull up. When she went to answer it, she found Wayne standing there in jeans and a Western shirt. Mufti.

"Where'd you come from?" she asked.

"When you drive a fire-engine-red vehicle like mine with a light bar, your doings are pretty well tracked," he said wryly. "The car's at my place. Do you want to walk around town or go somewhere else?"

"Aren't you about as recognizable as your vehicle?"

"Probably," he admitted.

"Then, come in. I don't want anyone to overhear. I'll make coffee and I have some fruit I bought yesterday."

"Everybody seems to know everyone's business around here," he remarked as he followed her to the tiny kitchen. "I don't usually mind it, but if you want privacy, good luck."

She laughed. "You've mentioned that before. But just think, everyone knows everything except who's committing arson."

"I know. That grabs you, doesn't it?"

She started the coffeepot, brought out the plastic tray of fruit with some napkins and led him to the living room while the coffee brewed. She devoted a whole ten seconds to drinking him in, then got to business.

"I have a friend who's an arson investigator with the Atlanta fire department. I called him yesterday."

Wayne sat up a little. "And?"

"He thinks the scenario we worked out is possible. And frankly, he called it terrifying. He asked that we not publicize it."

Wayne shook his head. "No way. Not a word goes past the sheriff."

"Have you talked to him?"

"That was next on my agenda." He slapped his hand on his thigh. "Whoever came up with this is too damn smart. He knows this animal."

Charity understood exactly what he meant. Most arsonists failed at massive destruction because they didn't understand fire well enough. The person who had done this did.

"So we're back to looking at my department."

"Not just," she was quick to say. "For example, there's a man right next door who knows fire, and probably others. You've got a community college, a great place to do research and gain understanding. You have opportunity in the form of the siding crew."

"I noticed that." His expression couldn't have been grimmer. "Do you know who they are yet?"

"Masters Construction."

His head jerked a little bit. "Luke's not the type. No way."

"He doesn't have to be the type. Somebody he hired is enough. Then my friend said something else. He said this guy had to have tried it out first. We need to be looking for where he practiced this method."

"How could anyone…" He stopped. "I'll try to avoid the stupid questions here. Okay, let me think."

She ached for him. She hardly knew him, yet she

could sense how troubled he was. This was his community, he'd undertaken to protect his neighbors, he seemed
to know most of them and he cared about them. Now
here he was, watching something ugly creep through
the community he had devoted himself to serving. That
had to hurt.

She rose and went to get the coffee, returning quickly
with two full mugs to find Wayne pacing the tiny living
room. He accepted the cup with thanks, sipped some and
continued walking in tight circles. The man was wired.

Not that she blamed him. She was a little wired, too,
and she didn't have a personal investment of any kind
here.

He waved his free hand. "Thousands and thousands of
empty square miles out there. And that's just this county.
Neighboring counties are about the same. There are line
shacks everywhere."

"Line shacks?"

"From back in the days when cowboys rode the range
all the time. It was a place to stay at the end of the day,
closer than riding back home. Some are still used, some
aren't. Point is, you could probably find more than one
isolated enough to practice some arson on, and if you've
got a couple of good extinguishers, you'd probably never
be found. Smoke might be noticed, but if it goes away
quick enough, everybody shrugs and thinks a neighbor
was burning something. As long as you keep control, it
might be years before anyone discovered the damage."

"And it doesn't even have to be in this county."

"No."

"Great," she said. She sat on the edge of the couch
and stared into her coffee mug. This was way beyond
her purview and her training, hunting for an arsonist.
Her mandate was to investigate the client, a long way

from a manhunt, usually. And always with all kinds of official resources to help.

The picture Wayne painted was dismal. At this point she could justifiably notify her company that the arson wasn't related to the owner and close the file. Nagging questions remained, but they didn't seem to point to Buell.

Right or wrong, however, somehow she had gotten more wrapped up in this. Fred Buell had touched her. Wayne had touched her even more. He was a man facing an impossible task, and the state couldn't even send him a trained investigator. The need to help in any way she could overpowered simple sense.

He stopped pacing and looked at her. "You could close this now, couldn't you?"

"What makes you say that?"

"I saw the way you looked after you talked to Buell. You don't think he had any part in this."

She hedged. "I still need to talk to his wife. To make sure the stories mesh."

He shook his head. "Charity..."

She decided she didn't need to be cagey with him. This guy was dealing with enough troubles given all the arson. "Honestly, no. I don't think he did it. I'm going to close the file as soon as I talk to Mrs. Buell."

"Then you can get out of here."

"No."

He simply stared at her, as if trying to puzzle it out. "This isn't your problem once you close the case. You should clear out before someone tries to burn your house down again."

"I'm not leaving." She bit her lip. "Don't ask me why, but this case is different. I don't know how much I can help you, but I'm going to try. I'll take some vacation and hang around. If you can stand me."

He shook his head a little and sat beside her on the couch. "The firefighter in you waking up?"

"Maybe. Or maybe I'm watching you worry about a whole bunch of people you want to protect but can't, and I talked to a rancher today who looked gutted but is giving thanks his family is okay. Call me a bleeding heart."

His thin mouth curved slightly. "I like your bleeding heart." Then the phone on his belt buzzed.

He blew air between his lips. "Never an uninterrupted conversation…" He put it to his ear. "Chief Camden."

He listened, then said, "On the way." He disconnected and stood. "Fire out at another ranch, partly contained. Wanna suit up?"

She drove him to his house to pick up his car. Unsure why he'd asked her along, equally unsure why she was going. Curiosity? Or an old instinct that hadn't died? A few minutes later they raced down quiet streets to the station. The trucks had already departed.

Charity waited in the car while Wayne ran inside. She was surprised when he reappeared wearing a turn-out suit but carrying another one. "What's the extra suit for?" she asked as they zoomed away.

"That's for you."

Her heart slammed. "Chief, it's been too long now. I can't fight a fire."

"Not asking you to. It's just protection if you need it."

Other thoughts roiled in her head. "Who'll be in charge of the scene until you get there?"

"Ken Banister, my assistant chief. He's good."

"But you still have to go?"

"Damn straight."

She decided to just hush. His face was set, and his mind was clearly on the fire ahead. As they reached the roads outside of town, they hit speeds that were close to the edge. She felt a surge of adrenaline, the excitement she used to feel as a volunteer. It ramped her up, stilled everything else and focused her tightly. Was it possible she missed this?

"We don't get this many calls in a month of Sundays," he announced angrily over the sounds of his siren.

She couldn't think of a response to that. Besides, she was sure it was an exaggeration brought on by his worry about the ranch and about another arson. Every place had fires, big and small. A bit of carelessness, a short in the wiring, a space heater placed poorly... Causes for fires practically grew on trees. They might get fewer of them here than some places, but fire was an inescapable beast. Man's best friend, yet his worst enemy.

And this was no time to be getting philosophical.

They caught up with the trucks about five miles out of town. These distances must be maddening for fire-fighters, she thought. All the time they were traveling, a fire was burning.

"These distances must be frustrating."

"No point in thinking about it. Work the problem. That's all we can do."

He was used to it, but she wasn't. Minutes were crawling by and she was mentally on the edge of her seat, a silent timer running in her head. Ranchers were prepared; she knew that. They might arrive and find nothing left to do but cool down the scene and investigate the cause. Still the timer ticked away.

Then she saw the wraith of dark gray smoke in the distance. She caught her breath as she caught sight of a second one. Not good. Two fires? Or the ends of one fire?

They careened around a corner onto a rutted road. Wayne seemed to know the exact capabilities of this vehicle. The fire trucks ahead lumbered; however, keeping them from going any faster.

She settled fully into the zone. Approaching a fire, ready for just about anything, full of enough adrenaline to keep her sharp, if not always careful.

They roared through a ranch yard, past the house toward the smoke. At last they pulled up on some pastureland, where a shed was being doused by the rancher. Men leaped off one of the trucks and began unreeling hoses almost before the trucks fully stopped.

Wayne climbed out, saying shortly, "Suit up. It's in the grass."

From where she sat, she couldn't see that, but she obeyed. Climbing out, she pulled on the turnout pants, adjusting the suspenders with practiced ease. Her shod feet jammed into boots quickly. The jacket slid over her shoulders with the weight of years past. She grabbed the helmet with a faceplate to protect her eyes from cinders and slipped back in time to another period in her life.

Fifty pounds of heavy equipment. Hot already. She wasn't used to it anymore. She shuffled a few steps over the uneven ground until she felt a little more at home and rounded the truck.

The fire had spread from the shed out along a fence line where a lot of tumbleweeds had caught. Apparently the tumbleweeds blazed fast enough and hot enough that there was now a line of ashes and then fire stretching far out onto the prairie. Old wood fence posts had ignited as well, and flames still licked some of them.

Suited or not, she had the sense to stay out of the way. She was rusty now, and besides, this was clearly a well-oiled team. One of the trucks raced down to the far end,

almost beyond sight, where more tumbleweeds were beginning to burn. So far the green spring growth hadn't
caught, but if the fires burned long enough, it could des-
iccate and ignite, too.

She hung back while Wayne took over direction of
the scene. She watched as they turned the shack into
sodden ribs of wood, but the work on the fire line was
more interesting. The trucks rode along from both ends,
using water cannons the entire length of the fire, while
the remaining firefighters walked behind with shovels,
checking for embers, turning a lot of earth.

"How come you're not working?"

She turned and saw the rancher, dusty and sweaty and
smeared with soot. Apparently he'd stepped back from
his efforts to let the pros take over.

"I'm not a firefighter anymore," she answered. "I'm
just observing. What happened?"

"Danged if I know. It's just a shed and I haven't used
it much since I got that steel barn. I was thinking of tear-
ing it down before one of the kids got hurt in it. They like
to use it for a fort, but rusty nails are starting to poke
out everywhere. Off-limits now. Anyway, it wasn't a big
deal until that tumbleweed caught fire. I guess I waited
just a little too long to get rid of it."

"I guess," she said. "How *do* you get rid of it?"

"Me and the hands burn it. Got a big concrete box behind the barn for stuff like that." He shook his head. "I
really need my butt kicked. Guess I got the kick."

He wandered off toward the house where she could
see a woman and three children standing on the porch.
At this distance, she couldn't tell their ages, but guessed
them to range from about eight into the young teens.

Prime suspects, she thought with grim amusement.
She'd almost bet that when Wayne started poking in that

shack, he was going to find matches or a lighter. Fooling around. The kind of fooling around that led to a lesson well learned...unless there was an incipient firebug in the group.

With all hands helping, the fire was soon out. Part of the rancher's fence was gone, too, but she suspected he dealt with that kind of problem on a regular basis.

Wayne left his crew, pulling off his helmet and tugging down his Nomex hood. He walked straight over to the family on the porch, and Charity, ignoring her own discomfort, moved close enough to overhear without being obvious. If she held her head the right way, the helmet acted almost like an amplifier.

"So," said Wayne, "if I go into what's left of that shed and look around, am I'm going to find signs that someone was playing with fire?"

The youngest spilled the beans instantly. "It was Brad. He wanted to make some s'mores."

Problem solved, Chastity thought. Concealing a grin, she headed back to the car and gratefully shed the turnout suit. The smell of wet ash stung her nose.

The fresh breeze felt good on her overheated and damp skin, a relief. She noted how quickly the firefighters did the same, removing their extraneous gear before making another check along the fence line.

Gradually the scene slowed down. Then one truck pulled out for town. The other remained. She stood alone by the car, realizing how much she missed the camaraderie after a fire, even more than she missed the adrenaline rush that went with it. Maybe she'd quit volunteering too soon.

Pointless thinking, though. She'd moved into another field, one that helped solve fires, one that often rescued insured people from the terrible results of accidents. Sometimes ordering a check to be issued felt a lot more helpful than running through a house with an axe ever had.

Of course, there was that time she'd saved a litter of kittens... A smile danced across her face at the memory. She'd never been at a scene where they saved a human life, but she hadn't volunteered for long. She'd known plenty of other firefighters who'd helped rescue people. Smoke detectors, though, had reduced the risk of death.

But kittens didn't know what that shrieking meant, and a scared momma cat could often take them to the wrong place trying to make them safe...until it was too late.

"Smiling?" Wayne asked as he joined her.

"Something made me think of a litter of kittens I rescued once way back when. So the kids did it?"

"Yeah." He doffed his gear into the back of his vehicle then they slid in. They weren't far down the road before he remarked, "I don't know who Les is angrier at, himself or his kids." He shook his head, still smiling faintly.

"Is school out today?" It was, after all, Thursday. Three kids could get up to a lot on a day off.

"They're homeschooled, but that didn't have anything to do with it. A pure craving to amuse themselves during some free time. Apparently they thought they'd put the fire out."

She smiled and shook her head. "Not quite."

"Evidently. Sometimes I think every kid needs to play with fire at least once. Most are simply lucky."

She grabbed the grip over the door as they hit an especially deep rut. "I was amazed by that tumbleweed," she said. "I've never seen anything like that."

"It was something, wasn't it? It's not usually a big problem because when it catches on a fence, there isn't a handy ignition source most of the time. Ranchers clear it out, of course, but it's not a huge priority unless there's a high fire danger. This was in a class by itself, though. That fence was buried in the stuff. Maybe from the high winds we had last month. Anyway, if the shed hadn't caught fire, it'd still be sitting there doing no real harm until he could get around to it. As it is, that stuff burns hot and fast."

She nodded. "I saw. Almost as bad as a dried-out pine."

"Close."

They reached the smoother county road, ending the bumpy ride. Charity cracked her window, enjoying nature's air conditioning. "I loved the way you walked up to those kids and questioned them. Once you asked them what you'd find, it was all over."

He laughed. "I try not to leave a whole lot of wiggle room. It saves time, and with kids, why prolong the agony for them? They knew they were in hot water. They were just wondering if anyone would figure it out."

She joined his laughter. "One of them would have let it out sooner or later."

"They usually do." He was still smiling as they drove along the road back to town at a saner speed this time. "So how did it feel to suit up again?"

"Is that why you asked me to ride along?"

He glanced her way, the corners of his eyes crinkling. "There's a lot bad to say about this job, but there's a lot more good. I figured you might be getting a little itchy to try it on again."

"I didn't do anything, kind of a fifth wheel. And I

didn't want to get in the way. Your people clearly know what they're doing. But suiting up again… It felt weird."

"Good or bad weird?"

She thought about it for a second. "I wish they'd come up with a more comfortable turnout suit. I know it's probably impossible, but all that insulation against the fire holds body heat in and it's awful."

"Can't argue with that."

"And it's heavy. I wasn't even in full gear and I felt as though I'd better get back in shape."

He laughed again then eyed her. "Nothing wrong with your shape."

She shook her head grinning. "Watch it, Chief. As for my shape, the other kind, I've never forgotten how heavy that equipment is, but I sure noticed I'm not used to carrying it anymore. Other than that… I got my adrenaline rush, I wanted to dive in and help, and I met all the old feelings that kept me doing it for over a year."

"Yeah?"

"Yeah." She leaned her head back, letting the breeze blow over her face from the cracked window. "It was great. Thanks. I tasted the rush again."

He was silent until the town began to rise on the horizon. "Now I'm in for it."

"In for what?" She turned her head to look at him.

"Bringing you along is going to make mc the butt of endless jokes and even a few questions about whether I'm thinking about hiring you. Heck, you might even hear some of it, too."

She hesitated before asking, "Can I hang around after we get back?"

He shot her a look. "No problem, but why?"

"Because I realized the thing I miss most was the camaraderie afterward."

From the side she saw him smile. "Hang around. I don't have to explain about strutting roosters, I guess."

"And teasing. I've been through it all. Say, is there some place I could pick up some baked goods for the guys?"

Chapter 5

Wayne wondered what was going on inside that woman. Her flirtation, waving her leg at him, had been obvious, but then she'd turned back to serious topics, like the possibility the arsonist had a practice site out there somewhere.

Then she'd decided to ride along with him and suit up. He'd hoped she would, but had expected her to beg off. But no, there she'd been, and she'd suited up, and now she was talking about what she missed about firefighting.

Had he been trying for that without realizing it? Man, he hoped not. This woman had a life elsewhere. He couldn't imagine she'd be happy in this sleepy county away from all the big city lights, and if she thought this many fires was normal out here, she was getting the wrong impression.

As he walked into the bakery with her, it occurred to him that he may have set up some unrealistic expectations. What did he think he was doing here? Yeah, he was attracted to her. Yeah, he could tell she was attracted to him. But attraction wasn't enough.

He'd learned from Lisa that even growing up around here wasn't a defense against the lures of a more populous area. Glenwood Springs had been enough to spoil her for this area, and from here she'd gone to Denver, a much bigger city. How could he expect a woman from a metropolis like Atlanta to want to hang around here?

Clearly he was not thinking with his big head.

"How many guys will there be?" she asked him. Then, without waiting for a response, she bought enough Danishes, doughnuts and cookies for a legion. Melinda appeared more than happy at this unusual purchase and threw in some extra crullers.

"You're going to make my crew fat," Wayne remarked as he helped carry the haul back to the car.

"They can use those treadmills," she retorted cheerfully. "Besides, if they're going to be merciless to you, they deserve the extra workouts."

He was still smiling by the time they got back to the firehouse. The first truck was already being prepped, turnout suits apparently having been checked and put into the laundry to get ready for the next rollout. The second truck still wasn't back, and Wayne knew they were making sure the fire was really out. That thing had been spreading like mad when they arrived, hot enough to leave dangerous coals behind.

Donna was off duty, her replacement for the next four days a mild-mannered older man named Hugh Gallan. Wayne introduced him to Charity.

"Arson investigator from the insurance company on the Buell place," he said. "Charity, this is Hugh Gallan. He's been with the department for nearly thirty years."

"Thirty? Really?" She shook his hand, offering him a warm smile.

"It's a great life," Hugh said frankly. "You go to bed at night knowing you've done some good for the world."

Wayne watched a thoughtful look pass over Charity's face. "Truer words never spoken, Hugh," she said finally.

"Hugh's a font of knowledge," Wayne said. "If there's anything he doesn't know about firefighting, I haven't found it yet."

Hugh grinned almost shyly. "Not true, Chief. I haven't found anything yet that you don't know."

Charity looked between them. "You guys play chess this way?"

Both men laughed.

"Come on, Hugh," Wayne said. "Charity brought a heap of goodies from the bakery. We can hear the alarm in the break room."

Apparently their 911 dispatch was properly set up, Charity thought as she walked back to the break room with the baked goods. The 911 dispatcher, wherever he or she was, would contact the appropriate department, setting off an alarm. A check of the computer or a radio call could get them all the info they needed in an instant. State of the art, and it meant that no one had to stay up all night here.

For such a small operation, this one didn't cut any important corners.

The second truck pulled in, setting off another round of activity. Then in ones and twos the guys began to drift into the break room. The instant they spied the assorted baked goods, the atmosphere ratcheted up from weary cheer to party mode.

Wayne hung back a little, waiting for the teasing to begin. Leaning against a counter, he folded his arms, smiling faintly as his crew dived into the baked goods. "Charity brought them for you" was all he said. The worst was yet to come. Or maybe not; maybe they'd restrain themselves in front of Charity because she didn't know them. She perched at one end of a bench, a leg tucked under her, and delicately ate a cruller. Fresh coffee had been made to wash down the goodies.

But something had shifted. They might not know Charity, but they zeroed in on her in a friendly fashion. She had turned out with them.

"So what did you think about wearing all that gear?" Hal Leas asked. Powdered sugar clung to one corner of his mouth.

"I think I need to get back in shape," she said honestly, but with a little laugh. "It's been five years since I wore that gear. I didn't even have the full turnout on and I was wondering if you guys had added lead to the pockets."

That brought a round of laughter, but nobody had missed the reference. Questions immediately bubbled around the table. Had she been a firefighter? For how long? Why had she left? Did she want to come back?

Well, thought Wayne, she'd gotten the camaraderie she had wanted. Knowing that she had once been a firefighter brought her right into their circle. Charity answered their questions easily and asked a few of her own. Circle closed.

Wayne slipped into his office to call the sheriff on the landline. With everyone laughing and talking in the break room, now would be a good time to get a few minutes.

He was put through to Gage immediately. "What's up?" Gage asked. "Don't tell me that fire that had you screaming out of here a couple of hours ago was arson."

"No, careless kids. But I want to talk to you about the Buell fire."

"Shoot."

"Charity Atkins talked to an investigator in Atlanta to try out a theory we had. I don't want to talk about it just yet, but the guy did suggest something interesting. He said that to carry off a fire of this kind successfully, he had to have practiced somewhere."

Gage fell silent, but even over the phone Wayne could hear Gage drumming his fingers. The first word that broke the silence was a curse, followed by, "One you wouldn't have been called to, I take it."

"Obviously. I'm thinking abandoned line shacks somewhere. If the arsonist kept it under tight control, smoke might have been noticed, but everyone who saw it would think it was a routine burn, especially if it didn't spread, and we weren't called."

"Got it," Gage answered. "You just put a helluva task on my lap. But I don't have to tell you that."

No, he didn't. They were both aware of the wide-open miles around them, the unlikelihood that even if they questioned people they would recall having seen smoke in the distance at this late date. Sooner or later someone might notice one of their long-unused structures was burned, but who knew when that might happen.

"All right, we'll keep an eye out, but I guess this has to be confidential. I don't imagine we want our arsonist to know we're looking farther afield."

"That's the thing, isn't it? I'm feeling boxed in, Gage. And that little display at Charity's place is bugging me. Why would anyone go for her?"

"Hank Jackson could have been the target, but damned if I can see any reason he would be. Or it could be kids."

Wayne couldn't deny the possibility, although something about the way it had been set up disturbed him. Whoever had done it had understood the importance of fuel in addition to the accelerant.

"Let me think on this," Gage said. "Say, is Ms. Atkins doing more than just clearing the table for her company?"

"Between you and me, yes. But I put it out there that she's a paperwork type of investigator."

"Good. I'm still trying to get you a state investigator. I figure they'll get so sick of my calls they'll get us one."

"I hope so." But it didn't seem so important now. With Charity having worked out a likely formula for the fire and Gage keeping an eye out, he was past wondering what an official investigator could tell him.

But he was worried about Charity. Her determination to stay might be putting her in harm's way. As much as he tried to make her seem unthreatening to an arsonist, there was no guarantee it would be believed.

At an impasse and hating it, he returned to the break room, aware that his absence would be notable if it extended too long. Charity was right about the camaraderie, but it had to be nurtured like anything else.

He walked in to a surprise: the crew were trying to persuade her to join them in a training exercise next week. What the…?

Charity was laughing and shaking her head. "No fair," she said. "I haven't been in training. You'd probably have to drag me around before long. Or I'd screw everything up for you."

"Hey, we get lots of newbies for training," Stan argued. "You're not quite a newbie. I mean, like, we don't have to explain to you how to navigate through smoke. Or how scary it can get. You wouldn't panic on us."

To his surprise, Charity looked tempted, really

tempted. "It's been a long time," she repeated. "Let me think about it. So you guys have a state-of-the-art training facility?"

"Well, I don't know if it's state-of-the-art," Ken answered. "But these days we don't have to wait to burn down a building someone wants to get rid of."

Charity nodded. "I knew you guys looked good when I watched you. Tip-top."

Which made more than a few male chests swell. Wayne wondered what was going on here. Men responding to a beautiful woman who understood what they did? Probably. He'd heard that before his time Donna had had some trouble breaking into this department. Guys generally didn't like girls in their clubhouse. But Donna had breached the wall through sheer determination, and maybe it had stayed down for good.

"So how long are you going to be in town?" Bill Husted asked.

"Not too much longer, unfortunately. I'm almost done clearing the Buell fire. After that, they'll send me someplace else."

"You ought to stay here," Randy Dinkum said. "Then you can complain like my girlfriend that there's nothing to do around here."

Everyone laughed and Randy got a few playful punches. "Just sayin'," he answered good-naturedly. "Shoulda dated Donna."

Ken laughed. "She'd wipe you off her boots, man."

Wayne's cell phone rang and once again he slipped from the break room to his office. It was his daughter, Linda.

"Hey, Dad," she said brightly, "I'm making dinner tonight and invited Jeremy over. That okay?"

"As if I have any choice when you already invited him?"

She laughed. "You don't like him."

"Do, too," he answered truthfully. Jeremy was the least of his worries about his daughter.

"Anyway, I wanted to know if you're going to be home so I know how much to cook."

"If you cook for Jeremy, you cook for an army." That kid was lean as a sapling but could eat like a lineman. "Hey, Lindy, can I bring a friend, too?"

A moment of silence. "For real?" Then she squealed. "Go, Dad!"

"You don't even know who it is."

"Female?" she asked, a teasing note in her voice.

"Yeah. Colleague."

"Female's enough. Bring her."

He wanted to roll his eyes when he disconnected. Linda had been pushing him to date for the past couple of years, but he just hadn't been interested. This wasn't a date anyway. Just a courtesy to a stranger in town.

Who the hell did he think he was kidding? Himself, of course. Never a wise thing to do.

Sighing, he returned to the break room to consider just how much folly he was in danger of committing.

Donna had appeared. Wayne smiled inwardly at the sight of her. He had more than one person who couldn't stay away from the firehouse during break, especially when there'd been a fire. She was getting all the details on today's activity while enjoying a cookie.

Again he hung back a little, watching. Because no matter how hard he tried, he was suspicious right now. Firefighter arson accounted for less than 2 percent of all arsons, but rural departments were the usual source, and boredom the usual cause. He had young guys who might have been getting bored.

So he kept a watchful eye for anything that didn't seem right, as much as it pained him. So far nothing had tripped any triggers in the back of his mind, but that didn't mean anything. Right now not one of them had a cause to complain about boredom. Three fires in little more than a week? Around here, that was a lot of action.

But the knowledge of the arsonist troubled him, too. He was as aware as anyone of how much you could learn online these days, and with a few practice stabs someone could have figured how to burn the Buell place that way.

And that didn't seem like a firefighter to him. Rarely did a firefighter ever set a blaze in an occupied building. Fred Buell and his family had escaped by the skin of their teeth.

"So how much longer are you gonna be here?" Donna asked Charity.

"Not long. I'm winding down."

Donna looked satisfied at that answer. He'd overheard occasional teasing that she was sweet on him, but he'd never seen any sign of it himself. As the only woman in the department, Donna was on the firing line for that sort of thing.

But finally Charity rose and announced that she needed to get back to her paperwork.

"What about the training session next week?" Randy asked.

"I don't know," Charity answered. "I might be headed back to Atlanta by then. I appreciate the offer, though."

"Keep it in mind," said Ken. "It's on Monday."

Charity nodded, smiled and waved to everyone.

Wayne straightened. "I'll drive you."

"Not that far, Chief. Hoofing it won't kill me."

"I'll take you anyway. I need to get something from home."

That caused a few knowing hoots, but he ignored them. Donna remained placid, her face revealing nothing. Okay, then. The rumors were probably just that.

"So what's up?" Charity asked as they wound through the streets to his home to pick up her car. She was capable of walking the few blocks, and it was a beautiful day, although clouds had begun to move in. She'd enjoyed her time with the firefighters, getting her dose of the camaraderie she'd missed. The surprising thing was how easily they'd welcomed her. She'd half expected a roasting, but they hadn't given her one. Maybe people here had better manners, at least with a stranger.

"To start, my daughter has invited you to join us for dinner. She's having her boyfriend over and was glad that I wanted to bring you. Are you on?"

Meeting his daughter? She should have shied away, because getting deeper into the growing quicksand with Wayne was clearly not wise. Yet she was curious about Linda and his home life. She could have groaned at herself. "That could be fun," she said cautiously, still hedging.

"It might be a little tense. Jeremy is new in Linda's life and he gets as stiff as a recruit in basic training around me."

She laughed. "Been there, done that."

"Haven't we all at one point or another? When I first started dating my ex, we were both seventeen and her father terrified me. I think he got a kick out of it."

"Entirely possible." So, high school sweethearts? She wanted to know more about that, but didn't want to pry into potentially painful places.

"Dinner?"

"Yes," she said, giving in to her impulse. A plane flight in her near future was beginning to look like her last lifeline.

"Great." He flashed her a smile that faded rapidly. "I talked to Gage about the possibility that someone practiced on abandoned properties for the Buell fire."

"That must have made his day. He's not going to share that, is he?" Mark Vincent had been very clear about not spreading ideas.

"No, he gets it. Now he's wondering how to check out possibilities without leaking anything."

Relief filled her. "I wouldn't be surprised if Mark, my investigator friend, sets up a similar fire to check it out. This is a new one. At least it's new when it's done on purpose."

"I know. Charity..." He hesitated. They weren't far from his house now.

"Yes?" she asked finally.

"Are you coming or going?"

The question nearly stunned her. The rules of engagement were clear. He knew that. Her job was back in Atlanta and her stay here would be necessarily brief. But her heart skipped a few times, and a dead hope sparked. "Meaning?" she managed to ask, although it was suddenly hard to drag in air.

"You keep telling everyone you'll be leaving soon, but you kind of told me you wanted to hang around. Which is it?"

"In theory I should leave as soon as I talk to Mrs. Buell," she said, aware of a heaviness inside her.

"In reality?"

"In reality I want to hang around. I still want to do more work on this arson, for one." She realized she'd just given him a huge opening. She was relieved when he didn't ask her other reasons, because she wasn't at all sure she could have explained. All she knew was that in a couple of short days she was developing an attachment to this town and to Wayne.

He pulled up into his driveway, and she prepared to climb out and get her own car. Just then a young woman in jeans and a T-shirt bounced out of the house, smiling broadly and waving.

The spitting image of her father, Charity thought as she climbed out. A beautiful young woman on the cusp of life. "Hey," the girl said, "you must be Dad's colleague."

Ignoring her father, she came straight to Charity. "He has good taste in colleagues. I was expecting squat and square with bad skin."

Charity couldn't help but laugh. "You look a lot like your dad. And he couldn't help it. My company sent me out here."

Wayne rounded the front of his truck, smiling faintly. "Behave, Lindy."

"I am behaving," the girl said cheerfully. "I complimented your colleague."

Charity wondered if she heard a slight emphasis on the word *colleague*. Maybe. "I'm Charity Atkins. Just Charity. And you're Linda, right?"

"None other. Say, why don't you come in and keep me company while I cook. Dad always has some other place he needs to be, but it would be fun to gab with you."

"Am I being sent away?" Wayne pretended to complain. "And Charity was saying something about needing to work…"

"Work can always wait a few hours," Linda said decisively. "It doesn't go away, you know." She eyed her father significantly.

"And some doesn't wait, as well you know, Lindy."

"Firefighters," she drawled, then grabbed Charity's hand. "Say you'll stay."

Charity couldn't resist. This girl was a pistol. "I'd love to."

Suddenly she felt as if she was being watched. Turning, she saw a car moving slowly down the street. Probably someone just checking out the stranger in town. She was turning away as she recognized the driver. Donna. The woman smiled and waved as she drove by. Charity waved back.

"I'll be back soon," Wayne said. "Assuming something else doesn't catch fire."

The house was warm and welcoming inside, a cozy place full of color and cheer and smelling wonderfully of roasting chicken. Clearly not a bachelor pad. Linda led her into a surprisingly spacious kitchen, and offered her a stool at the central island.

"What can I do to help?" Charity asked immediately.

"Just keep me company," Linda replied. "I like to talk while I cook. I don't get the opportunity often."

"Your dad works long hours, huh?"

Linda smiled and shrugged. "He has to. What he does is important. Besides, these arsons have him really on edge and I can't blame him. One of the Buell kids is a freshman, and I talked to him about it. That was a heck of a terrifying experience for all of them. He kept saying the ceiling was on fire."

"I heard," Charity said. "I talked to Mr. Buell."

Linda reached for a bowl that appeared to be full of lumpy flour. "I hope you like biscuits."

"I love them."

"Roast chicken, cream gravy, vegetables and biscuits." She laughed. "Dad says Jeremy eats like a linebacker. I guess he's right because I always need to cook like a crowd is coming."

"That sounds delicious. Already it smells wonderful."

"I love the smell of roasting chicken," Linda confided. "Or browning pork. I'm not so keen on beef, though, so I make Dad grill it outside when we have it."

Charity felt herself grinning.

"So you like my dad?" Linda asked.

Charity nearly froze. She hadn't expected such bluntness from this young woman. "I, um, well, I only got here a couple of days ago."

"It doesn't have to take long," Linda said with the wisdom of inexperienced youth. "You married or divorced?"

"No."

At that Linda frowned. "Guys must be all over you. You gay?"

That startled Charity into a momentary silence. She'd never been asked that before. This girl was blunt to a fault. But those dark eyes, so like her Dad's despite the color difference, were watching her expectantly. "Uh, you'd have to ask my last boyfriend."

Linda giggled. "Okay. None of my business. Dad would kill me if he knew I asked you, so don't tell him. Since Mom left, he's all about work and raising me. I'm leaving for college in August, and I worry about him."

Charity felt she had been caught flat-footed here. How could she respond to that? If Linda thought Charity was the one who would... What? What was Linda thinking? "Where are you going with this?"

Linda shrugged and went to wash her hands before she started kneading the biscuit dough. "I make drop biscuits, not the rolled kind."

"I like them better. More brown."

"Good. Where am I going? I don't know. I think I'm papering my dad with signs that say Eligible Man. Not that it's worked so far."

Charity was touched, but waded in cautiously. "It's hard to get rolling again when you've had a relationship sour."

"Have you?"

"Several. One just a few months ago."

Linda nodded. "What was the problem?"

"My job. I travel too much."

"My dad could say the same thing. The job part, I mean. When Mom left it was all about how boring this town was and how he was always working. I don't get the part about the town. I go spend summers with her in Denver every year, and I just don't get the fascination. Maybe there aren't as many activities here, but I have friends. That seems more important, to me anyway. And I don't get it about Mom. I mean, she grew up here. It's just not that bad."

"It seems like a very nice town."

"It is," Linda said firmly. "Anyway, sometimes I think Dad still wonders if something else was going on."

How awful, Charity thought. Her breakups had been bad enough, and she'd seen them coming with the increasing complaints about her frequent traveling, how it was impossible to make any plans and so on. How much harder it must have been coming from the mother of your child, someone you'd been with since high school.

If Charity sometimes wondered if her breakups had been about more than her job, how much more must Wayne wonder?

Linda began to drop sticky dough onto the baking

sheet. "I hope Dad's not late," she said in the tone of one who was used to it.

"His hours must be hard on you, too."

"Not usually. He made a point of being here more often when I was younger. And lately is no real example. I think I leave him in the lurch more often than he does me."

Another sad comment in a different way, Charity thought. "A girl has to have a life."

Linda looked up with a grin. "You got that right. You'll like Jeremy. I just wish he didn't get so nervous around Dad. I mean, Dad's an okay guy and he's never hard on my boyfriends. Well, except once. When I was fifteen I started hanging out with this guy my dad really didn't like."

"So what did he do?"

"Asked a million questions. The guy didn't like feeling as if he was under a microscope."

Charity smiled. "How did you feel?"

"Mad at first. It turned out Dad was right, though. Tom had never been in trouble that I knew of, so Dad must have heard something or smelled something. Who knows? Tom's in jail now and Dad was right."

Close call, Charity thought. And Wayne sounded like one great father. Apparently work didn't keep him from paying attention to what was going on at home.

And just listening to Linda spoke highly of Wayne's parenting skills. To be fair, she added his ex to the good-parent list, since the woman took her daughter every summer. A well-adjusted young woman chatted with her while making dinner and expressing her love for her father in multiple ways, including admitting he had been right about one of her boyfriends. Charity figured that was all pretty cool.

But Linda was worrying about her father's future. That touched her. Instead of being selfish in some way, she truly wanted Wayne to find happiness. Charity wondered if she would have been as generous at that age.

Deciding they needed to move to safer ground, Charity asked, "Are you excited about starting college this fall?"

Indeed she was. Linda was off and running about how she was going to Boulder, had arranged to room with a friend and was nervous about everything from classes, to homework, to being among so many strangers.

As open as a book, Charity thought as she listened with a smile. Bright, fresh and full of life. It was enough to make even a woman of her age feel old.

Well, not really old, but it got her thinking about Linda's joie de vivre and where she'd left her own. Had it been the boyfriends or the job, or a combination of both, that had left her less than happy with life?

It was definitely something she needed to think about.

The chicken got picked clean, the biscuits disappeared mostly into Jeremy's mouth and Charity enjoyed herself even though Jeremy was pretty quiet, as Wayne had warned her. While not saying much, his expression was friendly and open, and she suspected he'd be totally different if he weren't in terror of the fire chief.

Not that Wayne seemed to be trying to unnerve him. He made a few attempts to draw the young man into conversation, but didn't press him in an uncomfortable way.

Probably no need to, Charity thought. She'd bet Wayne already knew the family and had a fair measure of Jeremy.

He was quick to help Linda with dishes afterward,

and Wayne and Charity found themselves banished from the task.

"Time alone for them," Wayne murmured as they made their way to the living room with coffee. "The less of us, the better."

Charity laughed, suspecting he was right. "There's nothing quite like young love."

All of a sudden his gray eyes seemed to spark. "I wouldn't be so sure of that."

He struck the match as simply as that. In an instant, Charity became intensely aware of her awakening body, of the tingling that sprang to life between her legs. She felt as if every cell in her body was reaching out for this man.

"Don't do that," she said quietly.

His eyes danced. "I didn't do a thing."

"Right," she said sarcastically. If this guy was still mooning over his dead marriage, he showed no signs of it. As for her... Well, she ought to be careful. Only a short time after her breakup with Ted, she might be on the rebound. Hard to tell, except it still hurt sometimes to think of him. Or rather, to think of the way he had rejected her.

Wayne drew the curtains against the deepening twilight. She didn't sit, but walked around the small living room, looking at the prints on the walls. They were inexpensive copies of Monet, Chagall, Van Gogh and even a Picasso pen-and-ink of a toreador and bull. Beautifully framed, though. She mentioned it.

"On the rare occasions when I have time," Wayne said, "I like to work with wood. I made the frames."

"I'm definitely impressed."

He laughed. "Lipstick on a pig?"

She smiled. "Not many of us can own original art.

The frames are a beautiful touch, so no. Don't think of it that way."

He sat at the end of the couch. "Linda's my decorator. I like what she's done."

"She has a good eye." Charity turned slowly, taking in a room that had been filled gently with color and contrast in such a way that nothing overpowered anything else. "In fact, an amazing eye." Especially considering her youth. Teens were wont to overdo everything.

"I think so."

Jeremy and Linda made record time on the dishes and appeared to announce they were going to the movies. "I might be staying with Charlene tonight," Linda said. "I'll call and let you know."

"Okay. Have fun, guys."

"That was a great dinner," Charity called after her.

Linda winked. "The way to a guy's heart and all that." Then she and Jeremy were gone.

Charity turned and saw Wayne sitting with his face in his hand. "What's wrong?"

"Nothing," he said, dropping his hand. "It's just that she's too saucy by far and growing up too damn fast."

"She's sure on the lookout for you."

He sighed, but couldn't quite bury the smile. "She hasn't figured out that trotting various fillies nearby isn't sufficient."

Charity eased onto the far end of the couch. "Then, what is?"

"Friendship. A good person. Someone you can share with. Looks are only part of the package."

"I know," she said, feeling her humor fade a bit.

"Tell me?" he asked.

She shrugged and asked herself why not. As he'd reminded her, what happened here would stay here when she left. Although the idea of leaving was becoming less attractive with each day. "His name was Ted. We were together for nearly a year."

He nodded. "Nice guy?"

"I thought so, at first. And maybe he really is. I don't like jerks as a rule. But after we'd been together awhile he started complaining in little ways about how much I was gone. It wasn't as if he didn't know when we got involved." She shook her head. "I guess it doesn't matter. Actually living it didn't make him happy. I started hearing about how I was never there, we couldn't plan a date more than a day in advance…"

"Dang, I've heard all that," he said.

She glanced his way and saw him looking rueful. Some of the old tightness that gripped her heart every time she thought of Ted eased a little. "Yeah, you probably have. Anyway, it created tension, and finally a blowup."

"What did he do?"

"He worked for a big accounting firm. Not as though we didn't go through months of him never being around during tax season."

He sighed. "But that was different, I take it." He sipped some coffee then put the cup aside. "It's always the other person who needs to change. Never ourselves. The devil's in it when that starts. Any chance of a compromise goes out the window."

"I'm not sure either of us could have compromised without a job change," she admitted honestly.

"And you love your work?"

"It makes me feel good. Mostly. It's sometimes boring, and sometimes fascinating. But am I wedded to it?" She shrugged. "I honestly don't know. If something else came along that I really liked, I could change. So far nothing has. But you as much as said you're wedded to what you do."

"I am," he admitted. "Even my ex understood that. She tried getting me to move to a larger department in a bigger city, so I gave it a shot, but I couldn't bring myself to stay with it. It's not as if Glenwood Springs was a huge town. A little bigger than here, but not huge. I didn't want to do that anymore. While there were lots of things to do because of tourists, and it was beautiful, there was a downside to that. Small department, lots more casualties to deal with. Lots of auto accidents in the canyon, wildfires on the mountains, which are hard to fight because of accessibility. I honestly like the slower pace here."

"Except lately."

"Things come in bunches. Especially arsonists, it seems. Speaking of which, we need to go out to the Buell place for one last lookover tomorrow. The bulldozers will be coming in to clear the barn debris for the barn raising on Saturday. I've persuaded them not to touch the house yet, but I'm not going to hold that back for long."

"No, the Buells need to get going on a new house," she agreed. "We may never catch this guy. And frankly, that terrifies me."

"Me, too," he admitted. "It's one thing to have a stupid arsonist and keep putting out small fires. It's another to have a genius one. One who isn't afraid to kill people."

"I hear you." She sat somberly for a few minutes, then stood. "I guess I need to get back. I still have some paperwork to do. Any chance we can talk to Mrs. Buell tomorrow?"

"I'll give her a call and let you know."

"Thanks. I'll see myself out. And please let Linda know I had a wonderful time. She's a lovely young lady."

He stood, smiling. "I'm pretty proud of her."

Charity could certainly understand why. Still, she felt the emptiness of the house behind her as she departed, and realized she was going back to an emptiness of her own. If she had half a brain, she would have stayed. Or better yet, invited him to come over. It was, after all, what she really wanted: a fling with the fire chief before she went home.

But Linda rose in her mind, and she climbed into her car with determination. She might be leaving Wayne behind in an empty house, but she wasn't leaving any pain behind for him or his daughter.

Wayne watched her go with an ache that was the height of folly. They could flirt a little, but anything more than that might spell trouble for either of them. He knew he was in a dangerous position because Linda would be leaving in a few months. He was acutely aware that he was facing new silences, new gaps to deal with. A new kind of missing and grief.

Grabbing a light jacket, he went to sit on his small front porch. A few neighbors were out taking an after-dinner stroll in the twilight. He waved and chatted with some of them briefly. The Buell fire came up more than once, and he honestly told people they hadn't found out who did it.

Because no one believed it was an ordinary fire. As he chatted with his neighbors, however, he noted that there was an increasing anxiety in some of them. Well, why not? Three arsons in less than a year, and the last one could have killed a family. It wasn't as scary as when they had that serial killer stalking boys, but it was scary in a different way: anyone could be the victim of arson.

He'd bet half of them didn't believe the Mackey fire had been caused by grease.

Then his phone rang. It was Hank Jackson, the guy who was letting Charity stay at his rental house.

"Chief, you better get over here. It's not a fire, but I want you to see anyway. I think we're moving from arson to murder."

Chapter 6

When Charity got home, the house seemed warmer than usual. She checked the thermostat and saw that it had been turned up. Must have bumped it. She turned it down, then settled on the couch with her laptop, logged into the fire department's Wi-Fi and went to finish her investigation into Fred Buell's background.

His credit report showed him with the kind of debt that appeared normal for someone in his business. No new debt that seemed unusual stood out. No police record for any member of the family, unless there was something juvenile. Timely payments with just an occasional tardiness over the past seven years that had been quickly cleaned up. Most people had a little more dirt on their records than Fred Buell or his wife.

So a hardworking man who seemed to do everything right. Why the devil would anyone attack him that way? It seemed personal, as well as deadly, but she couldn't be sure of that. Things could be misleading. He might have just been a target of opportunity, what with that new siding and the people working on the place. She supposed she could get the police to interview everyone Masters Construction had put on that job.

But that was getting out of her line. She had one task and one task only: satisfy herself and her company that Fred Buell hadn't done this or arranged for someone to do it.

Not likely. He wouldn't clear his debts and house his family on the insurance proceeds. To do that, he needed to keep his ranch going. A good thing his neighbors were building him a barn. And she couldn't imagine the cost in lost livestock.

She remembered him sitting there in Wayne's office, twisting his hat in his hands, and didn't think he'd at all looked or sounded like a man who was trying to get away with anything. If he was, he deserved an acting award.

So she'd confirm his story with his wife in a separate interview and then go home.

Amazing how reluctant she was to do that. She had a hankering to stay here, maybe going to the training session with the fire crew on Monday. She had an even bigger desire to find this monster. A whole family could have died.

But she didn't have the resources, she reminded herself. She wasn't a cop. She couldn't even analyze samples and determine what accelerant had been used.

She wasn't that kind of investigator, and for the first time that really bothered her. A glorified paper pusher— that was what she was.

Sitting there in those stark moments of quiet, rubbing her temples a bit to ease a faint headache as the night deepened outside her window, she asked herself just how content she really was. And she remembered how good she'd often felt about herself when she was fighting fires. The feeling that she was really performing a useful service.

Watching those guys twice since she'd come to this town had reawakened a long-forgotten appetite. It wasn't just the excitement, although there was always a certain amount of rush involved in firefighting. But there'd been greater rewards. And, as Wayne had reminded her, ugly times, too. He spoke of bad memories, and she had a few of her own. They didn't keep her up at night anymore, but there had been spells for a few years when memory had overcome her at odd moments, triggered by something seemingly innocent, casting her back into one horror or another.

She'd been lucky, she guessed. She had recovered pretty well, but then she hadn't done it for that long.

Damn, she must be getting tense from all this heavy thinking. Her head was throbbing a bit now, and her stomach felt upset. She probably needed a long vacation, but how much better if she could leave herself at home. She almost laughed aloud at the idea.

She looked up at a sudden sound. Faint but annoying. A definite squeal. Crap, she knew that sound.

Pushing her laptop to the side, she went to find it. Sniffing the air, she couldn't smell any smoke, but she went room by room, checking for fire. Nothing and still the squeal continued. The two detectors in the hallway outside her bedroom and the two in the kitchen remained silent. She didn't bother looking in the basement because that was the worst place to install detectors. They were affected by temperature changes, and the furnace and water heater had to be down there, because she hadn't found them in a closet up here.

Looking up, she realized it came from the attic. It had to. She'd gone through every single room and found nothing, not even the source of the sound.

She hated to bother her landlord, especially since he'd mentioned a new baby, but she had no choice. The squeal was ominous, and needed solving.

Grabbing her jacket and her computer, she went next door and knocked. It took a minute, but Hank Jackson appeared, looking a little tired. A baby cried in the background.

"Colic," Hank said. "Sorry you had to wait, but I was helping Kelly. The baby's been at it for hours."

Charity wished she could tell him to forget it, but this might be as important to him as to her. "I really, really hate to bother you, but there's an alarm squealing in the house. I can't find it. I can't find any fire, either."

A new worry entered his weathered face. He half turned, grabbing a jacket from a peg. "Sweetheart, there's a problem next door. I'll be back as soon as I can."

His wife called back. "As if you being here is going to change one thing." She sounded both frazzled and amused. "Get going, cowboy."

He limped slightly as they crossed the grass back to Charity's place, pulling on his jacket as he did so. "An alarm you can't find?"

"It must be in the attic. I've been everywhere, and it's hard to lose anything in that house."

He gave a short bark of laughter. "True enough. Well, I put a carbon monoxide detector and a smoke detector in the attic when I was remodeling the place. Can't understand why the ones in the bedroom and kitchen wouldn't go off, though. They're supposed to have a feedback."

Which was the best setup possible, Charity thought.

But that was what you'd expect from a fireman. Every detector in the place should be squealing.

He stepped inside with her, and they both stood listening. "Yup," he said. "Attic."

But he didn't head straight for the attic access in the short hall leading to the bedroom and bathroom. Instead, he reached for one of the detectors in the kitchen. He pressed the test button and it beeped. "Fire's okay," he remarked. Then he pressed the button on a different detector. The test yielded no sound.

"Hell," he said. "Go around and open some windows." With that he gave a twist of his wrist and pulled the detector off its base. "Well, ain't this pretty," he said.

Hank climbed up into the attic while they waited for Wayne to arrive. He was just descending as Wayne walked in the front door.

"Well?" Wayne asked. The cool night breeze was blowing through the house, ruffling curtains. Charity shivered.

"Take a look at that carbon monoxide detector on the kitchen table," Hank said.

Charity joined him, knowing what he was going to see. "No battery. So…" He stopped. "Who cut the wires?" He turned instantly to look for the wall mounting and saw more of the same.

Hank joined them, another detector in his hand. "Somebody didn't guess I'd put one in the attic. Almost nobody does that." It had stopped squealing. "I need to see what's been done to the furnace and water heater."

The words chilled Charity even more. A disabled carbon monoxide detector did indeed probably mean someone had messed with the furnace. A silent, odorless killer, without a detector the gas would fill the house, put her to sleep, then suffocate her. The adrenaline rushing through her held her emotions at bay, kept her tightly focused. For now.

Wayne looked at Charity, and she saw that his eyes had narrowed and sparked with anger. "You'll be okay for a minute?"

"Of course," she answered. It would hit her later, she supposed, the fact that someone had tried to kill her. And might have succeeded except for one hypercautious landlord. Right now, numbness filled her. She couldn't even get angry yet.

With the windows open, the house was safe. Her headache and nausea were beginning to vanish, mostly likely because of all the fresh air. At loose ends, she followed and found Wayne and Hank airing out the basement by holding the door open.

"There's a window down there we can open," Hank said. "And a fan I can turn on."

Wayne looked at Charity again. "You should stay back. You've already been exposed, and more of that CO is likely coming up these stairs."

He had a point, and she backed up until fresh air blowing in through the bedroom window reached her. Her blood probably still contained a high level of the poison.

The two men headed down into a small, dank basement. From the head of the stairs she thought it looked more like a root cellar.

One yellow bulb lit it, but the two men picked up flashlights so they could see better. She waited, hating not being able to help, straining her ears to hear anything they might say.

Somebody had tried to kill her. It just didn't seem real. Not yet. But the indisputable evidence lay on the kitchen table with freshly cut wires and no battery.

She heard their voices, but couldn't make out the words. She hoped the fumes weren't thick enough to harm them. Then she felt another strong draft as the basement window opened, and the whine of a fan turned on. Okay.

Finally, cold to the bone, she went to the bedroom and got the comforter off the bed, wrapping it around her shoulders.

She had no doubt what was going on here.

After ten minutes, both men came upstairs. Wayne was saying, "You go home to the baby. I'm going to have the police and sheriff out here. We need some evidence collection."

Charity didn't ask the obvious question. Someone had apparently tampered with the furnace or the water heater as well as the CO detector. Murder, like Hank had said when he called Wayne.

Charity backed away from the door as Hank and Wayne reached the top of the stairs. Together they stood in the hall.

"Well?" Charity asked.

"Exhaust vents were disconnected." Hank looked pretty angry.

Wayne's face appeared even more grim. "It's a good thing you weren't here for long before that attic detector went off." His tone was clipped, almost sharp. "Wanna stay warm in my car while I call the police?"

A burst of resentment broke through Charity's numbness. She ought to be able to help with this. But she couldn't, because she was no longer even vaguely qualified. Just a paper pusher, really.

And she *was* cold. Colder than the breeze blowing through the house. Cold to the depths of her being.

"Thanks," she said finally. Feeling utterly useless,

she let Wayne escort her to his vehicle and turn on the ignition. "It should warm up quickly," he said. Then before he climbed back out, he shocked her by leaning over and kissing her cheek. "We'll get him, Charity. I swear."

She wished she believed him.

Twenty minutes later, the street seemed crowded. The Sheriff's Department had sent a crime scene van and the city police had sent two cars. And fury was at last beginning to bubble inside of her.

She'd come out here for one reason only: to ensure a man got his proper insurance payment after he'd lost everything, to ensure he wasn't involved in the arson. Apparently her presence here scared someone enough that they'd first sent a message with that heap of fuel and gasoline, but now they were frightened enough to try to kill her.

Because there could be no other reason for what had happened in that house. Leaving the CO detectors untouched would have been a warning. Silencing them had been a threat against her life. And it might have succeeded.

She had never thought that her headache and nausea could be coming from carbon monoxide simply because she had seen the house had detectors. But others never felt a thing and simply fell asleep. Either way she'd have been dead by morning except for a landlord who had taken the trouble to install a detector in an unexpected place: the attic. An unoccupied attic rarely got that kind of attention because there was no one up there to be harmed. So most detectors were placed in the living areas. And those had been silenced deliberately.

Nor did she believe this wasn't the arsonist. She hadn't

been here long enough to make anyone want to kill her. Hadn't had the time to anger or worry anyone else.

This guy had to be stopped at any cost. He'd definitely crossed the line, putting himself in a rare class of people who didn't just want the excitement of a fire, but wanted to kill.

The Buell fire had suggested a murder attempt, but there was no way to prove it. The speed with which that house had gone up might not have been intentional. This was intentional.

Another car pulled up. She recognized the sheriff.

Enough of sitting here. Reaching over, she turned off Wayne's engine, grabbed the keys and climbed out, wrapping the blanket around herself once more. Sooner or later fury would make her warm again, but it hadn't yet.

She stepped inside. Techs were examining the disabled detectors. Bright floodlights had been carried down into the cellar, to judge by the light pouring out the cellar door. She quickly stepped aside into the living room as a rubber-gloved tech moved past with a case.

She heard familiar voices in the kitchen and darted in there to find Wayne, the sheriff and a man in a blue police uniform. She edged up to Wayne and passed him his car keys.

Conversation stopped. Finally Wayne said, "Charity, this is our police chief, Jake Madison. Jake, Charity Atkins, the insurance company arson investigator."

Jake immediately smiled. "Nice to meet you. Obviously I would have preferred better circumstances. How are you doing?"

"I'm starting to get very angry."

Without a word, Wayne slipped his arm around her shoulders. "It's hitting," he said. "I thought you were too calm, woman."

Did she imagine the glances passing between the two other men as Wayne drew her against his side? Damned if she cared.

"Adrenaline," she said shortly. "But it works only so long. Do you think you'll find anything?"

"We're sure as hell going to try," Jake said. "We're sending everything to the crime lab, but the prints we lifted are probably all Hanks or yours."

"Why?"

"Because whoever did this was smart."

"Yeah, I've noticed. How did he get in?"

"The window locks can be jimmied from the outside with a spackle knife. All you need is some darkness."

Charity shook her head. "There hasn't been a whole lot of dark time when I haven't been here. And Hank's been keeping an eye out since the arson incident." Then she paused. "He's also dealing with a colicky baby."

"Folks go to work," Gage said. "They come home and focus on dinner. If someone didn't seem out of place… Well, we've got to check sightlines on the window that was jimmied. It might have created more opportunity."

"It wouldn't have taken a whole lot of time to do this," Wayne remarked. "In through a window out of sight, then out the front door as though it was perfectly normal. Who'd be paying attention?"

He paused, then dropped his next words like a stone. "Everyone knows why Charity is here. One of my crew wouldn't have seemed out of place."

The chill returned to Charity, trickling through her like glacial runoff, numbing her anew. She'd been with many of those guys just today. She couldn't believe any of them would have done this.

But maybe it was time to accept it.

* * *

Hank Jackson returned as things were beginning to wind down. "Am I allowed to fix that furnace now?"

Looks were exchanged. "I think we got all we can," Gage said. Jake Madison agreed.

"I'll do it first thing tomorrow," Hank said. "Before the colic starts up again." He looked at Charity. "I'm not sure it's safe for you here anymore."

"Or for you," she said, her lips feeling stiff. "I don't want to bring any more trouble your way. I'm sorry I've caused you this much."

"Hey," said Wayne. "You didn't cause this."

Hank nodded agreement. "I'm not holding you responsible for any of this. We got us a lunatic. The important thing is you being safe."

Agreeing they'd all meet again tomorrow at the Sheriff's offices, the last of them trickled out, except for Wayne.

"You stay at my place tonight," he said. "I'm not letting you out of my sight."

"I seem to be a flash point," she argued. "You have Linda to think about."

"Linda called when I was on the way over. She's going to stay with Charlene tonight. Regardless, if you think I'm going to let you go sit in a cheesy motel room across from a truck stop where anything could happen, you're out of your mind. Pack some stuff. I have a guest room."

The house had grown considerably colder since the furnace and probably water heater were turned off. The windows had been closed, but all that did was remove the outside air from the equation.

She packed quickly, running on automatic, as if she was getting ready to fly home. Leaving nothing behind.

The way, it suddenly seemed, that she had been living her whole life.

* * *

Wayne didn't say anything on the short drive to his house. There was nothing he could say that wouldn't be a useless eruption of fury. Work the problem. His mantra for many years, but it was wearing thin. First the appalling Buell fire and now what was clearly the attempted murder of a woman who was here only to ensure that Buell got his rightful compensation from insurance.

He couldn't for the life of him imagine how she threatened anyone. But he knew one thing for certain—no matter how much he might not want to see the last of her, he had to get her out of here soon.

Like tomorrow.

They reached his house and pulled into the driveway. When he turned off the ignition, neither of them moved or spoke. He felt the withdrawal in her, probably the main reason she wasn't erupting. Wasn't expressing anything, really. Under the circumstances, she seemed too calm.

Not good.

He climbed out and rounded the car to open the door for her. She looked at the open door for a second, then joined him. They grabbed her two suitcases and her laptop case and walked the short distance to his front door. He let them in, waving at her to go first. He grabbed the one bag remaining and followed her in.

"Have a seat somewhere," he said. "I'm going to make you something hot to drink. You look chilled to the bone."

Chilled to the soul more like, he thought. This was a woman who had fought fires and who must have faced other difficulties in life, but this was different. It was not every day that you narrowly escaped being murdered.

And they *were* dealing with a murderer. There was no question in his mind that somehow the arsons and this were linked. There could be no other reason to target this woman. None at all.

When he returned with cups of hot chocolate for them, she was sitting on the couch, still wrapped in the comforter she had taken, her jacket underneath. She stared at the cup he offered her, then blinked and took it.

"You're not okay," he said finally as he sat beside her.

"No, I guess not," she replied, her tone dull. "I feel awfully numb. It's as if everything inside me has just shut down completely."

"It's hard to deal with something like this," he said sympathetically. "Me, I'm mad enough to spit nails."

"I'll get there, I suppose." The comforter slipped from her shoulders as she cradled the mug in both hands. He wondered if he should pull it up again, then decided she might be too fragile for even a caring touch at this point.

He could only imagine what must be going on inside her.

"You know," she said after a while, "I've faced worse things than this. Roaring fires that could easily have killed me. Why does this feel different?"

"Because this time it's personal."

At that something moved in her face. She lifted the mug at last and sipped. "Yeah. It's personal. Hugely personal. It doesn't make sense, but why should it? None of this is making sense. Few arsonists can create a fire like Buell's. Few arsonists want to kill anyone. Few arsonists change tack and try to commit murder with carbon monoxide poisoning. And most arsonists know how unlikely they are to be caught if they keep their mouths shut."

"Maybe you're crediting arsonists with too much intelligence."

"This one is no slouch. And this one has slipped the rails completely." A long shaky breath escaped her and she leaned forward to put the hot chocolate on the coffee table, careful to set it on a coaster. Considering how many rings from old soda cans marred the top, the gesture was touching in a way. Or maybe a mark of her personality that even now she noticed little things.

Then he spoke the tough words, words that were surprisingly hard to say when he had known this woman such a short time. "You have to leave. Tomorrow. There's too much risk for you."

He couldn't have chosen better words to strike a fire. In an instant she sprang to her feet, leaving the comforter behind, and began to pace dizzying circles in his small living room.

"No."

"Charity, be reasonable! You've done ninety-five percent of your job. You can interview Mrs. Buell by phone. There's nothing left for you to do here, so why put your head in a guillotine?"

She faced him, planting her feet like a boxer in the ring. "Because this guy must be caught. You think he'll stop with me? What if he decides you're a threat? Maybe you aren't worried about yourself, but there's Linda to consider. There's also the possibility of future fires like the Buells'. More lives than mine are in the balance here. This is no typical arsonist and you know it."

"But…"

"But what can I do? I can stay here, that's what. We know I'm a target. This guy is going to slip up."

Her hazel eyes blazed, and he saw the fury in her. While fury was a far sight better than her withdrawal, it worried him in a different way. This angry, she might do something stupid. He hoped it would wear off fast.

But something else was rising in him, too. He cared about all the people he knew, would have protected any of them with his life, but this woman was somehow special, and damned if he was going to let her put herself needlessly in the line of fire. "We'll catch him. You don't need to put your head in a noose for us to do it."

"Ha." It was an angry, bitter sound. "Unless this guy was stupid enough to leave fingerprints all over Hank's place, I doubt you're going to get a clue. One of your firefighters? Maybe. But you can't put on blinders yet. Besides, you made a point of minimizing my role in arson investigation. They've all heard by now that I'm not here to solve this. So that tells you something right there."

In spite of his own tide of anger and worry, he reined himself in, gathered his churning thoughts. She was right. He'd done what he could to make her seem like less of a threat.

"So something else is going on here," she said.

"But what?" he demanded. There wasn't room for both of them to pace, so he stayed on the edge of the couch, his hands knotted together, his elbows on his knees.

She threw up a hand. "I don't know! How could I? It would require some kind of connection between the Buell fire and what he tried to do to me. I can't figure it. But it's sure as hell not limited to the orgasmic excitement of watching something burn and the fun of watching firefighters go to work. It's not boredom. There has to be something else going on, some link we're not seeing."

He supposed her anger was preferable to her earlier withdrawal, but he feared it just the same. Somehow it had to be tamped down, controlled, like the difference between a brush fire and a campfire. One wreaked havoc, the other was a useful tool.

"Charity...ease up for a minute. I don't blame you for being furious, scared or anything else you need to feel right now. But thinking is best done with a cooler head. You don't need me to tell you that."

It was a part of every firefighter's training, learning to resist the emotions of the moment and keep a clear head. He waited, hoping it would take hold. He knew she had to be capable of it, or she wouldn't have survived a year as a volunteer. They'd have benched her quickly.

For an instant she looked as if she wanted to take his head off. Then she visibly deflated, and came to sit beside him on the couch. "You're right," she said quietly.

"You can storm if you want. Cry, rant, whatever. I'll listen. I'll hold you. Get it all out. Only then can we go to work."

One corner of her mouth lifted a fraction. "You're not all that calm, either."

"No, I'm not. I told you how mad I am. But we both need to recognize that we need cooler heads. You might be right about some other agenda. You probably are. But we need to get through our gut reactions before we have any hope of getting anywhere. So have at it. I'll probably join you. The urge to kick something is pretty strong right now. There aren't words for what I felt when I saw the carbon monoxide detector had been deliberately disabled. There aren't words for how I felt when I realized how close you came to not waking in the morning. So do I want to shout? That's the least of it."

She blew a short, sharp breath. "Wayne? I think it's starting to hit me."

About time, he thought. She'd been too controlled for too long, and anger wasn't going to satisfy her. It simply couldn't be her only response to discovering someone had tried to kill her.

"Whatever he's trying to accomplish, this guy's a coward," she said quietly. "Dealing his blows stealthily, from a safe distance. He doesn't want to come out of the shadows. We need to make him."

She drank her cocoa and asked for more. Adrenaline used up calories fast. He was sure this wasn't over, and he kept waiting for the next bout as this mess continued to sink in.

He didn't hold it against her that it was taking time. Some things were so shocking that the brain simply rebelled, feeding it out in bits, letting it sink in slowly.

She was halfway through her second cup of cocoa when he saw her start to shake. She put her cup down quickly and wrapped her arms around herself as if that would stop it.

He slid across the couch and added his arms to hers, hugging her tightly, feeling the tremors rip through her.

"Just let it happen," he murmured.

Without any difficulty, he leaped back to the moment when his wife said she was leaving. He'd been in shock then, disbelieving then believing, a seesaw of emotions that took him from rage to anguish and back. He remembered the denial, the numbness that had held it all at bay, but not for long enough. He remembered it crashing in on him again and again, like huge waves battering a shoreline, battering him. Until finally he'd accepted the truth: he had lost his wife. Only then had he truly felt the failure, the grief, the emptiness in his life. But first he'd had to accept.

She spoke, her voice tight and shaky. "Monoxide is a horrible way to go."

"Yeah."

"People think you just go to sleep. But what if you wake up?"

He'd seen it once. An attempted suicide, but the car

had run out of gas too soon. The result had been horrifying. Neurologic damage had probably been the worst of it in the end, but there had been burns, too, a process he didn't fully understand. Sometimes there was violent sickness—headaches and vomiting that were often ascribed to something else, unless the exposure was already known. If more people had understood the possible consequences, they wouldn't begin to consider it a good choice for suicide.

But then, few methods were.

He rocked gently, waiting for her tremors to pass. He had no doubt Charity was a tough cookie when she needed to be, but this was an experience beyond what most folks would consider remotely normal.

"I'm being stalked," she said in that same thin voice.

"Which is why I keep saying you need to go home, be safe." He didn't want her to go, but even less did he want her to be hurt or killed.

"No," she said again, her voice a little stronger. "Somehow I became part of something bigger, and someone else might pay if I just leave." She looked at him from hollow eyes. "Two attempts on me, Wayne. The first a warning. This one could have been a successful murder. If anyone's going to draw this guy out, it's me. And we have to do it before he sets another fire like the Buells'."

He wanted to argue with her, but she'd put him at an impasse. If this arsonist had the ability and the taste for it, he could do the Buell job all over again. Not soon, maybe, but eventually. And maybe next time the family wouldn't escape. It was clear now that he didn't care if he killed someone. That made him all the more dangerous.

In the meantime, there'd be smaller fires, fires that caused property damage and all the heartache and fear that went with it even when no one was injured. People around here were getting nervous. He'd heard it earlier this evening. Any one of them could be the next victim. That was what they were thinking, with the Buell fire at the top of their minds.

Every single fire created risks with potentially deadly consequences. Even when a building was empty, fire crews could get seriously injured or killed fighting the blaze. There was no innocent arson.

Gradually her shuddering stopped. She didn't try to pull away, just leaned against him almost limply. When she spoke, she took the conversation in a totally unexpected direction.

"I told you," she said in a small voice, "that my boyfriends get fed up with my traveling, and we break up."

He waited, sensing that something important was about to emerge. "Yes." He kept the word quiet, hoped it was encouraging.

"Tonight when I was packing to come here, I packed everything, the way I do for a flight. It suddenly struck me I've lived my whole life that way. Ted was right."

He hesitated, then said, "Back up. Ted was right about what? And how could it be your whole life?"

"Because it has been. My dad worked for a huge multinational corporation, and he was some kind of troubleshooter. Sometimes he could just get on a plane and take care of things, but the truth is, I don't think we ever stayed in one place more than a year or two. Always on the move. Changing all the time. Never really fitting in. My mom treated it like an exciting adventure, but for a kid…"

He felt her shrug against his shoulder, and he was already aching for her. "Anyway. Then I got the job with the insurance company and seemed to be settling well enough when the opportunity to be an arson investigator came along. I jumped at it. I knew it meant traveling, but that didn't bother me. I enjoyed the arson academy and was especially excited when they agreed to give me a year to be a firefighter. Totally different. Then I left and returned to the company and this job."

"Okay." He was trying to piece it together, and hoped he'd get to what she was trying to say.

"Ted," she said, "got it right. He accused me of being unable to put down roots."

He didn't know how to reply to that. He couldn't even argue against it. He didn't know her well enough yet. All he knew for sure was that her words slammed him deep inside. But this was no time to analyze his feelings.

"So I was standing there packing tonight, and I realized I'd spent my whole life packing, and I even up and left the fire department when they offered me a career position. I didn't have to be a volunteer anymore. They wanted me. But no, I had to go back to a job that would keep me on the move. So Ted was right. I don't put down roots."

He really didn't have an answer to any of that. His own emotions were turning into chaos as he listened. *Take care*, he warned himself. He had to keep his own feelings out of this, whatever they were. "You could learn?" he suggested tentatively.

"Maybe. But I realized something else just now. I've never so much as hung a picture on a wall. I was admiring your prints earlier. My apartment is bare of them. Most everything I own other than basic furnishings and some clothing is in those suitcases. I'm always ready to leave at a moment's notice."

Wayne's heart squeezed. This picture of her was so sad, especially since she was the one looking at herself.

Facing something. Maybe dealing with something. He tightened his hold on her and wished he knew what kind of comfort she needed. "I guess you found a job that suits you, then."

He felt her pull back a little, then soften against him again. "I wonder if I have. What all those boyfriends were telling me, if not in so many words, is that I can't commit long-term. But whether I can or not, I've figured out in the past few days that I'm not happy in this job. I feel useless right now. I don't like that. The most useful, best time of my life was with the fire department. I didn't love every minute of it, but I felt as if I was doing something important."

She eased out of his hold and paced his living room again. He watched her gnaw her lip, her gaze distant as she thought about all this. "I need to make some changes," she announced finally.

"Is that the reason you're insisting on staying here? Because you don't need to be here to make changes. And you're putting yourself in danger."

She faced him. "No, it's not. I want this guy more than I can tell you. I'm frustrated that I can't do more, but I'll do whatever I can, even if it means putting my head in that guillotine of yours. Learning how to put down roots can come later. But right now I'm scared for other people in this county. I'm scared for you and your daughter. I give a damn that some lunatic is running around out there trying to destroy everything people have worked for." She shook her head. "I care about this more than anything I thought I cared about in the past. I *care*," she repeated. "I'm not leaving until we catch this guy."

"I get where you're coming from," he said carefully. "But you have a job…"

"To hell with the job. I learned something tonight. It's

time for change. I'm not sure where it's going to take me, but at least now I know what's wrong. And that matters, too, because I could have been dead before morning. Funny how that seems to bring clarity."

That part he got, for sure. "Yeah, it can. Just be sure the clarity is the right picture."

She stopped pacing. "You don't think it's a problem that I can't put down roots?"

"I'm saying that it's a problem only if it's making you unhappy. Some people really don't want roots. They don't like being stuck in one place."

And maybe his wife had been one of them, in a slightly different way. Maybe her need for a bigger city had just been a different expression. She'd become bored with the town she had grown up in. She needed the excitement of new things. But then he decided not to draw that parallel. It didn't approach what Charity was saying. Lisa had left, found her new life and settled into a new marriage three years ago. It wasn't as if she'd kicked the dust of Denver off her heels, too, and moved to New York or something.

No, Lisa had had a different problem, and there was no escaping the fact that part of the problem had most likely been him. He wished she'd just owned up to it because it had left him feeling as if he'd failed in some major way but didn't know how. And not knowing how, he had no hope of fixing it.

He sighed and rose, grabbing both their mugs. "More hot chocolate, or something else?"

"Chocolate is good for what ails you, right?" She smiled faintly for the first time since he'd arrived at her place to see that disabled detector. He hoped that was a good sign.

"So I've been told."

"I'd really rather have coffee, if you don't mind."

Wayne went to the kitchen to make it, wondering what was going on inside that woman. He seemed to do a lot of that. Right now she was looking as if her self-revelation had lifted a burden from her shoulders. Maybe it had, but given tonight's events he wasn't about to trust their emotions too far. He was just switching the coffeemaker on when she spoke behind him.

"Sorry for the confessional," she said.

He turned around and leaned back against the counter. She'd shed her jacket at last, and her boots, as well. Thick white socks covered her feet, and she still wore a white button-down shirt with her jeans. "No apology necessary."

She leaned against the door frame and folded her arms. "It was as if a whole bunch of puzzle pieces just came together. Now I get it. What I'll do about it remains to be seen."

"You don't necessarily have to do anything about it," he said fairly. Although secretly he wished she'd hang around for at least a while. He'd understood all along that she'd be leaving, probably sooner rather than later, but with each passing day she became more interesting to him. He wanted a chance to get to know her. He wanted to go to bed with her. All of it. Even if it went nowhere.

A dangerous state of mind.

Behind him the coffeepot hissed and burbled a bit, the only sound in a suddenly too-quiet house. This was a taste of silences to come after Linda left for college. He didn't like it.

He figured he and Charity weren't over the rough ground yet. Once again he wondered where her mind was going. He knew where his was. It was avoiding all thoughts of what had almost happened to her by focusing on her appeal. Even in casual clothes she looked sexy. It would be so easy to put everything else on the back burner and just make love to her.

In some corner of his mind he once again heard the sexy swish of her stockings as she had waved her leg flirtatiously at him. He wanted that woman to come back from the precipice where tonight had taken her, but he knew that was a foolish, selfish wish. She needed to deal, and he had to leave it to her to decide how.

The coffee was done. He turned and pulled down fresh mugs, filling them.

Suddenly she was beside him, taking one of the mugs for herself. A dizzying scent of woman reached him, along with the last, lingering sting of fear.

She had been afraid. That made her want him to wrap her up, but she was already heading back to the living room. He followed, feeling like a ham-handed fool who didn't know what to say or do. Give him a fire and he was in his element. Give him a car accident, an injury, a heart attack, and he knew how to handle it.

A woman? Not so much. He had clear evidence of that.

Again they sat on the couch while he waited for the next round.

"So Linda's definitely staying with Charlene tonight?"

"She called when I was on the way over to your place. I know it's a school night, but…"

Charity smiled. "But she's seventeen. More freedom is better. Soon you won't be there to make sure she gets enough sleep."

He felt the pang again. "Too true."

"You've done a good job, Wayne. She's a great young woman. Did I already tell you that?"

He tensed, wondering if she was about to lose it again.

But she sipped her coffee and remained outwardly composed.

"Thanks. So did you go to sleepovers, too?"

"Only once. Like I said, I was usually the outsider. I think it's great that Linda got to go through some of the most important years of her childhood in one place. She probably has lots of really good friends."

He nodded. Only one sleepover. Man, even as a *boy* he'd done that, although for guys it had often involved a tent in the backyard or somebody's fort. She had sure missed any sense of belonging. He couldn't imagine it.

"I was impressed when I went to talk to the sheriff about the Buells. He didn't have to pull a file or hunt up anything on his computer. He knew everything about them off the top of his head. Is everyone that well informed about their far-flung neighbors?"

"Maybe not everyone. But most. And Gage is a latecomer. He arrived here a little more than twenty years ago and married the local librarian."

"So he rooted."

"Firmly," Wayne agreed.

"It's not too late, then."

God, this was beginning to concern him. She seemed stuck in a loop. It might be an important loop, but she couldn't mount up and change it all tonight. Or maybe she had focused on something even more important to her than her brush with murder. Hard to imagine it, but it was possible.

Finally he said, "Charity, do you have any idea how much time I spend wondering what's going on in your head?"

Again a faint smile. "Maybe you shouldn't bother. I have a short horizon."

"What's that mean?"

"I don't look too far down the road. Never have. The longest range plan I've made in my life was investing in a 401k. But how can you make plans when everything will change in a day, a month, a year?" Her smile faded. "Today is it. Tomorrow may never come. And I'm sitting here thinking about how rootless I am and how if a murderer had succeeded it wouldn't matter a damn. I don't even leave footprints behind me. My apartment could be rented fully furnished and they'd only have to remove some clothes and toiletries. Maybe a few coworkers would come to my funeral."

"Stop this," he said, feeling his chest tighten with concern for her. "Stop now."

She tilted her head. "Why?"

"Because you're talking yourself into believing you're pointless. You're not. You're just as important as everyone else walking this planet, rootless or not. And by the way, roots don't have to be in a place. They can be in a job, a friend, a lover when you find the right one. The only thing any of us is really rooted to is ourselves. That always comes with us."

Finally she broke down. Huge silent tears welled in her eyes, then ran down her face.

He couldn't stand it another minute. He reached for her, leaned back until she lay half on him, and held on tightly.

However she looked at it, this woman had nearly died tonight. That was a helluva lot to deal with.

Chapter 7

Charity had no idea how long she wept. She never made a sound, but she'd learned early in life to keep silent when she cried. Other kids picked on her and she hid her reactions. Her mother expressed impatience, always wanting to know what could possibly be bad enough for tears.

It wasn't that her parents hadn't loved her. She knew they had. But in retrospect she had often thought their lives must have been more stressful than they let on. Maybe her mother hadn't found all that moving to be an adventure, but had been weeping silent tears of her own. She'd never know now. They'd both been killed in a flood along the Amazon. An adventurous life. She wondered if her mother looked on her death the same way. Somehow she doubted it.

So an upbeat mother and a busy father had made the best of it, and didn't seem aware how it was affecting their daughter. Or maybe they couldn't do anything about it. Regardless, she'd grown up to be a gypsy, always moving on, unable to stay long. She'd experienced her own adventure as a firefighter, then had chosen a relatively safe job, one that gave her a sense of continuity, at least. Wherever she might be at any moment, she still had the same job.

Like her dad.

Wow.

She realized that her tears were easing. Wayne's shirt was soaked beneath her cheek, but she could hear his steady heartbeat, his regular breaths, and felt his arms snug around her. He wasn't complaining.

Nobody had ever done this for her before. His arms around her seemed to create a cocoon of safety, however illusory, and she didn't want to lose the feeling. The look she'd taken at herself tonight had been as shattering as the attempted murder, as crazy as that sounded. She was a cipher, moving through life, staying always on the safe surface of it.

Tonight had changed that drastically. Tonight had dragged her into the trenches, had slapped her with reality, and now she was going to need to deal with it. Unless she ran back to the security of never really connecting.

She doubted she would ever again like herself if she did that.

That craziness earlier when she'd wanted to hang out at the firehouse with the guys, feel that camaraderie again… She *had* missed it. Maybe the only time she had ever felt she really belonged had been during her stint as a volunteer. After a few months, a few fires, she had been fully accepted. Nothing else in her life had ever felt that way.

So she had sought it again today, even knowing it

would be transitory. Apparently she needed more out of life than she was getting. Fleeting thoughts of wishing she could stay here, even though she was probably more an outsider than she had ever been in her life. Not just the new kid on the block or in the school, but someone who was just blowing through, not worth the effort of getting to really know. Not worth any effort at all.

Yet today she had been welcomed, and she had pulled away from it sooner than she'd really needed to. Why? Was she afraid that if she tried to make those roots they'd only wither?

God, she was a mess. She sat up abruptly, wondering if she'd ever settle inside herself. Aware that turning to Wayne might bring grief. Not trouble. Grief. She'd let him know right up front she wasn't a stayer, but that hadn't kept a few guys from trying anyway. She'd laid it out to herself and to Wayne more clearly than she ever had. He was on notice.

But notice didn't necessarily mean anything. A handful of guys had hooked up with her anyway, only to move on when they realized she wouldn't change.

Could she change? She didn't know.

Wayne sat up, too. "Coffee's cold now," he remarked. "I'll go get some more."

"I'm sorry I soaked your shirt."

He surprised her with a half smile. "I'm not. Shirts can be changed."

This time she remained where she was. She listened to him entering his bedroom. A few minutes later he was back, wearing a blue sweatshirt. He picked up their mugs, carried them to the kitchen, returning with fresh coffee.

This time she drank hers. So good, so hot. "I really dumped on you," she said eventually.

"I get the feeling you don't dump often. I don't mind." He leaned forward, setting his cup down, resting his elbows on his knees. He turned his head so that he was looking at her profile next to him. "So you're a gypsy at heart?"

"Guess so."

"But it's not making you happy."

"Not anymore," she agreed. "It really struck me, obviously. I've been running on automatic, kind of afraid to let anything really touch me."

"I gather you learned that young."

"So it seems." It was a truth, painful or not, that she was facing. "I don't really blame anyone for it. My parents probably never imagined that I'd turn out like this. Why would they? The world is probably full of kids who would thrive on the kind of traveling I did."

"Where are your folks now?"

"They died in a flood when they were in the Amazon."

"Good reason to stay home."

She gaped at him, astonished by the truth in his remark. All of a sudden the unintentional humor of his words struck her, and she laughed, feeling as if some kind of knot inside her let go. "I guess so. I don't know why I never thought of it that way. I always think of them as having lived such exciting lives."

"It sounds as if they did. We're so tame around here. A lunatic arsonist, a serial killer last winter… I could go on. We seem so peaceful, like if you let your eyes close you might go to sleep like Rip Van Winkle. You'd wake up in twenty years but you wouldn't have missed a thing."

She wiggled around on the couch until she had one leg stretched out and was facing him. "Are you saying that isn't so?"

"I'm not saying we're excitement central. But the fact is, people here are mostly nice, mostly friendly and mostly go about their business without causing unnecessary grief. So yeah, it's a nice place, a great place to live. But like any other place, trouble finds us, or some of us make it. Like folks everywhere, we want our lives peaceful and trouble-free. But wishing and reality are two different things. Life doesn't leave anyone alone forever."

She turned that around in her mind, trying to get what he was driving at. Was he asking her if she was a gypsy because she wanted constant change? She didn't think she did, but she kept moving around anyway. Was she afraid of stasis? If so, he had it right when he said life didn't leave anyone alone for long. Troubles came in all kinds.

Or was she just afraid that if she stayed too long she might discover all over again that she didn't fit?

She shook her head a little. "This is a bit self-indulgent of me. We've got a dangerous creep out there. My problems can wait."

"Well, I disagree," he said gently. "You've had a big shakeup tonight. You're dealing with it in the ways you need to. Let 'er rip."

He leaned back, putting his feet on the coffee table. "There's my little rebellion."

"What?"

"My ex would have killed me for putting my feet on that table. I do it all the time now. And you probably noticed all the rings on the table."

She smiled wanly. "Sort of."

"They're there because I refused to yell at Linda for not using a coaster. Heard enough of that. It's just a piece of furniture, not an heirloom, and certainly not some ridiculously expensive piece. I don't care how battered it looks. It's there to be used."

"I can agree with that."

He glanced her way. "It's like life. You get dinged. Unavoidable. But dinged or not, that coffee table is still useful. Linda and I joke that we're turning it into a unique piece of art. Maybe it is. I bet nobody else has a coffee table that looks quite like this."

She laughed. "I'm sure you're right." But her laughter faded as his message reached home. "I'm like a piece of furniture in a showroom."

"No, you're not. You've been dinged, too, and as much as you might try to avoid getting dinged some more, you're still accumulating new dents and scratches and watermarks. I saw the way you looked when you mentioned being dumped by Ted, or whatever his name was. You might be trying to avoid it, but it's happening anyway. So you need to figure out what you really want and go for it. If it's joining the circus, I'll come to the show when it's in town."

She'd liked him from the outset, had felt attracted to him enough to flirt, something she rarely did, but now she felt an overwhelming wave of warmth. Knowing all her warts, or the worst ones at least, he was telling her she was okay. Likening her to a unique work of art.

"Damn it, Wayne, you're going to make me cry again."

He gave her a crooked smile. "If you need to, be my guest. I didn't mind the first round."

But instead of crying, she put her mug down again, not on a coaster this time, and slid over toward him. He twisted immediately, welcoming her with an open arm. She curled into his embrace, loving the sound of his heartbeat in her ear, loving his particular masculine scents. "You're a remarkable guy," she said.

"Not really. I managed to utterly blow my marriage. And don't tell me it wasn't my fault. Best case is that we were both at fault. Nobody's perfect."

"But she left you because she hated this town?"

"She said it was driving her crazy. I never quite got clear on that, but she didn't offer anything else, so I guess I must have been boring her to death. It wouldn't surprise me. I work a lot, and more so after I became chief."

"That's part of the territory. I know."

"I know you do. But Lisa was sitting home all day with a child. Most of her friends were busy with their families. I'm not sure what she needed, but she seems to have found it now. And I've made a good life here with Linda. I wish I knew more."

"Maybe not," she said, absently running her fingertips over his hard chest. "Those scenes can be devastating. I speak from experience. Someone you've let inside even a little bit can leave you gutted."

"I suppose. I was gutted enough." He laid his hand over her roaming fingers. "You keep that up, woman, and you're going to be fighting a fire of another kind."

"Maybe that's what I want."

"And maybe you've just been to hell and back and want to forget it for a while. You might not be happy in the morning."

A few seconds later, she abruptly sat up, and soon he was so grateful he had drawn the curtains early tonight. She reached for the buttons of her shirt and began undoing them.

"As we both discovered tonight," she said steadily, "there might not be a morning."

He was sure his jaw must have dropped a little. Never in his life had a woman sat in front of him and started removing her clothes. Some part of him screamed that he'd better stop this now because if she wound up hating him…

But then the buttons were undone and she shrugged the shirt from her shoulders, tossing it. "You liked it when I flirted with you this morning," she said with a knowing smile.

"Yeah. I'm never going to forget it, or the sound of your stockings. But Charity…"

"Oh, hush. I think you want this as much as I do."

He couldn't deny it as he stared at her breasts, cupped in the kind of lacy confection he'd hitherto only seen in a catalogue or a movie. Women actually wore that stuff? Pristine white, but lacy and silky looking. The mounds that filled it promised to be full and gorgeous. His blood began to thunder in his ears.

She touched the front of it, twisting her fingers just a bit, and the bra fell open. She spilled free, firm round globes tipped in pink with generous nipples that were already engorging.

His groin throbbed so sharply it almost hurt, and his jeans began to feel way too tight.

Then she stood. He held his breath as she unbuttoned her jeans. The sound of the zipper drawing down seemed loud, the only sound in the world except his own rapid heartbeat, his speeding breaths.

Shimmying slightly, she pushed the jeans and her undies down, stepping out of them and kicking them aside. Standing there in an unclasped bra and socks, she was absolutely the sexiest thing he had ever seen in his life.

If the phone rang, he was going to kill someone.

She smiled at him, running her tongue over her lips.

Then she lifted one of those beautiful long legs and wiggled it at him as she had that morning, this time exposing the delightful secrets between her thighs. "Socks," she said, her voice husky. "Not nylons. Sorry."

There were a million sensible reasons why they shouldn't do this, but if he voiced a single one of them right now she'd be hurt. Badly hurt. She'd exposed herself, and putting her off would be the cruelest of rejections. His clarity of thought was fading anyway. Pounding desire was taking over, within moments of drowning him in need.

She cast the bra aside, then twisted around, giving him a view of a perfect rump, and one second later she dropped into his lap and leaned back. He nearly groaned as his staff throbbed in reaction.

"You should have been named Lilith," he muttered thickly, and gave up the battle. His mouth closed over hers hungrily, tasting her and a hint of coffee. His hand closed over one of those incredible breasts, squeezing gently at first, running his thumb over her nipple.

The shiver that passed through her was of an entirely different kind than earlier. He felt her passion as he felt his own, a moment of coming together that transcended ordinary reality.

She reached up an arm, winding it around his neck, deepening their kiss with a small moan in the back of her throat. His desire for her became a galloping stallion, racing across summer-heated fields, unstoppable and full of joyous life.

He squirmed a little beneath her, increasing the pressure of her weight on his erection. Already he felt close to exploding, but he wanted to drag out every single second of this encounter.

She moaned, encouraging him. He squeezed her

breast harder, pinching her hardened nipple until a soft cry escaped her. Then, impatient beyond belief to know every part of her, his hand started to drift down to the nest between her legs.

The doorbell rang.

He swore as she jerked back. "Damn it," he said thickly. "I can't ignore it. It could be a cop. It could be about Lindy."

Her gaze snapped quickly into focus, all the haziness of pleasure disappearing. He didn't want to let go of her, but when she tugged, he did. He saw concern in those hazel eyes, a shift. "Sometimes I hate reality," he muttered.

She quickly gathered up her clothes and headed for the bathroom, a quiet laugh escaping her. "You're not going to get off so easily, Chief."

Man, he hoped not.

As soon as he heard the bathroom door close behind her, he opened the front door. He fully expected to see one of the cops standing there, most likely to give him a little more information about the incident at Charity's place. He was fairly certain it had nothing to do with his daughter because the movie wasn't even over yet.

Instead, he was astonished to see Donna Willem. She was off duty for a few days so what business could she possibly have?

"Hi, Donna," he said. "What's up?"

"Just wondering about Charity Atkins. The guys kind of like her and we all know about the carbon monoxide thing. I said I'd come ask, since they're all stuck at the firehouse."

She couldn't have called? Any one of them could have called. He stood there, feeling caught flat-footed, although he couldn't say why. As far as anyone knew, he'd offered Charity the use of his guest room for a night or two.

"She's fine," he said. "Fortunately. But she can't stay in Hank's rental until he fixes the furnace, so she's going to use my guest room."

Donna smiled and nodded. "I'll tell the guys everything's okay. I guess they're kind of feeling left out."

Or Donna was, he thought. Weird. He was looking at her, and for the very first time wondering about her. She was such a levelheaded presence. Calming usually. Of all his crew, he most counted on Donna to remain cool. So why not a phone call?

He heard the bathroom door open behind him, and couldn't help but turn, fearing what he might see. But there was nothing to fear. Charity looked neat as a pin, right down to every last hair on her head, all primly pinned up right now, and carrying her laptop. No one could ever guess where they'd been headed just a few minutes ago.

"Hi, Donna," Charity said brightly. "Nice to see you. I was just going to ask Wayne if he could make some more coffee." She held up her laptop. "Work never ends."

"I guess not," said Donna. "Well, I didn't come to bother you. The guys were just worrying."

"Aw, that's so nice," Charity said pleasantly. "I like the guys, and you, too. I'm going to miss you all when I go home. But as you see…" She held out her arm. "Trying to wrap things up is all."

Wayne figured he might be missing something here. He didn't like that feeling. "Why don't you come in, Donna? You can have some coffee and call the guys from here."

Donna hesitated, then shook her head. "Thanks, but I said I'd come back. There's a great poker game going

on right now. I don't trust them not to heist my chips."
She gave a little wave and headed to the car she had
parked out front. Wayne watched her drive away before
he closed the door.

"Weird," he said aloud this time.

"You have a watchdog." Charity sat on the couch and
put the laptop on the coffee table.

"Oh, come on."

"Seriously. That wasn't about me. Not really. It was
about you. I think that woman has her eye on you."

"She works for me! And she's never done anything..."

"Coffee every morning," Charity said. "Even though
you've asked her to stop. How many other little things?
She won't cross any lines unless you invite her to in some
way, but she didn't stop here to make sure I wasn't dead.
She wanted to know if I was staying with you."

"So now she knows." And so would everyone else in
town, but he'd known that would happen anyway. Secrets were hard to keep around here.

"Sorry. I can go stay at the motel."

"Hell no. Absolutely not." Anger began to stir in him.

She looked at him kindly. "Wayne, you have a daughter to think about, and a future here as fire chief. Do
you want the whole town gossiping about how you had
a fling with me?"

He snorted. "Lindy's hoping for exactly that, the
minx. As for the rest of the town... If there's one thing
I've learned living in a place like this, it's that you just
have to live your life as you choose. If you start wondering what'll be passing around the rumor mill, you'll
never leave your house."

He paused as a thought struck him. "Hell, I wonder
if that was what was getting to my ex. Not just that she

found this place boring, but the knowledge that there was no way to kick up her heels without everyone knowing."

He sat suddenly on the end of the couch. Had Lisa wanted to have an affair? Had she realized that if she did he'd hear about it before long? Had she been pining after some other guy? Just the thought felt like a gut punch even after all this time.

"You don't know that, Wayne," Charity said quietly. "So don't imagine it."

"Well, she left a great big hole to fill with imaginings," he said a bit bitterly. "I've been wondering if being bored with the town was code for being bored with me. Tired of me. If I did something wrong. If I failed to do something."

"Probably all of the above," Charity said bluntly. It startled him out of his descending spiral of thoughts. "We all screw up sometimes. Guess she gutted you anyway, Chief."

He looked at her, wondering at the shift in her. This woman had been lying naked in his lap fifteen minutes ago, and now she was cool and reserved again. Had Donna's appearance reminded her that she was only here temporarily? Had she changed her mind once she had a few minutes alone to quiet the emotional storm?

If so, he was glad. He certainly didn't want to be some kind of painkiller she'd regret taking in the morning. On the other hand, he was sure he was going to regret never having made love with her. It had been a very long time since he'd wanted a woman the way he wanted this one. As if his heart had been on ice, or maybe he'd been aware he had a daughter to raise and needed to set a good example.

Change was as inevitable as breathing, though. Linda

was leaving in a few months. He was going to have to change one way or another, start building a new life.

Given what Charity had confided about herself, he guessed she wouldn't be the best person to do that with. But a fling? Well, it would have to remain one to be safe. What if it didn't?

And once again he was wondering what the hell was going on inside Charity's head. She'd been vamping him a short while ago, and now she was cool as a cucumber. Donna had definitely altered some delicate balance.

Or maybe she was still on an emotional seesaw because someone had tried to kill her. He wasn't aware of any manual that said a person had to react in certain ways and in any certain order. Anyone who thought they knew how someone should handle a shock clearly didn't know how wildly different people could be.

He opened his mouth, deciding to take the bull by the horns when his doorbell rang again. "Oh, for the love of Mike," he said irritably. It didn't help to hear Charity giggle softly as he went to open the door again. Or to hear her begin tapping at her computer keys.

"Grand Central Station," he muttered as he reached for the doorknob. He opened the door, and to his relief he found a deputy this time. Sarah Ironheart. A little taller than average, with long gray-dashed black hair, wearing her deputy's uniform.

"Hey," she said. "Sorry to bother you, but Gage got to worrying. He does that sometimes."

"Come on in and join the party," he said, trying to sound pleasant but feeling far from it. Stymied sexual needs were goading him, leaving him feeling cranky.

Sarah leaned in a little and waved to Charity. "That's Ms. Atkins?"

Wayne stepped back. "Come on in. Really." Might

as well deal with the whole mess right now. At this rate, he might have the city council on his doorstep in the next hour.

Sarah stepped in, introducing herself to Charity. Wayne went to make more coffee while the two women chatted casually. While it brewed, he returned and joined them.

"Actually," Sarah said, "I'm not just here to check that Charity is okay. Gage is really concerned about this, so we're setting a watch on your house tonight, Wayne."

"A watch?" He sat on the couch. "This person isn't attacking me." But even as he spoke he knew he'd brought the danger home with him. She was sitting at the other end of the couch, with a laptop on the coffee table in front of her. "You're right," he said before she could answer.

"I think we've moved past the point of a firebug who might have underestimated what would happen in the Buell fire. Don't you?"

"I've never underestimated this guy," he said flatly.

Charity spoke. "But until tonight… Well, most arsonists aren't murderers. They like fires. Most deaths associated are incidental to the fire."

"Collateral damage." Sarah nodded, her dark hair swaying slightly. She usually kept it pinned up and out of the way, but tonight it hung like a veil. She must have been called in suddenly. "I get it. But we've moved past that, obviously."

Wayne sighed impatiently. "I hate this. Catching an arsonist is never easy. One like this even less so. Charity and I were talking earlier about how this seems to be about something more than getting a thrill from a fire. Something else is going on."

"And someone," Sarah said, "is clearly nervous about what Charity might discover. I guess the title of arson investigator leads to all kinds of concerns for an arson-ist. But that's not really what you do, is it?"

Charity explained once again. "Mainly I'm hunting for evidence that this fire might have been set to gain fraudulently from the insurer. I'm not equipped to hunt for the arsonist beyond a paper trail that might indicate the ranch's owner could gain from this. You and the fire department do the real work. And as far as I can see, Mr. Buell stands to lose any way you slice it. We don't usually see owner-instigated arson that results in losses. Mr. Buell isn't the type of man who is going to be able to write this off to save himself from a code violation or whatever."

Sarah shook her head. "No, he's not. I've known him since he was a kid. He's put his heart and soul into mak-ing that ranch work for his family. It's all he knows. This has to be killing him."

"I think it is," Charity said.

Sarah looked at her. "But you get some kind of train-ing for this, right?"

"I went to an arson academy way back. I didn't focus as much on methods as on motives. The chief here has more training in identifying the actual causes of arson than I do."

"MMO," Sarah said. "Any investigator's triad. Means, motive and opportunity. I guess you're still work-ing on the means, Chief. The motive is unclear. The opportunity…"

Charity answered. "Happened every Sunday morn-ing when the Buells left the ranch to go to church. There was also opportunity when the new siding was put on the house."

Sarah nodded. "I remember that. A few houses had roof or siding damage from that hailstorm last fall. Fred was cussing because he felt wood siding would have stood up better, but the insurance would only pay for that metal stuff."

Charity perked. "How mad was he?"

"Oh, not that mad. He just felt the money could have been better spent on something sturdier. According to him, the insurance was wasting its money. Maybe he's right, I don't know."

"That isn't an unreasonable opinion," Charity responded. "Sounds like a man thinking of a better way to prevent future losses. But there's something going on here that doesn't just have to do with fire."

Sarah agreed. "I've seen a lot, all these years as a deputy. Motives are often muddier than they seem at first. But this time...this isn't just about setting fires. Anyway, the guy has a new target. The target is here. We're going to keep a sharp eye out tonight. I just wanted you to be aware of it, Chief, so you weren't wondering about prowlers. The city cops don't have any overtime, so you'll see deputies if you see anyone." Sarah rose.

"You haven't had your coffee yet," Wayne objected.

Sarah smiled. "I'm one of your watchers tonight. Gotta get to it."

After she left, silence filled the house once again. Charity was no longer tapping at her computer, or even really looking at it. Wayne was twisting the pieces of this mystery around in his head like one of those old wooden puzzle boxes.

"None of this is making any sense," he said.

"No, it isn't."

He hesitated, then said, "Coffee?"

"Thanks. I might actually get to drink it this time."

So the interlude was over. She'd enticed him like a siren, fueling desires he'd been ignoring and burying for years now. Living like a monk didn't exactly suit him, but he had a daughter and he had a public position. Plus, during so many years of monogamy, he'd never once felt a strong urge to kick over the traces and sample around. He guessed he was one of those one-woman men, so what the hell had he been thinking earlier?

Donna wafted into his mind as he filled the mugs yet again and carried them back to the living room. So Charity thought the woman was sweet on him? Man, he didn't want that. He was her boss, and anyway, Donna had never caught his attention that way. That was one spark that hadn't flickered even briefly.

They sat on opposite ends of the couch and Wayne realized he felt ready to spring. Waiting for another knock on the door? Waiting for something? Maybe a solution to drop in his lap from the heavens?

"I'm sorry."

He turned his head toward Charity. "For what?"

"You want the whole laundry list?"

As frustrated as he felt, he couldn't contain a smile. "After only a few days, it can't be much of a list."

"It's long enough." She clapped down the lid on her laptop. "I brought danger your way."

"You're just doing your job. You didn't cause any of this, and considering that I'm heading up the investigation at this point, I might have been a target anyway."

She turned on the couch, stretching out one leg and leaning back against its arm. He liked it when she sat that way. Snug denim reminded him of the incredible legs beneath it. He hadn't seen many women in his life who had legs that would look great on a chorus line.

"Then," she said, "I've flirted with you beyond belief. I'm usually more professional." A tiny impish smile appeared on her face. "You're certainly the first guy I ever stripped for."

His heart slammed. He cleared his throat, suddenly caught up again in the musky tendrils of desire that had been winding around them such a short time ago.

"No answer for that?" Her smile widened a shade. "You do things to me, Chief. Can't explain it, and I'm not going to dissect it. Maybe I got a little carried away. It's the first time someone's actually tried to kill me. Plenty of threats, but no action. So maybe I decided I deserved to have some fun."

He felt himself hardening again, and shifted so she couldn't see it. He was beginning to have some doubts about whether either of them could skate through this as a one-night stand. He wasn't at all sure he was built that way. As for her, he didn't know how much she might be riding the edge of shock and fear and trying to avoid thinking about it.

He was sure of one thing, though: she was opening up and he was finally getting a peek into that complex head of hers. And maybe, in some way, he was finally getting a peek into his own. So many things he hadn't done and hadn't allowed himself the space and time to think about since his divorce. Maybe he'd buried himself in being a dad and a fire chief to the exclusion of everything else.

"I was thinking," she continued, "while I straightened myself up in the bathroom so I wouldn't embarrass you, that maybe I went too far. I mean, I'm not the only one to consider here."

He cleared his throat again. "You know I want you." Did she color faintly?

But her answer was blunt. "That I do. But there's always the morning after. You said I should have been named Lilith. It was flattering in a way, but it got me to thinking. I don't want you to feel like the victim of a drive-by later. I have a tendency that way. I told you. I don't want to leave any wreckage in my wake here."

As much as he wanted to deny it, to claim he could handle it, he couldn't honestly say that. He had no experience of drive-bys, or one-night stands or whatever. He just simply had never done that. He'd married almost right out of high school, and within a short time had had a brand-new daughter. Not even the bit of college or the fire academy had put the brakes on Lindy's conception and arrival.

She leaned forward a little and drew absent patterns on the sofa fabric with her fingertip. "I've never been much interested in one-night stands in the past. I can't tell you how I'd react. For me, there were three long-term relationships. I got to know the guy first, we dated for weeks or months until I thought I'd found something steady, all before we did more than kiss. Didn't help much in the end to be so cautious at the beginning, but that's always been my approach."

"So this is not you? Is that what you're saying?"

"I'm saying I don't know if this is a part of me or a moment of near hysteria. Either way, I'm not a good bet. And now I know why."

Now the picture was coming together for him. Now he was understanding her, and he felt a heaviness in his chest. She'd reached out for something she wanted, then withdrew into her shell at the first opportunity, to protect both of them. Damned if he knew a way around that. All he knew was that he felt bad for her.

"So anyway," she continued a little too brightly, "I'm sorry I was a tease, and I'm glad Donna showed up to make sure we weren't in bed together."

That hit him like a punch. Was that really why Donna had showed up? He'd be the first to admit he didn't pay attention to such things, and his mind didn't run along those paths, but as a woman, Charity might have sniffed it out. She might have caught on to something he didn't know how to detect.

"You really think that's why she was here?"

"Telephones exist," she said drily. "She wanted to know if I was here. She wanted to see with her own eyes that I was still being businesslike. A phone call would have satisfied nothing. I guess I must be pinging her threat meter, even though I won't be here long."

Then she turned, putting both feet on the floor and opened her computer. "We need to work, Chief. There's something going on here and we need to nail it down."

He didn't know how her computer was going to help much with any of this, but it was probably safer than looking at each other.

He might understand a little better what was going on inside Charity, but he didn't have a clue as to what was happening with the arsonist.

And that was beginning to terrify him.

Chapter 8

They sat staring at a list of possible motivations built from their own experience and from searching the web. It wasn't a very long list of motives for arson, topped by an attempt to defraud and at the very bottom, jealousy and revenge. The latter two seemed to be the primary causes of arsons committed by women, which were rare to the extreme.

"And we can cross them all off," Wayne said, "because of what happened to you."

Charity shook her head slowly, carefully avoiding Wayne's gaze. "Maybe not. We might be making a mistake to link what happened to me to the other arsons. Think about it. Just because someone put a fire starter out behind the house doesn't mean they're the same person who torched the Buells. It might be a copycat or someone with an entirely different motive. And I'm going to get a headache."

She flopped back against the sofa and blew a long breath. "I can't imagine any woman being jealous of Fred Buell. Or wanting revenge."

"Why not?" He sounded defensive.

"I don't mean there's anything wrong with Mr. Buell. But he's got a family, he never goes anywhere and he works his butt off. Does he strike you as the type who would fool around even if he could find time?"

"Well, no," Wayne admitted.

"Exactly. I've heard not one critical word about that man here. Assuming one of his kids didn't tick someone off, or his wife isn't having an affair when she goes to church with the family on Sunday."

Wayne laughed. It sounded reluctant, but it emerged anyway. "Sorry, I know this isn't funny, but…"

Charity shrugged and smiled back. "I meant it to sound funny. But seriously. I doubt that family drove anyone to those lengths. They don't have time and they live too far away from the neighbors. It's not as if there's a problem with a barking dog or something. And I assume if his livestock strayed into someone else's land, he'd be called and asked to recover them."

"I can't imagine any rancher wouldn't do exactly that. If the problem became frequent, they might ask the sheriff to stop by, but my guess is if Buell had a fence down his neighbor would be helping to patch it."

"That's the sense I get, too, but I haven't been here that long." She sighed, ran her hands through her hair, pulling half of it out of the neat chignon, paying it no mind. "The box is too small."

"Box?"

"We're looking at typical arson motivations. We're linking two incidents that may be separate."

He rose and returned quickly with two fresh mugs of coffee. She took hers with thanks, and drank.

"So you want to go outside the box?" he asked. "That widens the field, all right, but makes the problem a whole lot bigger."

"True," she agreed, "but right now the box we're in isn't helping at all. There's nothing *typical* about any of this. If there is, it's buried beneath something else."

He sat thinking for a minute or so. "Okay. It can't hurt. We're not getting anywhere this way. So let's start with what's outside the box."

"The Buell fire was no typical arson. It appears to have been well planned. No simple crime of opportunity. It could have killed five people in addition to the livestock. I gather that around here killing a man's livestock is tantamount to murder."

"Pretty much anywhere that would be true. It's his livelihood. It's his treasure, and his family's future."

"Which could put this in the category of a whole lot of anger against Buell. But that brings us back to an inoffensive man. We need to dig further into his past."

He arched a brow. "How so?"

"I don't know. Let me think about that. It may be a very old grudge. We need to think about how he might have unintentionally hurt someone way back."

"This is revenge in slow motion if that's true."

"I know. It's just an idea. All I know is this person's motives are muddy. They don't fit the usual, so we've got to look at everything." She shook her head, and for the first time truly noticed her hair had fallen. Impatiently, she pulled the rest of the pins from her head and let it all tumble down. She scattered the pins on the table, then stared at them. This whole investigation looked like that.

Absently, she reached out a fingertip and began to

move them around. "Say the stuff that's happened to me has been done by the same person. We've been supposing that, so maybe we ought to suppose it for a little while longer until we can disprove it."

"I don't think we should rule out the connection too quickly," he said firmly. "The first incident was too much like a warning. The second…"

"Was attempted murder. The Buell fire may have been, as well. But if we keep coming back to that, we're inside the box again, and this box isn't fitting."

She continued to avoid looking at him, mainly because she was a little embarrassed. What had gotten her to pull that striptease earlier? That wasn't like her. A moment of wildness because death had come so very close? Or her attraction to this man, which was strong? If she could just be sure what had been going on inside her, she'd feel a whole lot better. It seemed she had a sexy imp buried within. Another revelation to add to the list tonight.

He wasn't the only one, she thought ruefully, who couldn't figure out what was going on inside her head. She darted a glance at him, but he seemed to have let the earlier interlude slip into the past. He was intensely focused, his clipboard in front of him, scribbling notes here and there as they talked.

"I should just go back to firefighting," she remarked. The words startled her even as she spoke them.

He smiled faintly. "I thought you were ready to move on."

"I thought so, too. But I missed it more than I expected, and you know what?"

"What?"

"It was a hell of a lot simpler than this." She gathered her hair with one hand and began to twist it back up onto her head.

He spoke. "Unless it's driving you crazy, leave it down. You have pretty hair."

His words sucked the air from the room. "Wayne…"

"I know. Neither of us really wants to play with that kind of fire. I get it. But let me enjoy the eye candy."

She felt her cheeks turn red-hot. No man had ever before said she was eye candy. Her blush didn't keep her from smiling, though. She liked it. "Tsk," she said, then laughed. "You're eye candy, too, Chief."

His smile widened. "Okay, you wanted to get back to business. I'm old enough to behave. I get having a taste for firefighting, obviously, but have you been that miserable in your job?"

"Why, do I have to be miserable to remember I once took greater satisfaction from something else? And it was satisfying in a way this job will never be." She tossed the pins back on the table. "I'm kinda between worlds in this job. I have to let you guys and law enforcement do ninety percent of the real work, and then I piece it all together. I get some satisfaction from clearing an owner and getting him his money. I get some real satisfaction from preventing fraud. But it's not the same, and I'm feeling so hampered right now it's not funny."

"You wouldn't be any less hampered if you were one of my crew."

"I know. But at least they get to help people in important ways, even if they don't get to do it as often as they'd like." She fell silent, thinking about what she'd just discovered about herself, and wondering if it was a temporary aberration. Given her penchant for moving on, she couldn't really trust herself, could she?

Wayne tossed down his pencil. "Just for a moment,

let's put the Buell fire back in the target-of-opportunity box."

"How so?"

"Well, say we have someone who likes to play with fire. Maybe he's been experimenting to amuse himself. Trying out different ideas for creating a fire. Maybe he just tried this one out, but never thought he'd have a chance to really do it. Maybe never intended to really do it. Just had kicks trying it. And then Buell is having that siding put on, and all of a sudden there's an opportunity to try it full-scale."

Charity stared at him, everything else forgotten. "You're giving me a whole different kind of willies here."

"Me, too. It doesn't explain the barn, but that could be explained just as a way to muddy the whole thing if it worked. And if it didn't work, he'd still have the barn fire to amuse him."

"God!" She was appalled, although why this seemed more appalling than the other scenarios they'd discussed, she couldn't imagine.

"Worse," Wayne continued inexorably, "what if it worked better than he expected? What if he didn't expect the house to go up that fast? Fire's an unpredictable animal. I know I keep saying that, Charity, but you and I both know how fast it can get out of control. What if he thought it would be nowhere near as bad, that maybe the Buells would get out, that they'd save the animals... or what if the house didn't go up when it was supposed to? What if..."

She tripped over his words. "What if the house took longer to ignite than expected? So the fire happened after the Buells were in bed, too late to save the livestock, with barely enough time to save themselves? But what does that tell us?"

"That we're back to an arsonist who wasn't out to kill an entire family. One who maybe didn't even want to kill the livestock." He shook his head. "Circles."

"No, no. That could be important." Her mind was racing now.

"But how?"

"I read the description of the house. Plaster walls. Those contain gypsum, a fire retardant. So the fire probably worked its way up through the walls, which mostly likely were hollow and pretty oxygen deprived except for those small holes we found. So it would most likely have smoldered for a long time. The gases had to reach the attic, at which point they went into flashover and from there it was fast. God knows what was in that attic, but probably a lot for the fire to feed on. Old furnishings, old letters and boxes? And plenty of oxygen once it got there. Attic vents. The mix would have been explosive. It could have found its way down through the ceilings through light fixtures. Heck, the burning on the ceilings they saw could have been paint or wall paper responding to the excessive heat above, not the plaster. The roof would have gone up like tinder. The attic floorboards, too. After that, the rest was inevitable and fast."

He cussed quietly and nodded. "I can see it. The arsonist might have even thought it wasn't working if it was slow enough. Which brings us to the barn. The house wasn't burning, so light the barn, which would have been easy enough."

"Too easy."

"But a big fire." His nod became more emphatic. "I hate to say it, but this is starting to make sense."

"Or the arsonist may have thought all those plaster walls and ceilings would stymie the fire. How many times did they tell us that, Wayne? How many walls and ceilings have you had to axe open to make sure fire wasn't brewing behind them?"

"Plenty," he said heavily.

"So maybe a slow fire was expected. A controlled one. The barn was lit when nothing seemed to be happening and boom, it all happens practically at once. If I were the arsonist, I'd be scared crazy about what I did. Because it wasn't what I intended at all."

He sat quietly for a minute. "So an arsonist who had a cool idea, but it played out differently from what he expected. Maybe he practiced, maybe he didn't, but he sure didn't expect the buildup of gases in the attic to cause a flashover. Maybe figured the accelerants he pumped in might not even get there in a large enough quantity to cause that kind of result, or that the attic vents would let enough of it escape. Maybe even figured smoke alarms would warn the family before it got out of hand. Then… nothing happened. So he spread a little accelerant in the barn as his consolation prize and…"

"And," she agreed. "Here we are."

He turned sideways on the couch, looking at her. "Line shacks aren't very sound structures, and few have been weatherized. No need. They're basically a place to get out of the wind and rain, and use a camp stove to cook. To know what would happen in a house, you'd need a house to practice on, which I should have heard about if it were anywhere nearby. So an attic flashover could have been unexpected."

"And a fire smoldering for lack of oxygen even less so. I mean, even if you found an abandoned house or shack to practice on, it wouldn't be the same as a lived-in, cared-for house."

"Not nearly as weatherproof," he agreed.

She thought a light had come into his gray eyes, a

flicker of excitement, as if he knew they were on the trail. It still wasn't much of a trail, but it might explain some of the perplexities of this situation. It made sense of the Buell fire, which until now had seemed utterly senseless.

"So now," Wayne continued, "you've created a catastrophe so big that even a fire department response couldn't save a thing. Seems like you'd want to lie low for a long time."

"Until an arson investigator for the insurance company shows up," she mused. "Do you know how many of us deal with most of this over the phone, and with the records sent to us? A lot of companies don't even send an investigator to the scene unless one is nearby. We rely on you guys and law enforcement, and spend a lot of time trying not to step on your toes so we don't shut down the information flow. But we depend on *you*. We don't have the authority to do what an official investigator can do."

"I made that clear at the firehouse. I'm sure word got around, since everyone's talking about the Buell fire."

She shrugged. "Maybe the arsonist didn't believe it. Or maybe my suiting up at that fire with you changed a perception. Or someone's after me for another reason. Take your pick."

"Or you hanging out in the break room afterward," he reminded her.

"There is that. But how to tie it all together in a useful way?"

"That's the question," he agreed. His phone buzzed and he lifted it off the table to answer. "Hi, Lindy. How's it going?"

Not wanting to eavesdrop, she headed for the bathroom. Some freshening was in order, and a splash of cold water on her face felt like heaven. When she no longer heard the faint sounds of Wayne's voice, she returned to the living room. He stood facing the window, even though the drapes were closed.

"Something wrong?" she asked immediately.

He turned with an odd smile on his face. "I think I just got lectured by my daughter."

"Really?"

He laughed. "Yeah, really. She called to tell me she's going to stay with Mo tomorrow night—that's another one of her girlfriends—so she'd stop by tomorrow afternoon just long enough to pick up clean clothes. Then I teased her by asking if she was sure she wasn't going to stay with Jeremy Dalton."

"Wait. Jeremy is Gage's son?"

"One of them."

"Wow." She absorbed the tight knitting of this town once again. "And?"

"She told me she remembered every single word I ever told her about puppy love, and how people who are seventeen still haven't found themselves and really don't know who they want to spend the rest of their lives with, and, oh, by the way, unless I'd forgotten, she had a prime example of that mistake in her own life."

"Ouch." Charity actually winced.

"Well, I have lectured her on that. Wonder why." He shook his head a little, looking rueful. "She's right, of course. I just didn't know if she really heard me. I guess she did."

"I guess so." Charity smiled and stretched a bit. She enjoyed the way his gaze trailed appreciatively over her, but resisted the urge to stretch again. No more teasing.

"She's glad you're here under the circumstances because nobody would stay at the La-Z-Rest if there was another choice."

Charity laughed. "She's something else."

"It didn't end there. She told me she wouldn't look into the bedrooms to see where we'd slept."

Charity felt her cheeks heat again. "She didn't!"

"She did." He looked as if he was trying awfully hard not to laugh. "So of course I scolded her. Which earned me one of those huffs of impatience teen girls are so good at, and she wanted to know if I thought she was born yesterday."

Charity sank onto the edge of the couch and put her face in her hands. She had the worst urge to laugh, too, although she didn't know if it was from near hysteria.

"I know," he said. "The odd thing is, it *feels* as though she was born yesterday. Clearly not."

"Clearly," Charity said, her voice muffled.

"Cheer up, you're leaving soon."

At that her head snapped up. "Meaning?"

His smile faded. "I don't want you to go. But you have to. And the sooner the better. I'd never forgive myself if something happened to you."

"We've beaten this horse already. Let's not kill it. I'm not going anywhere. I might be your only link to this arsonist."

She stared at her laptop. Did he really just want to get rid of her? Or was he truly concerned about her safety? If she had any sense, she'd be concerned, but right now she wasn't feeling sensible. She wished she could read his mind. "Back to the fire," she said in a businesslike voice. "What if those holes we found weren't used to introduce accelerant?"

"We won't know until the lab results come back. What are you thinking?"

"Not sure, except that eight holes seems like an awful lot, and there might have been more we didn't find. I'm having trouble imagining someone having the time or interest to pump in a whole bunch of accelerant through holes that size."

"But we know the accelerant had to be there."

"Yup. Circles again." She tapped on her keys, bringing up the assessor's records. "Okay, this house was built in 1922. Back in those days, if they included any insulation, they used newspapers."

"Stacked newspapers don't burn well."

She nodded, but raised her gaze to him. "But who can speak of newspapers a century old? Very brittle, very dry, and while they might have done some sagging initially, some would still be hung up throughout the walls."

"We don't know what was in there."

"No," she admitted. She tapped some more and brought up the description of the siding job that had been done only a couple of months ago. "Says here that the old siding was ripped off and the new siding applied to plywood already in place. That's no help. Plywood began to be used in construction in the US all the way back in 1865. Chances are, nobody has seen what was inside those walls since the place was built. Plywood, studs, lath then plaster. All of it combustible except the plaster."

"And electrical wiring was added later. I remember seeing it when I was out there once."

She nodded. "That answers my next question. I was wondering why, if there was a slow smoldering fire, they wouldn't have had electrical problems to warn them."

"They wouldn't have had any. Conduits ran through the house at the corners of the ceiling as I recall. More conduits to bring plugs down to a useful level. In some places the conduit had just been papered over."

She laughed a little. "I've seen that. I guess nobody was going to move electrical wiring just to get the wallpaper under it. For a long time it was that way in a lot of places, I guess. Nobody wanted to tear out walls to wire, nobody wanted to move wires. So were you out there to inspect?"

He nodded. "Sometimes we get asked to do it when people change insurers. Other times we do it simply because the owner asks. As near as I could tell, the Buell place met code sufficiently because of the conduit. No exposed wires."

She sighed. "This gets us nowhere."

He stirred, taking a few steps around the room. "Okay, that's it for tonight. I'm getting brain fried, which is never a useful place to be." He faced her. "You've had a long day. Time to hit the hay, especially if I'm going to make it out to the Buell place ahead of the bulldozer in the morning for one last check."

She nodded agreement, even as her heart began to skitter. Was he going to make a pass? If he didn't, could she stand it? If he did, how would she answer?

Sick of her own maunderings, she closed the laptop and picked it up. "I need to plug this in."

"Plenty of sockets. Help yourself. Anyway, go change into your sleeping togs, then we'll say good-night."

That struck her as a slightly odd way of ending this. Why not just say good-night here?

But she *was* feeling frayed and worn-out, and trying to sort out something so insignificant seemed like a waste of the few brain cells she had left.

She went to the guest room, dug out her charger and plugged in the laptop. She changed into her T-shirt and yoga pants she slept in and put ballet slippers on her feet.

Then off to the bathroom for a washup and teeth brushing.

When she emerged, she found Wayne a few feet away,

wearing a navy blue fleece jogging suit. He stared at her for several moments, moments that seemed to stretch almost endlessly. Her body awoke despite her fogged brain, responding to an ancient call.

Then he astonished her by reaching for her hand and leading her farther down the hall.

An instinctive protest escaped her lips. "I told you I can't make promises."

"I don't remember asking for any."

"But…I hurt people!"

"Been hurt before, and you're jumping your fences." His room was dimly lit, a golden glow from a bedside lamp. All the interior decoration in this house was elsewhere. This room looked like a monk's cell except for the large bed. Basic, colorless, a place to sleep and nothing more. That tugged at her somehow, as she imagined the ex removing everything and him not bothering to replace anything but bare essentials. And Linda had decorated everywhere else, according to what Wayne had told her. Apparently he'd never given her rein in here.

Before she could think of any sensible protest to utter, he pulled down the comforter and sheet. She considered backing out of here now, but before she could unfreeze her leg muscles, he swept her off her feet and laid her on the bed. Once he'd tugged the covers over her, he lay behind her on top of them, and drew her close into his embrace.

"Just sleep," he said. "I don't want you to be alone if today hits you again."

The light remained on, as if to comfort her and guide her. His warm, hard strength pressed to her back felt like a bulwark. Astonishment woke her fully. He couldn't really mean to hold her chastely all night just in case she needed someone.

But soon she heard his breathing deepen and become regular as sleep overcame him. He *did* mean it. One lone tear rolled down her cheek as her heart squeezed with understanding. This man's capacity for caring exceeded any she had ever known. All he wanted was to ensure she wouldn't wake alone in a strange place, afraid and without anyone.

Bighearted didn't begin to cover it.

Slowly, she, too, relaxed, safe in the protection of his arms, and sleep led her into the quiet places.

Charity awoke suddenly. It was still dark outside, the inky night held at bay only by the dim glow of the bedside lamp. While she'd slept she had become tangled in both covers and Wayne. He now lay on his back, she half across his chest with her blanket-wrapped leg tucked between his.

His chest rose and fell in a slow, steady rhythm. His mouth was slightly open, but he didn't snore. His heartbeat was a slow thud beneath her ear. A day's beard growth shadowed his chin and jaw.

Comforting. Amazingly comforting. Intimate without being too much so.

She snuggled a little closer and his arm tightened around her shoulders, welcoming her, but he didn't wake. She wondered what time it was but couldn't even guess. The time zone change, compounded by the latitude change, gave her no clues by which to judge. Her internal clock had been slightly off-kilter since she arrived.

As near as she could tell, the sun rose here a half hour earlier than Atlanta at this time of year by the local clock, but then there was the difference between Eastern and Mountain Time, two hours. Her head whirled with calculations she wasn't awake enough to do, and she gave up.

What did it matter anyway? The fact that she had awakened probably meant it was close to her usual waking time at home. Which would make it about 4:00 a.m. local time. Good enough.

She realized she was trying to ground herself in some way, not that it would do any good. She'd spent her whole life trying to ground herself in a world that kept changing. Jet lag, followed by new time zones, days of different lengths, different climates, new faces, new sights, new rules, new problems. Often even new languages. One teddy bear she refused to part with even though it was excess baggage, a favorite T-shirt she outgrew too rapidly. Until she finally felt she couldn't land at all. The sun would rise and the sun would set, and with each move that would vary, altering even the lengths of her days as horizons and latitudes changed.

Alaska had scared her a bit, with a sun that almost never set in the summer and almost never rose in the winter. After that, Norway had seemed almost familiar, although everything else had changed. Sometimes living in a walled compound and never seeing what was beyond the gates, locked in with a bunch of other misfits like herself, who didn't even band together because what was the point when they'd be leaving soon?

Sometimes having a bodyguard, because executives from big companies and their families were targets for kidnapping. One year they stayed with her aunt Maria because it was too dangerous to go with Dad, and then Aunt Maria had gotten sick and everything had been turned on end again.

She'd gone through life floating like a leaf on the rapids, moving swiftly, sometimes nearly submerging, but always bouncing back somehow until she couldn't imagine living any other way.

She considered herself settled in Atlanta, but how could she be settled when she was almost never there? She hadn't been kidding about her apartment. She might have been going home to it for the past five years when she wasn't on the road, but it still felt like a way station in her life. It might have been a motel.

Now she was here, temporarily of course, and felt long-forgotten stirrings of a need to actually belong somewhere. To have a community, to settle in and put down those roots she probably could never grow.

She thought she'd made peace with the way she lived and who she was, but somehow this town, this fire chief, had unsettled her. The man was as rooted as they came, and she had felt twinges of envy. A home, a daughter, friends, a place in a community and doing a very important job.

Sitting with those firefighters yesterday afternoon, she'd felt a belonging she hadn't felt since she'd been a volunteer. That community had wrapped around her once again, letting her know how much she had missed her brief sojourn in it.

But maybe she should be wary of that feeling. The instant her old department had wanted to put her on payroll, she had decided to resume her job with the insurance company. She'd fled.

Maybe she found some kind of security in moving all the time, although she couldn't imagine what. Unless maybe she was avoiding pain by refusing to attach. Everything went away sooner or later.

Wayne's divorce proved that. Rooted though he was, he'd suffered abandonment by his wife, and now his daughter was moving on. No escaping it.

But moments like these, moments where she felt cared for, came rarely when you kept moving on. She was living life the way she had always lived it, but for the first time she now questioned whether this was her choice or simply a habit. Some psychological thing that was working beneath the surface, always goading her.

If it was, maybe she needed to start living her own choices, not the choices she'd had no say about when she was growing up.

"You're awake," Wayne murmured.

"Did I disturb you?"

"You haven't moved. I was listening to the changes in your breathing. Either you were awake or dreaming. You okay?"

"Yeah. I always am." She always was, too. Eventually.

He stirred a little, lifting his head. "Just after four."

"I thought it might be. I guess I'm still on Eastern Time. You go back to sleep. Maybe I'll get up and make some coffee."

"Not alone, you won't." His hand slid down her back, caressing her bottom briefly. "Ah, woman, the things you do to me."

The things she did to *him*? How about the things he did to her? One sweeping touch and she felt like a torch.

She tilted her head instinctively, seeking his mouth with hers. She needed this contact, needed this man, and she didn't care what it cost.

She felt the briefest moment of hesitation from him, then he rolled slightly, propping himself over her, taking her mouth in a kiss so deep it seemed to reach her soul.

Nerves that had been quietly humming suddenly started to sing. New aches welled in her body, calling her to transitory joy. Reaching up with her arms, she pulled him closer, hating the blankets, the clothing, between them, yet they hardly seemed an impediment to all that was blossoming inside her.

For the first time in forever, she felt a softening, an opening, a need for a man to love her, fill her, possess her. She was melting into a hot puddle of molten metal.

His tongue toyed with hers, each brush against sensitive nerves wakening her to an awareness of the moment with intense clarity, the clarity of passion.

He shifted again, sprinkling kisses on her face and throat. His hand found its way beneath blankets and stroked her breasts until her nipples grew so hard they ached. All of her ached. With each touch, she felt the yearning grow between her legs, a throbbing so strong it nearly hurt.

He lowered his head, finding her nipple with his teeth through her shirt, nipping gently. His hand swept lower until it cradled the nest between her legs. At first he just rubbed lightly, then he squeezed, a pressure she desperately needed. She arched into his touch, her entire body begging for more.

Then, slowly, he eased his hand away and lifted his head. Staring down into her eyes, he smiled. "Appetizer," he said huskily. "I hope. But not yet."

Disappointment crashed through her. "Why?" she whispered.

He leaned in to give her another kiss. "I want you more than I can say. But I don't want to take advantage of you."

"But…"

He laid a finger across her lips. "Shh, before I forget my good intentions. Wait until last night really settles in. Please."

A long sigh escaped her. Her frustrated body screamed once and then began to relax. Brain cells fired in response to reality, and she acknowledged the justice of his concern.

He cupped her face, sprinkled it with kisses. "I want a medal."

A startled short laugh escaped her. "What?"

"I just did the hardest thing I've ever done."

He sat up, and she struggled against the covers until she could, too. "The hardest? Really?"

He glanced over his shoulder. "Really. It's easier to walk into a burning building than to walk away from a burning woman like you."

She kind of liked that, and it eased her disappointment.

"I need to clean up. See you in the kitchen."

Considering how close they'd come to making love last night when she'd sat naked on his lap, Charity wondered if she had blown her one chance with Chief Wayne Camden. Her withdrawal when Donna showed up at the door must have looked to him as if she was sealing herself behind concrete walls. Maybe he was still concerned that she'd back out. And maybe she would have. Last night she hadn't behaved like herself, and he might be justifiably concerned that her reactions were arising from shock.

She swept hair from her face as she listened to the sounds issuing from the master bath. She guessed she had blown it, and wondered how many other good things she had blown by skipping away from them. Not just a couple of boyfriends, she was sure. She never really let anyone in.

She padded down the hallway to the other bath, pausing only to grab some clean clothes, then spent some time showering and brushing out her hair to dry it a bit. There was a blow-dryer nearby, but she didn't like the way they made her hair more flyaway. Finally, she pinned the damp strands up and went out to make coffee.

Wayne had beat her to it. He had on his uniform pants and a white T-shirt, dark socks on his feet. She had chosen jeans and a blue button-down because he had said they needed to go out to the ranch today, before the bulldozers arrived.

He put a mug in front of her before opening the refrigerator. "Are you okay with eggs?"

"I love them every which way."

He brought the carton out and set it on the counter. "Then you get one of my famous omelets."

"Famous?"

"That's what Lindy calls them. She always says it with a perfectly straight face."

She studied him. He'd shaved, his dark hair was damp and he looked utterly scrumptious. "Why wouldn't she?"

He shrugged. "I don't know. It's just that sometimes when she says things like that I don't know if she's funning me. Certainly there's nothing famous about this omelet. Promise you'll let me know if it's awful."

She laughed quietly. "Want some help?"

"Thanks, but I'm a solitary cook. Just keep me company." Cheese joined the eggs, what looked like some leftover ham and a green pepper. "If you see something you don't like, holler."

"Everything looks good so far."

He cleaned the green pepper, then paused to look at her. "How are you this morning? Really?"

"Fine." She knew he was referring to last night, to the attempted murder, but this morning it seemed like a bad dream. Far away. As if it had happened to someone else. She wondered if that would wear off, or if she had assimilated it somehow. It seemed rather soon, yet the aura of unreality clung. It wasn't as if she'd been hurt in some way. "The only thing that fits what happened last night with the arsonist is that he's a coward."

"Agreed. And if he'd succeeded, it sure wouldn't have looked accidental when we investigated. So there wasn't a hope of him trying to cover his crime."

"No." It most certainly wouldn't have. The disabled carbon monoxide detectors ruled that out. If she'd been found lifeless this morning, those detectors would have been examined. She opened her computer to check her email. One from work caught her attention.

"Oh, hell," she said.

"What?"

"My boss wants to know how I can be sure Fred Buell didn't do this himself. He reminded me that a lot of people commit arson to get community support. And it's true that sometimes poor people do it for specifically that reason. To get out of a lease they can't afford, to get old furnishings replaced, to get donations."

He had just finished dicing green pepper. Forgetting everything else, he joined her at the table. "What are you going to say?"

"What I'd like to know is how he found out about the barn raising tomorrow."

Wayne arched a brow. "Why should that be a secret?"

"It's not. I just didn't tell him about it, but he mentions it here."

He shook his head. "Why would someone be getting in your way? Or is he having you checked up on?"

"I don't know." Feeling suddenly frustrated, she slammed down the lid of her laptop. "There's a barn raising, so? That's not going to make up for the lost animals, the terrified family or anything else. These folks will be lucky to get enough out of the insurance to rebuild their house."

"Is that what you're going to tell him?"

"Among other things. I've been doing this for five years now, Wayne, and my record for sniffing out fraud is higher than most. He has no reason to be questioning me."

"Unless someone planted a poison pill."

Her head jerked a little. "Someone sure as hell wants me out of here. And the irony of it is, I can't do one blessed thing to catch this creep. All I can do is make sure Mr. Buell and his family get what they deserve from their insurer." She tapped her fingers impatiently on the table and put her chin in her hand. Anger steamed through her veins, hot and uncomfortable. "The murk is getting thicker."

Then she rose and went to the bedroom she hadn't used last night, grabbed her cell phone off the charger and dialed her boss as she returned to the kitchen.

"Alex? Charity. What the hell is this crap about the barn raising? No, I don't care that you're still at home. I'm in a different time zone. It's four-thirty in the morning here, and I'm already working."

Alex said impatiently, "I got an email suggesting that Buell might be defrauding us, that he's going to get a brand new barn out of this for nothing."

"Well, your informant is wrong, and I want a copy of that email. You know what the truth really is, Alex? This man not only lost a barn, he lost expensive livestock and his entire house. He almost lost his family. If *we'd* been doing our jobs, we would have raised his coverage over the years. But we didn't bother. So guess what? This guy is seriously underinsured. *Seriously.* He won't gain a dime from this. He's losing. This ranch is the only thing he knows how to do, and he can't support his family without it. No way."

"But he could bankrupt his debts and…"

"A court would take every penny of the settlement we give him to cover that. What's he supposed to live on? How's he supposed to feed his kids?"

"The land…"

"What's left of it after a court settlement of his debts, you mean? He might get a little cash if the court seizes it and they get a decent price at auction. How likely is that?"

This time Alex didn't argue. Charity waited impatiently. Finally he said, "You're sure about this?"

"So sure that I was sick when I looked at the assessor's evaluation and compared it to his insurance coverage. So are you going to screw him even more because his friends want to help him out? Crap, Alex, they're talking about living in the barn with the animals."

"All right," he said after another pause. "I thought it was kind of odd to get that email."

"You better believe it's odd. We've got a serious arsonist out here, and last night he tried to kill me. So please, put your suspicions away and let me do my job."

Alex's voice rose. "Tried to kill you?"

"You got that right. I'll send you the police report when it's available. If you don't trust me to do my job right, then send someone else. I can have my resignation in your email box in the next thirty seconds."

"No," Alex said swiftly. "I don't want that. I got that email late last night and it just raised questions. I'm not familiar with the whole situation. Charity? If someone's trying to kill you, you need to come back."

"I'm not leaving until this gets figured out. This is one dangerous arsonist. I'll keep you informed, but after my last interview today, I'll be sending you my report and a request that the check be issued. After that…well, I'm hanging around for a while. It got personal."

Alex sighed heavily into the phone. "I can't let you stay somewhere you're unsafe."

"No one is letting me do anything. I'll seal this case and take some vacation days. You and the company will be off the hook. And send me that damn email. I'd like to know where it came from. Or maybe the sheriff would."

"All right, all right. I'll forward it. Just be careful."

She disconnected and paced the kitchen a few times before settling. "How about that omelet?"

Wayne smiled. "Coming up. And I liked the way you handled that. But is it really personal? Maybe…"

"Don't even say it. It's personal, all right. And I'm the worm dangling on the hook for a very frightened arsonist. How about we dangle me some more when we go out there today?"

Chapter 9

Wayne made the omelet with practiced skill. It was one of Lindy's favorite weekend breakfasts, topped only by cinnamon buns from the bakery.

Dangle her like a worm for the arsonist? He didn't like that, but he honestly didn't know how he was going to stop her short of asking Gage to throw her in a cell. She really had her dander up, not that he could blame her, and even though he feared for her, he admired her gumption and determination.

He spoke, aware that he might be igniting a firestorm. "You know that thing you said about not being able to commit?"

She looked at him over her cup of coffee. "Yes. Unfortunately. I've been doing a lot of thinking about that."

"Well, whether you know it or not, you just committed in a big way. The biggest. You're willing to put your life on the line for this one."

He waited for it, sure she was going to dismiss him, or tell him he didn't know what he was talking about. But instead a small, slow smile dawned on her face.

"I guess I have," she said finally.

"And what's more, you committed every time you answered the call to a fire. Think about it, Charity. That's all I'm asking. Maybe you just need the right things to make that commitment to."

"Maybe. But I did run away when the fire department wanted to hire me full-time."

"Maybe it wasn't running away. Maybe it was going back to what you believed was an important job." He hesitated, then began scooping half the omelet onto each plate. "Sometimes things look one way, but if you turn them just a bit they can be very different. I somehow think that when the time is right, the reason is right, you'll put down some kind of roots. And like I said, it doesn't have to be in one place. There are other kinds of roots."

He watched an array of emotions slide across her face, all of them unreadable to him. But in the end, they apparently didn't trouble her, because she smiled faintly and began to eat.

"This *is* a famous omelet," she announced after a mouthful. "Linda isn't funning you."

"Thank goodness. Considering she wants them every weekend, I'd hate to think she was pandering to my ego."

"She's not," Charity announced, and continued eating with a healthy appetite. "I love the white cheddar, too."

"Linda doesn't like the orange stuff."

"This beats it by a mile." She cleaned more than half her plate before asking, "What's the agenda today, Chief?"

"We'll leave for the Buell place about six-thirty. The

sun will be up by the time we get there. We should have a couple of hours before all the heavy equipment moves in...if we need that much time anyway. I doubt we'll find anything new. Then we'll come back and speak with Mrs. Buell. After that..." He shrugged.

"You need an arson dog, Wayne."

He shook his head. "One was supposed to come with the missing state investigator. I wonder if he's actually on leave or something."

"You only have one?"

"There are more, but each has a district. Maybe I should've rattled some bars to get someone from another district, although at this point I'm not at all sure he'd find anything you and I haven't."

"There's not a whole lot left to look at," she agreed. "That's the really mind-blowing part of this—nothing is left. I've been to so many arsons, and there's usually a lot more to check out. What have we got except a heap of ash and plaster?"

"Not much," he said. "That was the most disturbing thing of all. Not much."

Wayne didn't know what to make of the changes he saw taking place in Charity. The woman was a puzzle, all right, and now he wondered if she was always this mercurial or if the case had gotten to her somehow. Somehow beyond the attempts to kill her.

Or maybe there were just some things she didn't like and refused to allow pass. That he could understand. Which didn't mean he liked the idea of this arsonist taking another swipe at her.

That email seriously troubled him, and he mentioned it again as they were washing up after breakfast, and making more coffee. "Why would anyone send an email like that? I don't think Fred Buell has that kind of enemy."

"It was directed at me," she said firmly. "And no, I don't think I'm the center of the universe, but I've got somebody so scared or mad that they're willing to attempt murder. The carbon monoxide failed, but an email suggesting fraud might have been another way to get me out of here. My bosses might question my judgment and send someone else in my place."

"But they didn't."

"They want me out of here, but not for that reason." She filled two mugs and carried them to the table. It was still too dark outside, and too early to leave for the Buell place. Time to talk more.

He was glad of that, because he needed to understand some things. "They don't think you're falling for a fraud, do they?"

She shook her head as she sat. "Wayne, I've been doing this for them for five years. My fraud-proof rate is higher than anyone else's. Simply, I don't skim these things, I look really close and sometimes I learn things that others might miss. In that sense, I'm golden. I also have an instinct for this, a nose, if you will. Things will niggle at me until I get to the root of it. This time there's no niggle. Fred Buell didn't commit that act. Not any of it."

Wayne nodded, sipping his own coffee. "Seems as though if he had a hand in this, he would have increased his insurance."

"Exactly. Maybe not all at once, but gradually over a couple of years. The thing is, we should have been paying attention to the property appraiser's records. Someone at my company screwed up. Maybe they went to sleep after the housing bubble burst and everything was overinsured for its value for a while. I don't know. I just know that the pattern for an arsonist is to get more than enough insurance."

He nodded, thinking over the things he'd learned from her. "But then there's poor folks. Someone like Fred Buell who might think he could get a new barn for nothing."

She shook her head. "Then, he'd have burned the barn, not a house with his whole family in it. And I doubt he'd have left the livestock in it. Even if he didn't care about his stock—and everyone tells me he did—he's not covered enough on the barn to handle his losses in livestock. Seriously, this fire has put him in a world of hurts. And I'm probably discussing his financial situation too openly."

Wayne shook his head. "Nothing I didn't guess from the moment you said he was underinsured. The situation is the same for a lot of ranchers out here. They make it only if they keep going. They walk a line so narrow that one bit of serious trouble can put them under. Oh, we have a few who are doing well, but most are like Fred. Keep taking the next step so you can barely keep your head above water. It was bad enough when the economy tanked and people stopped buying beef. Then feed prices went through the roof, commodities speculation drove it even higher and there are some out here for whom the loss of a single steer could make the difference between a profit and a loss. Seems hard to believe, doesn't it?"

She shook her head. "Actually, no. A lot of small businesses, single-owner type deals, run on very thin margins. No room for error or trouble."

"Well, Fred's not that close to the edge from what I hear, but he's not raking it in, either. His kids get home-schooled in part so they can help with chores. It's the way folks used to live all the time. Some folks are still living that way."

Wayne paused, thinking about all of it. "So you really don't think that email was an attempt to get at Fred?"

Charity shook her head. "Not likely. Another investigator would find exactly what I've found. You know, this all makes me hopping mad. An innocent man targeted for some reason. Why? Why ruin Fred Buell's life? For a thrill? As much arson as I've dealt with, I still find it hard to believe. I've seen apparent arsons that turned out to be accidents. I've seen arsons for gain. I've seen arsons that initially look like accidents. I've seen arsons as the result of a dispute. But the ones that really get me are the ones for a cheap thrill."

He smiled crookedly. "Some of them get off on it."

"There are other ways to get off."

He couldn't disagree with that. "Charity, will you be honest with me?"

She looked surprised. "I'm always honest."

"Except when you don't share."

He watched her bridle. "What do you mean?"

"Just what I said. You shared some pretty personal stuff with me last night, but I'm sitting here once again wondering what you're thinking. You want to risk your life to catch an arsonist."

"And a potential murderer."

"True, but you're the one at risk for being killed. You turned all stubborn about this for some reason. You're not a detective. You're not in any position to investigate this, so why hang around to give the guy another opportunity? You just said someone else could finish your job. You even said you think you'll have it finished today. This person has threatened your job and your life and you're digging in your heels."

"I'm a stubborn person."

"Maybe that's how you got through your rambling childhood. I don't know. But you say you can't commit, now here you are committing your life to a dangerous game that should be left to the proper authorities. I'm not criticizing—" although he guessed he was in a way "—but I need to understand. Is there something pushing you besides your desire to catch this creep?"

He watched her look down at the mug between her hands and he waited, coiled tight as a spring. He already knew he was coming to care for this perplexing woman in dangerous ways, that when she left he was going to miss her like hell. But he'd rather see her leave here alive and safe. "You keep too much inside," he said finally.

"I thought I was letting it all hang out," she said. Slowly her gaze lifted and met his. "I'm confused, Wayne. I know that. I'm trying to sort out some major life issues all of a sudden. It finally stood up and bit me on the butt. I'm a runner."

"I sure don't see any of that here. That's what's got me wondering. I can't stand by while you do this if I don't at least have some understanding."

"What are you going to do? Throw me out of town?"

He sighed and rubbed his chin. "Really? Let's not go there. Try respecting the fact that I have some feelings and opinions here."

She averted her face, but he caught a glimpse of her embarrassment. "I guess I've been selfish."

"No, I wouldn't say that at all. It's just that you're all locked up so tight in yourself. I'm honestly proud that you felt you could tell me so much last night, but then you shut down again. Was that necessary for survival when you were growing up?"

She hesitated, still not looking at him, then nodded.

"I guess so. I never had a confidant. A few times when I tried, I was laughed at or criticized. I'm different."

"Different how?"

"I guess I'm not like other people."

Something inside him suddenly hurt so badly he thought it was going to crack wide-open. "So people shut you down when you tried to open up?"

"Yes." The word came out clipped.

"That is so freaking sad," he said. The pain inside him, pain for her, made him want to slam something.

"It's the way it is. My mother told me not to be so dramatic. She said I exhausted her. My first boyfriend told me he was sick to death of hearing about my feelings. Clearly there's something wrong or different about me. So you're right, I don't share easily."

"God." He pushed back from the table and reached for her. At least she didn't resist when he tugged her into the living room and sat on the couch with her close beside him. He wrapped his arms around her in what he hoped was a gentle but unbreakable grip.

"You listen to me, Charity Atkins. You're not different. You're a human being with human feelings and needs, and anyone who wasn't willing to listen to you wasn't worth your time. And that includes your mother."

"But…"

"I don't care what they said, any of them. They were being selfish. You think I haven't listened to hours of teenage angst from Lindy? Of course I have. You want to hear some of mine?"

She remained stiff in his arms but gave a little shrug. He took it as a yes.

"I still don't know why my wife left me. You'll never know how many nights I've paced this place and wondered what I did wrong. I kind of intimated that I'd made peace with it, but the truth is I haven't. All she ever said was she was going crazy in this town, but that doesn't answer many questions, does it? I still wonder, I'll always wonder what lay behind that. She grew up here, Charity. She had friends here. Why should a few years away change all that? She claimed it did, but you know what? Glenwood Springs isn't much bigger than this town. It just has more attractions because it caters to tourists. So maybe more things to do, but was that all of it? I wonder. I'll always wonder. She didn't even try to take Lindy with her. I wonder about that, too. Didn't want her except for summers and every other Christmas. But she was Lindy's *mother*!"

She was softening as she listened, no longer as stiff as wood. "That's awful, Wayne."

"Damn straight. At least if she'd cut me to pieces I'd have answers about what the hell is wrong with Wayne Camden, wrong enough to leave even her daughter."

She shifted a little, her head turning toward him, just a little. "Maybe it wasn't you," she said quietly. "Maybe it was all her."

"Maybe. And maybe you ought to consider that about the people who made you feel you had to be a clam. If they didn't care enough to listen, then they *didn't care*."

She lowered her head. He hadn't really been able to see her face since they'd sat on the couch, but reading her face was seldom useful. She'd not only closed up when it came to talking, but she'd shielded her face, as well. He caught flickers, just glimpses, of what she might be thinking or feeling, but they vanished quickly.

He hoped that he'd once again see the woman who had busted out so briefly yesterday, flirting in his office, confiding in him last night, doing that amazing strip-tease. Inside her a woman waited to be set free.

Of course, he could be totally deluded, but he didn't think so. The real Charity was in there somewhere, and he suspected she'd be full of excitement, joy, raw sexuality and delightful secrets.

Every so often, she tried to reach out, like at the fire station yesterday, like last night. Then she pulled back like a startled turtle, walking herself once again into a solitary existence, everything on the surface, everything safe. Protected. Where no one could hurt her in the ways that really mattered. Where Charity couldn't be dismissed yet again.

Yet now she wanted to put her head in a very real noose, and he needed to know why. Was it her need to prove she had some worth as a human being, a worth that others had denied her? Or was it something else?

"I'm angry," she said quietly. "Really, very, truly angry. Something happened when I talked to Fred Buell. That man's pain was palpable. He's close to broken, Wayne."

"I know."

"I hate arsonists, but this time…when I saw what it had done to Fred, it became personal. Really personal. I don't usually do personal. But I guess this time I am. I looked at that man, all but crushed, and still managing to give thanks his family had survived. That's real courage. Maybe it taught me a lesson, I don't know. But this is deeply personal to me now. More personal than just the attempt to kill me. Maybe that sounds weird but…"

"It doesn't sound weird," he said when she stopped talking. "It makes sense to me. Someone else's pain being bigger than your own? I get it. I do."

At last she twisted enough to look at him. "I think you do."

He hesitated, but decided that confiding more might

help her to do the same. "Last winter we had a bad accident out on the highway three miles out of town. Friday night. Four high school students heading home from a football game. Black ice on the road. Too much speed. You were a volunteer. I don't need to paint the ugly details."

"No. Don't. I've seen."

"Anyway, I knew all those kids. I knew their families. I helped pick up the pieces and afterward the only thing I had to be grateful for was that I wasn't the one who had to notify their families. I came home and hugged my daughter until she couldn't stand it anymore, and I don't think I had a solid night's sleep for weeks. She also got pretty mad at me because I took the car keys away for a few days. Thing was, mad or not, I could see in her eyes that she understood. They'd been her friends."

"Oh, dear Lord." She turned fully into him and wrapped her arm around his waist.

"I lost two good firefighters that night. That was it for them and they quit. I can't say I blame them."

"But you stayed."

"I stay because sometimes I can make a real difference. Someone has to."

She grew still against him. A look at the clock on the cable box told him they were fast running out of time. He hoped she'd offer another piece of herself, a bit of understanding, but he guessed she was lost inside her own thoughts, even as she returned his hug. He was savoring this time, maybe too much, but it had been so long since he had enjoyed holding a woman, being held by one, in moments of quiet.

Minutes passed, and just as he was thinking it was time to suggest they leave, she spoke.

"I thought I was making a difference doing this job.

I mean, catching fraud is not just about saving my company money. It's about saving our clients money, because premiums increase more slowly if we're not paying out huge sums on fraudulent fires. And it feels good, sometimes, when I have a case like this one where I can help a client get his due when he's been wronged by someone. But it's not like what you do. What I did with the fire crew. It affects lives, but not in the same way."

"Don't put yourself down. It's like I said, someone needs to do it."

"I get that," she said. Then she sighed. "But maybe it's not enough for me." With that, she pulled back a little. "Time to go?"

"Getting there. It'll be chilly still, so wear something warm."

Charity went to the guest room to get a sweater and her jacket. She even messed up the bed and remade it inexpertly, figuring that Lindy *would* look—curiosity was normal—and she didn't want to cause Wayne any unnecessary teasing, especially when all he'd done was comfort her through the night. And Linda, evidently, wasn't one to exercise discretion in her comments.

In the past twelve hours, she'd told Wayne things about herself that she'd never shared with anyone, even the whiny stuff about having her feelings dismissed. Oddly, she felt she'd found a safe confidant for those truths about herself. She knew one thing for sure, they might not be truths in the objective sense, but they were true for her emotionally, and she had trusted him with them.

For the first time in years, she'd opened up to someone, exposing what she believed were her deepest flaws. Being different in some way, a way that made others just want her to be quiet. Maybe she obsessed too much when her feelings were knotted, or when she was stressed. Or maybe she just confided more than people really wanted to hear from anyone. Maybe at times she was too self-centered. She didn't know.

Or maybe she'd just overreacted to normal human impatience. Regardless, she couldn't escape the fact that it had altered her, left her scarred in some way. So much so that she never entrusted her deepest thoughts and feelings to anyone.

So what was wrong with her? She figured she'd never really get an answer. She didn't know what had possessed her to open up so much to Wayne. Maybe the realization that after a few days she'd never see him again? Would never have to deal with that inevitable complaint about her feelings?

But then he'd told her he was having a similar experience over his divorce. Not exactly the same, obviously, but wondering what was wrong with him. Always wondering. She could definitely sympathize with that.

She emerged from the bedroom ready for the day, and found Wayne dressed in his blues—the comfortable shirt and pants that could be worn under a turnout suit—and a matching jacket for warmth. On his head sat a white ball cap emblazoned with the department's seal and the word *Chief*. His jacket sported a badge, too. His shirt had an embroidered badge, but the one on the jacket had been carefully etched in brass and silver.

All very official. She felt anything but official in her jeans, work shirt and boots. Dressed down, but necessary for what they were about to do. Of course, she wasn't really *official* in any meaningful sense of the word. She was the private employee of an insurance company, paid to do a job that often brought her across the path of public servants who did it for much nobler reasons. Sometimes they helped, the way Wayne and the sheriff were helping. Sometimes she was treated as an unwanted outsider and had to find a way to grease the skids, as it were. Get herself taken seriously. Or at least treated as if her access to information mattered.

She often wondered where the hostility lay. After all, she wasn't questioning the word of the professionals, she just needed information from them. It wasn't her job to second-guess a professional arson investigator. But sometimes she got treated like a spy from the enemy camp.

"What are you thinking?" he asked as they climbed into the car and headed for the Buell ranch. The first signs of dawn might just be barely visible to the east. But only barely.

"I was just thinking about how helpful you've been. A lot of fire and law officials I work with resent me. I guess they see me as an interloper. A bean counter who might just get in the way. It's not always easy."

"I'm surprised anyone would react that way. You didn't come here to hamper anything, merely to collect the facts."

"You'd think. But apparently someone already thinks differently about what I'm here to do." She shook her head a little. "I don't get it, either. I can't pin the arson on anyone. That's the job of the fire people and the law. At best I can raise suspicions. The sharing goes both ways, although I'll be the first to admit more of it comes my way."

"Well, you've certainly helped me. I'm glad you found those holes, and the scenario you developed explains a lot that had me scratching my head. That's a good thing."

"It may be a good scenario, but it doesn't explain

enough. Like who and when. Is the sheriff going to keep an eye out?"

"For practice sites? He said he would, but on the qt. You should have heard him groan."

She laughed quietly. "I can imagine. I'm starting to appreciate the size of his jurisdiction."

"Well, at least some of the mountains fall to the Forest Service, but not all. He might ask ERT to keep an eye out."

"ERT?"

"Our emergency response team. Years ago it started with one medevac helicopter, a pilot, a mechanic and a nurse. Now it's a whole lot bigger. More helicopters, a few small planes, more medical personnel and a lot of volunteer rescue searchers."

"How'd you manage to avoid growing an arsenal?"

"When the defense department started handing out free goodies, our sheriffs were more interested in building up our search and rescue capabilities than an armory."

She thought that said a whole lot about this community. "Other than arson, does anything bad happen here?"

"All the time. I think I mentioned the serial killer we had this past winter. Over the years, we've had our share of bad guys, big and small. Even a drug operation being run by one of our prominent ranchers. So yeah, it all gets to us one way or another."

"But you still focus primarily on people helping people?"

"We try to. There are a lot of rugged individualists around here, but the odd thing is, even rugged individualists sometimes need neighbors, or a rush flight to medical facilities. Nobody really goes it alone."

She liked that philosophy. Sooner or later everyone

needed help of some kind. It was true, she thought as she looked out the window at the passing dark countryside. You might have to be pretty self-reliant out here most of the time, but every so often…every so often you'd need neighbors to hold a potluck and a barn raising.

Or a helicopter to swoop in and pick up someone who was injured or sick.

"Living in a big city, I guess I take that for granted," she said. "Help is always three digits away."

"It is here, too. It just takes longer."

She twisted to look at him. The light from the dashboard painted his face with a soft glow. Handsome, but more important a good man. He'd accepted her ugly little secrets and put them away somewhere inside him. He wasn't pressing her, or dismissing her in any way. She wouldn't have blamed him if he had done either. Voicing her hurts out loud sometimes made her feel very small and petty.

So what if she'd been dissed by people who didn't care to hear her thoughts or feelings? Why had she taken that so much to heart? Why had she let it cripple her? Why hadn't she done exactly what he'd suggested? If they didn't want to listen, then move on to someone who cared enough to listen.

Instead, she'd crammed herself into an emotional box that she almost never opened, not even to herself. As if she was afraid of the things that roiled there. As if they were monsters that needed to be contained.

What if they were?

This time it was almost as if he sensed the direction of her thoughts. "You can talk to me," he said. "I'm not afraid of your feelings."

Afraid of her feelings? What an odd way to phrase it. But maybe that was what had happened those other times. What if her feelings had been perceived as threatening? Then, that made them wrong, didn't it?

But what about the boyfriend who had just said he was sick of hearing about her feelings? He hadn't felt threatened, just tired of it.

"Charity?"

"Just thinking."

"I can tell that all the way over here." The car jolted a little as they rode over a rough spot on the road. "Share?"

"I'm thinking that maybe I'm whiny."

"I'm thinking that maybe you're sensitive. Not all of us are born with armor-plated feelings. We can be hurt. Quite easily, too. A couple of words can leave a scar as real as any knife."

She shifted again, easing a stiffness that wanted to creep into her shoulders. "I was always told that old saw about sticks and stones."

"I'm not buying it."

Surprisingly, a small giggle escaped her. "How'd I know that?"

"Maybe because you know it's true. You can break a leg and heal from it good as new. Heck, you can even crack your skull and survive it all right. But a few well-aimed words? They can't be erased. And if they hit just right, the scar remains forever."

"Possibly. Did it happen to you?"

He laughed quietly. "I think I was a freshman in high school. Something of an instigator for pranks and things. Anyway, a teacher told me I had a chip on my shoulder. I still remember my reaction as if it happened yesterday. I didn't see myself that way at all. I was having fun, not trying to start fights but, man, did that hit me hard. I spent days, maybe weeks wondering if she was right. It was as if my head got knocked around a hundred and eighty degrees. True or not, it affected my behavior and I've never forgotten it. Maybe the teacher did me a favor."

"Or maybe she was wrong."

"I'll never know, will I? I can't see myself through anyone else's eyes. But it sure made me reevaluate myself."

How he knew where they were, she couldn't imagine. They were out so far that all she saw was an occasional sign designating the county road number. But he knew where to turn, and as they did she saw the gray light of dawn limning the mountains to the east. Now they were on the ranch road, bouncing quite a bit and moving slowly.

"We'll be a little early, in terms of the sun," he remarked. Then he added, "I only heard that criticism once, but it stuck with me. I can only imagine how I'd feel if I'd heard it from more people than that teacher. I'd probably be absolutely convinced there was something wrong with me."

She drew a deep breath, liking him more than ever, and admitted, "There's something wrong with me now, that's for certain. Even if there wasn't before, there is now."

"You've tried to shut down?"

"Exactly."

They jolted along for another minute before he spoke. "Well, I'm only a fireman, not a psychologist. But I happen to like you a whole lot, and other than trying to find a chink in your armor so I can get to know you, I don't have any complaints. You're safe with me, Charity. That much I can promise."

Oddly enough she believed him. What did that mean? She ought to know by now how unsafe it was to trust anyone, but here she was, trusting Wayne Camden. She hoped she didn't learn another painful lesson.

At last they reached the site. The morning had just begun to take on a rosy glow; the sun still hadn't quite crept above the mountains. Despite the hulking black skeletons in front of her, she saw past them.

"This is beautiful country," she remarked as they pulled up closer to the ruins.

"It is," he agreed. "Come back this summer and I'll take you camping in the mountains. You might freeze if we tried that now."

"Good point. I haven't acclimated yet." As they climbed out, she was reminded how true that was. The wind that never ceased out here nipped at her ears and tried to find its way into the collar of her jacket.

The greening spring grasses silenced their footsteps as they headed over toward the barn. The peaks of the western mountains were already brightening with daylight. It was odd, she thought as she stood there waiting, to watch the light creep down the mountains toward them, as if it would arrive from the west.

Then everything changed as the sun poked above the eastern horizon and bathed the world with warm light. Almost moment by moment she could see the contrast increasing as day conquered the world.

Wayne didn't say anything, simply standing beside her as she soaked it in, as if he understood her appreciation. As if he shared it.

But then it was time to start work.

This place was as unique as any she had ever lived. She kept looking out and around as they walked over the ash and charcoal of the barn remnants, seeing a wild, open kind of beauty unlike some of the supposedly ex-

otic places she had lived. She was beginning to understand why people loved this place.

"What are we looking for?" she asked.

"I'm pretty sure kerosene or gasoline was the accelerant. I believe the lab tests will confirm it. I guess I'm
just hoping something got overlooked."

"You want a clue?" She couldn't help it; she laughed.
"Look around, Wayne."

He flashed her a grin. "Hope springs eternal. You
know how weird it is the way some things don't burn? I
can hope, at least until we walk away and the bulldozers arrive."

A couple of supporting posts on the south side of the
barn hadn't burned through, indicating that they had
probably been farthest from the fire. A nail poked out
of one, about the height for hanging something. Here
and there she caught traces of larger pieces of blackened
wood and something that looked like roof tiles. From the
burn marks she could see the outline of stalls, maybe
some small rooms near one end. A piece of leather tack
looked surprisingly untouched. But overall it looked like
the inside of a fire pit that had burned itself out.

She scuffed a little at the ground, stirring up the ashes
and dead coals, wondering what might be buried beneath. Once the roof collapsed, it might have snuffed
out some of the fire beneath it, although that had probably happened too late.

Metal tubes of unknown purpose were scattered
around, blackened like everything else but still whole.
She tried "softening" her focus, hoping that she'd be
more likely to discover something that wasn't just more
of the same black.

Wayne was poking around near the floor with a tele-
scoping rod, stirring things around. Probably a pointless

task, she thought. While he was right that the weirdest things somehow survived a fire, how likely was it that they'd find a clue?

"Don't come over here," he said.

"Why not?"

"I found at least one calf. You don't want to see if you don't have to."

She didn't want to. The dead animals weren't covered by the property insurance, so she had absolutely no need to check into any claim about whether or how many head Buell had lost.

Finally she walked upwind, escaping the acrid smell and other unpleasant odors. She recognized some of them, but she didn't need to swim in them. Burned flesh, burned hair, other things.

She turned to stare over all the destruction, the house, the barn. It still didn't make sense. Would it ever? A family in the house, animals in the barn. An extremely murderous arsonist. And even if the barn had been a "consolation" fire when the arsonist thought the house might not burn, why make it impossible for the animals to escape?

The house. She stared at it, more troubled than ever. A family of five sleeping inside, saved only by recently installed smoke detectors. Even if the arsonist had miscalculated the extremity of a flashover in the attic, it was still risky from start to finish. Murder was a much bigger deal than arson, criminally speaking, and any time human lives were involved you moved into the territory of attempted murder.

Of course, after yesterday, there was no reason to think they weren't dealing with someone perfectly capable of murder.

The question that kept gnawing at her was who would

be next? Because someone like this wouldn't just stop. They had to *be* stopped.

Eventually Wayne joined her. "Nothing," he said.

"That's the thing about arson. The evidence usually burns up. Gotta look anyway."

He nodded, his eyes narrowed as he scanned the scene. "This is just too damn clean. You can tell accelerant was used at three different places in the barn, all along one side, but that's it. The dust caught, the hay caught and zoom. Buell would have aired the place out over the day, but toward evening he'd have been pitching hay and feed into the stalls for the animals, making more dust. He said there was hay in the loft. Then you close up for the night, and that dust might have settled except the cattle were probably restless. Maybe because someone they didn't know was moving around outside or inside. Or maybe because kerosene had already been spilled. Restless, they stir up the dust, lots of it."

"And the air becomes essentially flammable."

"Then you have all that old dry wood, and whatever else in there that might burn easily." He sighed. "So, all right. The dust might have flashed, singed some hair, but it might not have started a big fire except for accelerant. But once that dust flashed, the accelerant catches, the hay catches and that's all she wrote."

"Or the accelerant ignites the hay, the dust flashes extremely hot and the fire spreads fast."

"Either way," he agreed. "But too damn hot to leave evidence behind."

A distant rumble drew her attention. She looked toward it and saw heavy equipment making its way up the ranch road. "Time's up," she remarked.

He strode toward the remains of the barn again, then stood there with his hands on his narrow hips, studying the scene as if it would speak to him. As if some message were writ there.

All of a sudden, he straightened. "Charity?"

She trotted over to him.

"Do you see it?" he asked, pointing.

"See what?

"Can't you see the pattern? Some of those stall doors were open."

Wayne held off the dozers and the trenchers for about an hour as he and Charity strung a tape measure and started mapping the remains of the barn. The ranchers who had brought the equipment stood around impatiently, then finally started helping by holding the tape, calling measurements out, while Wayne sketched. Charity did her best to take GPS readings of every important location on Wayne's satellite phone.

When he was done mapping it, he took a bunch of photos. With the light still at an angle from the rising sun, the demarcations of all the interior doors and walls seemed to stand out.

At last he appeared satisfied and told the workers he was done. From there he marched back to the house and stood looking at it, but this time he didn't seem to see anything unusual. He paused once again to look at the small holes just above the foundation, but didn't remark on anything.

"We can come back to this," he said as he and Charity walked toward his SUV.

"Wanna tell me what you're thinking?"

"Not here."

Chapter 10

Wayne didn't say another thing all the way back to the station. Once there, he parked in his place at the rear of the bay, took his clipboard from Charity's lap and tucked the map of the barn remains down under the very bottom.

"Let's walk over to the diner and grab some real coffee. Edna Buell should be here in about twenty minutes."

Still curious, but almost able to feel the way his mind roiled, she didn't ask him again about why the barn was troubling him now. What those open stall doors might mean.

He paused long enough to let Donna and the crew know where he was going. When orders flew his way, he laughed and suggested he was going to need more than two sets of hands to carry that much latte. Donna and Jeff immediately offered to join them. Wayne waved away offers of money.

Donna limped a little as she walked and fell in beside

Charity. "Last night must have been terrifying for you. I was out there this morning so I can write my report. I can't understand why someone would try to do that."

"Me, either," Charity answered. "But maybe someone misunderstands my role here."

"Maybe so."

Jeff, striding along beside Wayne, looked over his shoulder. "So are you going to join us for drills on Monday? The guys were serious, you know."

Charity gave a little negative shake of her head. "You guys just want to show off and remind me how much I've forgotten."

"Naw," said Jeff cheerfully. "Well, maybe partly. A fresh audience is always good. Chief here stands around barking when he's not in the burn room with us. It'd be nice to have someone applaud."

Donna spoke. "How can you be sure she'd applaud? She's done this before. Maybe you'll all look like a bunch of hicks."

The tone was teasing, but Charity couldn't let it pass. "I saw the crew in action twice since I got here. What I saw was a very professional team."

"See?" Jeff said to Donna.

"And all because I bark so much," Wayne joked. "Maybe I should bellow more. And where's Randy today? I thought you guys always shared shifts."

"Ken tapped him to help get the burn building ready for Monday. He says he's got some new stuff up his sleeve."

"Which won't be much of a secret if Randy knows about it," Donna remarked.

"That's what we're counting on," Jeff laughed.

As they were walking back, carriers full of lattes with Charity carrying three whole pies she'd bought from

Maude, Charity asked, "How is it you guys have a burn building? I've seen a lot of small departments that have to resort to burning buildings that are slated for destruction because of budgetary restraints."

"Three counties put their budgets together," Wayne answered. "It's near us because we already owned twenty good acres for it. Until then, we'd been putting together structures of our own. I don't have to tell you how unsafe that can be."

"As unsafe as a real fire."

"Exactly. So a bunch of us went in together to put in a really good training building. Safer, and what's more we can use it to simulate two story structures with attics or barns." He shook his head a little. "It's nice, and we can get some really long burns."

"And we get worn-out," said Jeff, grinning.

Charity laughed. "Just like the real thing."

"I hear we might put some more burn buildings out there," Jeff said.

"How can we do that if the county cuts our budget?" Donna asked.

Wayne looked at her. "They threaten that every few years, Donna. It's part of the game. And somehow in the end they never really cut anything important."

Back at the station, they left the coffees and the pies with everyone in the break room. Wayne headed for his office, and Charity and Donna trailed him.

"So you'll be done today?" Donna asked.

Charity hesitated. In theory she would be, but she hadn't forgotten her own determination to dangle herself like bait by hanging around. If they were ever going to catch this guy, they had to make him slip up.

"I'm not sure," she answered. "I might be a little longer."

Donna put her cup on her desk, then rounded it to take her seat. "Be gentle with Edna. She's been through hell."

Charity eyed her. "What makes you think I wouldn't be? I'm not a prosecutor. I just need to hear her story."

Donna nodded, and Charity continued into Wayne's office. She could understand Donna's protectiveness. After all, she'd told Charity from the start that Edna had been her friend since they were kids.

When Edna Buell entered Wayne's office, she didn't look any better than her husband. This fire, the scare, the aftermath, had all taken a real toll on this family. Charity felt badly for them. She hated to have to do even this much.

The woman, thin as a bird, sat on the chair. She had brushed her hair into a bun, she couldn't have been much older than thirty-five, but right now she looked about fifty. Wind, sun and suffering had carved themselves in her face, and the dress she wore looked a least one size too big.

Wayne made the introductions and asked after the children.

"They're okay. I lost all their school books in the fire, so they're in school with the other kids."

"How do they like that?"

"I'm not sure. It's different and I think they feel a little lost, but the teachers are being nice, and so are most of the other kids. They know most of the kids from Bible school."

"Of course," Wayne agreed.

Edna shook her head a little. "First time I've been asked for a pink backpack, though."

"Probably wouldn't have much use for that at home," Wayne remarked.

"None," Edna said. "I'm talking to Fred about it,

though. I know he needs the help, but maybe if I drive them we can manage to keep them in school. I could do more, then, around the place."

"A ranch is a lot of work," Wayne said gently. "And this fire didn't help anything. You want to talk to us about it?"

"Not really." But Edna's eyes moistened. "I've never been so scared in my life. As long as I live and breathe, I'm never going to forget the way the ceilings were burning."

"Everywhere?" Charity asked quietly.

"Just in patches at first. Fred says it must've been the old wallpaper. I don't know why, but some folks papered their ceilings. He can't recall it, so maybe it was his great-grandparents who did it. Anyway, some of it was painted over, some of it was the same as the walls. And it burned. Why would the ceilings burn?"

Wayne and Charity exchanged looks. "We're working on that," he said.

"And the smoke. By the time we'd grabbed the kids, we were choking. It was thick upstairs, not so bad downstairs, but by the time we got 'em all down, the front porch was burning. It looked like a window on hell. What if we hadn't been able to get out the back?"

Good question, thought Charity as she watched the woman pull a wadded handkerchief out of her purse and wipe at her eyes. "Every time I close my eyes, I see that fire, that smoke, those ceilings." She dissolved into tears while Charity watched helplessly. Nothing she could say or do was going to make this any better for Edna Buell.

When she could speak again, Edna said, "The kids are having nightmares. Every single night. I don't know if they'll ever feel safe again. Ever. I don't think I will."

She cried some more, but kept talking through her

tears. "I don't know what I would've done without Fred. He kept it together. Kept us moving. Found the way out. Then he saw the barn, and that's when he lost it, and it's all my fault. All of it!"

Charity felt shock rip through her. Aghast, she stared at the woman then looked at Wayne. He had to ask the next question since he was the official here, but she didn't want to hear the answer.

"Edna," Wayne said gently, "did you set that fire?"

"No, no, no! But my wishful thinking… It was my punishment."

"Punishment for what?"

"I wished I wasn't stuck out there all the time. Every day was the same, nothing ever got better, always wishing next year we'd do better and maybe be able to have a little fun, and we never can. I was complaining all the time and I wonder Fred didn't throw me out. Stupid, stupid, stupid! I made it happen because I couldn't stand it."

Silence filled the office. "So," Wayne said, "do you think Fred set the fire?"

Edna's head snapped up. "No way! He loves that place. He's proud of it. He wouldn't have a life without it. And he wouldn't risk hurting his kids or animals. I'm such a fool. I have the kindest man in the world for a husband and I was wishing it all away because I was tired of it. Well, I'm not tired of it anymore! No, sir. I know what's important now. It's those kids and my husband. That's all I want. But my stupid, wishful thinking… I brought it on us. I got my wish and now I wish I'd died."

Charity couldn't stop herself. She reached out and gripped Edna's shoulder. "Your wishing didn't make this happen. If wishes were horses, beggars would ride. You know that saying. If wishes made things happen, we'd all win the lottery or something."

"But I was evil inside!"

"You were worn-out. There's a big difference. Somebody else did this to you, and you shouldn't feel guilty. You didn't set that fire."

"No. And if I wished for it all to burn up, it would have been on a Sunday morning when we were all in church, not during a night when we were all in our beds and could have died." Edna sniffled and wiped her eyes again. "I don't wish my family dead. I don't!"

She broke down again and Wayne passed a box of tissues across his desk. Charity pulled a few of them out and pressed them into Edna's hand. Her hankie was soaked through.

"I feel so ugly inside," Edna confessed tearily. "I lost sight of what really matters and got so selfish. I don't even know how I turned into that ugly woman."

Charity patted her shoulder again, then leaned back. "Sometimes our thoughts get stuck in a rut and start to reinforce themselves. Unfortunately, sometimes it takes a shock to shake us free of that."

"I had a shock, all right. Thank goodness Donna helped Fred put in those smoke alarms when I asked." Edna sniffled and wiped her face again. "I won't be thinking that way anymore. Do you need me for something else? I gotta help my sister buy groceries. She can't afford to feed all five of us and she's waiting out front. The potluck helped. It really helped."

As Edna was leaving, Wayne asked casually, "Any reason Fred would leave stall doors open?"

Edna paused and turned. Above her reddened eyes, her brow knit. "Of course not. If you knew how hard he was on the kids about that and leaving gates open... Just two weeks ago he was all over the youngest for not

closing a stall door and a mare got out and into the oats.
Lucky we didn't lose her."

"Thanks," Wayne said. "I didn't think he would."

"Oats?" Charity asked after Edna had closed the door
behind her.

"Gassy food, those oats. As I understand it, you can't
feed too much at one time."

"Oh." She sat there both perplexed and certain, an
odd combination. She was certain that the Buells hadn't
caused the fire, but she was still perplexed by all she
didn't know and understand, not the least of them about
the stall doors. "Why are those doors so important to
you? You mapped it, but you haven't explained a thing."

"I know. I've been thinking about it, but I'll ask you to
hold your curiosity a little longer. I want us to be somewhere we can't be overheard."

She started. "You're worried about ears here? In your
office?"

"I'm worried about ears anywhere right now. We don't
know who this guy is."

He had a point, she thought. She looked down at the
scuffed toes of her boots, saw the dark streaks from the
ash. "I'm going to stay and participate in the training
exercise."

"How'd I know you'd say that?"

She looked up, drinking in his now-familiar face and
thinking how much she liked just looking at him. She
wished they were far away and enjoying a different kind
of privacy, the kind they had almost enjoyed early this
morning. Some part of her seemed to have developed a
perpetual ache to feel him hold her, surround her, enter
her.

"I'd much prefer you get out of here today," he said.

"I know. And I told you why I'm not. What better chance do we have?"

She watched him frown, oddly discomforted to be making him unhappy. Why should that matter? They had a problem to solve, they both knew it, and she seemed like the best route to a solution. This should all just be a matter of logic.

But she recognized that feelings had entered into it. She cared how he felt, and he seemed to care about her. Enough to hold her through the night so she wouldn't be alone after what had happened. Enough not to try to take advantage of her in even a small way when she probably would have crumbled like a house of cards if he'd tried to make love to her.

She looked down at her boots again. "I should get a room at the motel. People will talk."

"I don't give a damn. Let 'em talk. I'm not letting you out of my sight unless I'm sure someone trustworthy is around. Are you ready to file your report on the fire?"

"Pretty much. The Buells should get paid. I'll try to expedite the check, but I'm not sure how much I can speed it up. I've never had a case quite like this before. But I know we should be paying some living expenses for them in the meantime, and there's no reason that shouldn't come fast."

"So no problems?"

She looked up, feeling a small touch of amusement. "I didn't say that. I'm not sure they're used to paying homeowners who don't have a mortgage to deal with. They're more used to sending out estimators for repairs, and then stalling the big mortgagors for a while. This is going to blow their minds, paying the whole sum to the householders."

One corner of his mouth lifted. "Told you Fred was a careful man."

"Clearly. He made sure nobody could take the homestead without going to court. He's used his herd as collateral, I see, but never his house or land."

"So no matter what, he'd have the basics to get back on his feet."

"In theory. It's not looking so good right now." She rose and stretched. "Guess I'll go into the break room, then, and see how much I can get done."

"The guys'll bug you to death."

"That's fine." She shrugged. "I know how to turn down the volume."

The hard parts of being a firefighter, she had often thought, were the hours spent sitting around the firehouse waiting for something to happen. There was only so much you could work on equipment, and work out. Although as a volunteer, she hadn't had to do it often, she had heard about it plenty from the career types.

The guys were watching a movie on the flat-screen TV on the wall. They paused it as soon as she entered.

She looked at the screen. "An arson film? Really?"

Six men laughed. "We're not going to watch a kiddy movie," said Jeff.

"So you watch a movie about a firefighter arsonist?"

"Damn," said Hal Leas. "Isn't he stupid? So convinced a firefighter would never get hurt. Besides, it's fun to kibitz the way these guys fight fires. Most of 'em would be dead before they finished arguing with each other."

Everyone laughed because it was so true. Thirty seconds in black smoke without a breathing apparatus could kill even the healthiest of men, never mind one of those fires where the temps were obviously as high as a crematorium and one breath would have seared the lungs.

"It's a fun movie anyway," Jeff argued. "And you could understand the arsonist. He was after that nasty politician who wanted to cut the department and was risking the firefighter's lives."

"He should have looked further," Hal retorted. "He killed firemen."

Charity put her laptop on the table farthest from the screen. "Doesn't every life matter?"

Immediately they all chimed agreement. "Of course," one of the others said. "But it's just a stupid movie."

"About a really stupid firefighter," said Jeff, giving the other guy a little shove. More laughs.

"Mind if I work back here?" Charity asked. "You can keep watching. It won't bother me."

"We'll try not to get too noisy," Jeff answered. "And thanks again for the pie."

"Happy to do it."

She settled on the bench and opened her computer, waiting for it to boot up. Too many questions were swirling in her head, and nobody was off her mental hook.

An arsonist who knew what he was doing, or an arsonist who had made a mistake, underestimated what would happen and nearly cost a family their lives? Right now she was having trouble thinking any part of that burn had been accidental. After all, it seemed this guy was willing to try to kill her.

Freaking coward, she thought, as she connected with her files at the company and began entering her final assessment, which basically amounted to: pay the homeowners. Dealing death at a distance or indirectly was a whole lot easier than doing it face-to-face. Although a detective she knew had told her that once you killed someone, that line would never be there again. The next one got easier.

But she didn't see any sign of that. Burn a family out of its home, possibly killing them? Screw with carbon monoxide to kill her? Cowardly maybe, but not dumb. And definitely, it hadn't gotten easier for the arsonist, not yet. He was still staying at a distance, with a possibility it wouldn't work.

Her head snapped up as she thought about that. What did it mean, if she was right? Risk-taking while hoping the full consequences wouldn't occur? She was an arson investigator. Everyone in town probably knew that by now. What if she had been expected to recognize the effects of the carbon monoxide?

Would she have? She'd been getting a headache but hadn't felt any drowsiness yet. Anyway, everyone reacted differently. Some people seemed to feel nothing. Others reacted quickly and badly, including nausea and vomiting. The killer wouldn't know what type of reaction she would have. Had he been betting on her knowledge?

Her eyes strayed to the big screen, and she saw one of the climactic scenes beginning to play out. Back draft, one of the most dangerous situations a firefighter could face. A closed space heated to ignition or higher, but unable to flame once it had burned all the available oxygen. Then you opened a door or a window, letting in air, and the whole thing exploded. Firefighters had to be careful to check around doors and windows for smoke stains, indicating that the fire inside was trying to get oxygen. That it was fighting for its life, waiting for air to breathe. A deadly situation.

But the Buell house had been a flashover. Maybe a back draft situation had built in the walls, but the attic had plenty of oxygen, and the fire had exploded in a critical flashover as soon as ignition temperature was reached. Instant ignition of everything in the room, every single surface.

Too bad the walls were gone now. She'd have loved to be able to look around at some nail holes to see if the signs were there.

Then she thought of the photos she had taken of those holes at the bottom of the house. She called one up, magnified it and studied it intently. The spray of black emanating from it could suggest a fire that wasn't getting enough oxygen. It was sending out tendrils of smoke, because one of the weirdest things about a back draft was the way the nearly airtight space seemed to breathe. In and out like a bellows as it tried to burn, then gain oxygen. She'd even felt it once while touching a sooty window, a minor vibration, like a quietly growling beast.

A warning, one no firefighter ever ignored. The minute sufficient oxygen reached the overheated room, it would explode.

So a combination of factors at the Buell house? A back draft situation in the walls that the arsonist didn't fully understand, one that maybe hadn't worked as planned? Then a flashover in the attic because a volatile mixture of accelerant and air were ignited? And anything could have ignited it, even the heat building in the walls with the back draft.

Crazy. Amazing. Shouldn't even be possible. But clearly it had been. But the more she thought about it, the less likely she believed the outcome had been planned. It had been an accident of structure, chemicals and heat all coming together in an explosive instant.

Nobody could have planned it that way.

But somebody could have believed they knew more

about fire than they did. Someone could have thought events would play out very differently. That the Buells would have had more time. Or maybe that the fire had failed completely.

She finished her writing, but wanted to wait a bit before sending her report, to read it over once more. Besides, since talking to Edna, she was wondering. Wondering if Edna's complaints had driven her husband to try to torch the place, the only possible way out.

And Wayne was worrying about those open stall doors.

All of a sudden her perspective shifted, and she realized it was possible that Fred Buell had done the whole thing, not realizing how fast the house would burn, opening stall doors in the hopes animals would escape.

Her heart quickened. Talking with Edna had given her the first real intimation of a motive for Fred to do this. Inexperienced with fire, it all might have escaped him. He could have set the fires without guessing the attic would flash over. He could have opened the barn so the animals would escape, but maybe that had burned too fast as well, and cost him some livestock. Had anybody actually asked how many animals he had stabled versus how many had died?

Of course not. It was all so freaking clear that Fred wouldn't do this to himself or his family.

Feeling sickened by the turn of her own thoughts, she tried to rein them in. Reminding herself that she wasn't supposed to solve this, but merely to find evidence of fraud, and she had no evidence of fraud. None. Nothing but an ugly, niggling suspicion. God, she was going to have to run through this all again. And how did it tie to the attempts against her? Something wasn't right.

She still had time to think; no decision had to be made today. Since it was Friday, it wouldn't slow down the payment any. Just as she was closing her computer, one of the guys spoke.

"So are you coming to train with us on Monday?"

With a start she realized the movie had ended. "I think I will," she said. "Not much, I don't want to get in the way, but it'd be fun to suit up again."

All the guys seemed to think that was great. Then one asked her, "You ever seen a real back draft?"

"Yeah, once."

Of course they all wanted to hear about it, and about how it had been handled. "You need to go high," she said. "As high as you can to let the heat and smoke escape upward. We took off the roof and worked our way down."

"Wow," said Jeff. "People forget that smoke burns."

"Yeah, they do," she agreed. "It's funny in a way."

"How so?"

"Well, I deal with arsonists. Most of them can't make a big fire for anything. They don't understand it. But then people forget what can really burn, including smoke, soot and carbon monoxide."

As soon as she spoke the words, something inside her stilled. Carbon monoxide burned.

Just then Wayne appeared. "Charity? The sheriff wants to finish his report. Can you spare a few?"

"Sure." She hopped up, grabbing her computer and her jacket. "See you guys," she said.

"Like Monday?" Hal asked, and laughed.

"For sure Monday," she agreed, laughing back.

She climbed into Wayne's car once again even though the sheriff's office wasn't far away.

"You don't look so good," he remarked.

"Carbon monoxide burns."

"Of course." Then he hit the brake as they were backing out of the bay. He looked at her. "My God."

"Exactly. Let's go. I don't want anyone wondering what's going on out here."

He finished backing out and headed toward the sheriff's office at the center of the town. "Immediate explosion," he muttered.

"If it got dense enough. Admittedly, the likelihood is probably slim, but there were ignition sources in that house. I just question whether it would have been enough."

"Thank God we'll never know. Still, any way you look at it, you were sitting there in an extremely volatile mixture."

"Well, it just struck me, but it's probably too far out there. Nobody would plan to start a fire that way. The likelihood of success is too slim."

"But it fits with our semicapable arsonist."

She almost snickered. "That's a good description. I was thinking about what we know about the Buell fire again, and I can't imagine that was planned to happen the way it played out."

"I'm having trouble with that, too. But FYI, when you were in the back working, I managed to get hold of Fred Buell. The all-important question was answered. The walls were originally stuffed with newspaper, as far as he knows."

"Which would have settled and become less flammable as a result."

"Which would have created a smoldering burn in the presence of an accelerant."

She sighed. "So we've got our method. Now we just need our man." And Fred Buell was once again on her list.

* * *

The sheriff wanted to know if they'd learned anything else that might lead him to the arsonist. They huddled together in his office with the door closed, and at last Wayne explained about the open stalls and showed him the map.

Gage shook his head. "Doesn't make sense."

"Unless the arsonist was hoping the animals found a way out of the barn."

"Like people, animals don't always think clearly when they're terrified. From what you said that fire happened fast. So what the hell does it mean?"

"I wish I could read minds," Wayne answered. "For a little while I feared it meant that Fred had left the barn open for the animals to escape, but after talking to his wife…no way. In the first place, he could have just taken the animals out of the barn for the night. In the second, he was in bed with his wife when the alarms went off, and I don't think he's the kind of man who would have risked his family that way, or burned his livestock alive."

"I don't, either," Gage agreed. "Not unless his mind snapped more than I can believe possible. And if it had, I think we'd be seeing some signs of it even now."

Charity remained silent, keeping her questions to herself. As quickly as Gage Dalton had come to Fred Buell's defense, she figured that raising questions about him would get her exactly nowhere. It was the kind of thing a person in her position had to avoid: stepping on the toes of the officials involved.

Gage looked at her. "Are you about ready to close up shop?"

She shook her head. "I need a few more details and then I promised to drill with the crew on Monday."

Gage half smiled. "Glutton for punishment?" he asked.

"Maybe just missing something I used to enjoy."

He nodded understanding. "Oh, the state investigator ought to be out here on Tuesday. About time. Maybe we'll get some answers for everyone."

Charity doubted it. While she was sure the state investigator had a lot more experience than she did, she'd also seen the scene and knew how little was left.

Unless something turned up fast, she was going to be ordering the check for the Buells early next week.

Because there were always questions left, unless you caught the perp. And that was rare enough.

Wayne had the weekend off. He finished up at four in the afternoon, and he and Charity headed back to his house. He was trying to think of something fun the two of them could do that evening. Kind of a date, he supposed.

But in all honesty he wasn't sure she was in the mood. She'd been looking troubled since before they went to see Gage, and he wondered what was bugging her. It wasn't written all over her or anything. Little was. But she was quieter and graver than he was used to. As if she'd doubled down on her poker face.

Well, he was a little troubled himself. That map of the barn was burning a hole in his clipboard and the back of his brain.

Sighing silently, he pushed all thoughts of a fun evening away. He suspected the two of them were going to be working.

Even as he had the thought, however, it struck him that in all the years he'd been doing this job, he'd never been able to bring it home with him. Lisa hadn't wanted to hear about it. Linda had to be protected from most of it. So he'd had no one to share his preoccupations with. It was different with Charity, and he kind of liked it. If something was bugging him, he didn't have to leave it at the station.

On the other hand, tonight he would have liked nothing more than to light some candles, share an intimate light meal, then make love to the woman beside him until she was moaning helplessly with delight.

It was like being a teenager all over again, he thought with amusement at himself. All these years spent growing older and, he hoped, a little wiser, yet here he was feeling like a kid on a first date wondering if he could get to first base. And no cautions about how short a time they'd known each other were going to help. He'd known Lisa nearly the whole time they were growing up. There'd been almost nothing he didn't know about her...until the day she'd dumped him.

So much for lengthy courtships. You could hardly do any worse by falling in love at first sight.

If Charity wasn't right there, he might have laughed out loud. Love? Nowhere near, he assured himself. Desire... Oh, yeah. Plenty of that around.

Once they were inside, she wanted to go shower. He sent her on her way while considering the problem of dinner. He had to feed her something, and he wasn't going to run the risk of taking her to Maude's again, because she was right. Everybody was already probably talking. Bound to be. Something new and different in this town gained everyone's attention.

A while later, while he was still pondering his own emotional state, he heard the familiar sound of his car engine pull up and soon Lindy bounded through the door, schoolbooks in one arm, backpack over her shoulder.

"Hey, Dad," she said, and gave him a quick kiss on the cheek. "Where's Charity?"

"Taking a shower. We were out at the scene again today."

"Filthy stuff, fire," she said, wrinkling her nose. "I told you I'm going to Mo's tonight, right?"

"Yeah, you did."

"So I'll just go pack." Then she paused. "You guys can manage dinner?"

Wayne feigned offense. "Do I look helpless?"

She gave him a sidelong look. "Considering some of the meals I had to eat after Mom left…"

"You little…"

"You love me," she interrupted brightly. "There's one of those frozen Italian meals in the freezer for emergencies. And a loaf of frozen garlic bread. Add a little Parmesan and it's a gourmet meal."

He scowled.

She laughed again. "Okay, I'm outta here. Just gotta grab a change of clothes."

Just then, Charity emerged from the hall bath with her head wrapped in a towel, and her body wrapped in a green terrycloth robe. She saw Linda and her face brightened immediately. "I thought I'd missed you!"

"No such luck," Linda answered cheerfully. "I was just giving Dad dinner instructions."

Wayne rolled his eyes. "You'd never guess I made it thirty-six years without much help."

Linda retorted. "You'd never guess how much he learned the hard way after Mom left."

He didn't appreciate hearing Charity's giggle.

"Anyway," Linda continued breezily, "I just need to grab some clothes and I'll be out of your hair."

"Great," he said, sounding to his own ears like a sullen teenager.

Linda glanced at him. "Sorry, did I embarrass you?" Then she rushed on before he could answer, "I won't be back in the morning because tomorrow is senior picnic, so a bunch of us are going to be making potato salad to take, and maybe some rolls, and…" She hesitated. "Dad?"

He softened. "What?"

"The girls were thinking about staying at Dineen's house after the picnic tomorrow. Will that upset you?"

"You mean I won't see you again until Sunday?"

Linda nodded.

He sighed. "I'm getting used to it. Go. Have fun. Stay out of trouble."

"Jeremy makes sure of that," she answered, wrinkling her nose. "That's the problem with having a dad who's the sheriff."

"Or a dad who's a fire chief," Wayne replied, unable to keep a tremor of amusement from his voice.

"Like living under a microscope," Linda said, then darted toward her bedroom.

He saw Charity look after her before coming farther into the living room. "Handful," she said.

"Slightly." He smiled. "Well, that leaves the two of us. I thought I'd make dinner, with or without Lindy's instructions, unless you want to go to the diner."

She gave a slight shake of her head. "I'll help make dinner here, if that's okay. But first I need to dress."

The words were out almost before he knew it, quiet and a bit husky. "No. You don't."

He watched with pleasure as her cheeks flamed. She looked down then met his gaze again, and he saw a smile fluttering around the edges of her mouth. "I guess I don't."

Passion slammed him like a freight train with the worst possible timing, since Lindy came down the hall again, carrying a tote and a backpack. "Behave, you two," she said as she reached the front door. "Don't do anything I wouldn't do." Her laughter trailed her out the door.

Wayne stared at the closed door. "Should I worry about that?"

Charity giggled again. "I don't know. No experience here."

"There are quite a few things a father would rather not know." He returned his attention to her.

Her smile remained. "I'm sure. Don't worry, she'll tell you all about it when she's thirty."

"I can hardly wait. Are you hungry?"

"Starved."

He held out his hand. "Then, let's go rustle up something."

The feeling of her delicate hand resting within his much bigger one tugged at him. He hadn't held hands with anyone since his wife, and come to think of it, they'd stopped holding hands years before she left.

Only now did he realize how much he missed that friendly, caring contact. Maybe Lindy was right to warn him. Charity would leave. The question was what she would leave behind.

Then he decided he damned well didn't care. Whatever life might be gifting him with this weekend, he needed it. He wanted it. To hell with the aftermath.

He could have just taken Lindy's advice, but he didn't want to unless he couldn't figure out something else. Seemed kind of cheesy to pull a frozen dinner, even a good one, out of the freezer. He was being a bit silly and knew it. This wasn't a date or anything, so why try to impress her? But for some reason he wanted to prove he was good for something besides his job.

Together he and Charity scoured the cupboards and the fridge. Sometimes when she moved he caught a glimpse of the curve of her breast when her robe gaped a little, but she seemed either not to mind or to be oblivious to it. He enjoyed the view either way.

"I think I need to go grocery shopping tomorrow," he remarked when they'd taken inventory. "The larder's looking bare."

"You should see mine. Cans of soup, a few things in the freezer and if I buy any fruit or veggies they'd better get eaten immediately."

"You really are home that rarely?"

"Yeah. And I never know how long I'll be there when I am."

He leaned back against the counter, looking at her. "I'm asking seriously here. Are you happy with that?"

She hesitated, and for the first time he saw her bite her lip. Unidentifiable feelings danced across her face only to vanish before he could read them. "I don't know anymore," she admitted at last. "I just accepted it. Now... It sounds awful, doesn't it?"

"Not if it makes you happy." Hard to say, but true.

She looked down. "I don't think it does anymore. I've been blaming the boyfriends, but now...I blame me."

"I don't think there's any blame," he said quietly. "You are who you are."

"But is it really me?" Her tone conveyed a surprising anguish, and he came closer. She sat at the small kitchen table and folded her arms in front of her.

"Are you okay?"

"No," she admitted.

He squeezed her shoulder, deciding the safest thing was to sit across from her. She needed some space to talk right now, and he didn't want to do anything that might silence her. But all this time he'd been looking at her as a bright butterfly who was flitting through his life, he'd never really considered that she might not be a butterfly at all. Not even after what she had told him last night. He figured she'd take that new understanding home with her, but he had no way of knowing what she might do with it. Would she change? Would she be able to? He didn't figure he'd ever know.

"Since coming here," she said quietly, "I've been facing a lot of things I've been missing. Like hanging out at the firehouse with good people. Then I see you and Linda and I know what else I'm missing. I'm so busy running I never stop long enough to build anything. Maybe I can't put down roots. But now I know what I'm missing."

He waited a moment. "I'm sorry."

"No point in being sorry. It's the way I chose to live. I could have put a halt to this merry-go-round any time after I grew up, but I didn't. My choice. Now maybe I need to make another choice."

"It can be really hard to make a major life change."

She lifted her gaze. "Not if you know what you want."

He felt her words like an electric shock, then wondered if he was misunderstanding. Their eye contact was palpable, charged with meaning. He opened his mouth to say something, to tell her not to leave. Or ask her what she meant. Before he could decide what to say, she changed the subject. "Enough of my confusion. I vote we go with Lindy's suggestion for dinner. Easy and uncomplicated. Then tomorrow I'll go grocery shopping with you and we'll get the biggest, juiciest steak we can find. I hear from Linda that you grill them."

"I do."

"And baked potatoes." She rose and went to the freezer, pulling out the packages. "So, Wayne, when are you going to tell me why those open stall doors trouble you?" He tried to get another look at her eyes, but the shades were down again. Would they ever stay up long enough for him to get inside?

Chapter 11

"Let's talk about it after dinner," he answered, working to keep his cool. With practiced skill he pulled out the deepest sauté pan and turned on the oven. They'd gotten close to something, and then she'd pulled a disappearing act. For the first time he felt some genuine sympathy for her exes. Guys weren't necessarily known for their emotional IQ, but to never be allowed to get close? That would be a bigger problem than her travel.

He'd gotten past that shell a couple of times, but it seemed to snap back fast.

Dinner was almost ready. He gave the chicken Florentine another stir and checked the timer. The bread would be out of the oven in a minute. He even found a bag of precut salad to go with it, along with some bottled dressing. And he'd included the Parmesan Linda had insisted on, apparently forgetting that he'd been the one who had taught her that. As always, thinking of his daughter made him smile.

Charity didn't have any kind of family, no attachments, nobody to make her smile at a simple thought. The pain he felt for her was huge, but if she didn't stop darting away she'd never have any of it. Danged if he knew how to pin her down, to get her to deal with it. Wasn't his place anyway.

Just as the timer dinged, she astonished him. "I'm sorry, Wayne. I did it again."

He bent and pulled the baking pan out, putting a split loaf of garlic bread on the counter. "It's okay."

"No, damn it, it's not okay. Even I can figure out that much. I've shared things with you that I've never shared with anyone, and then I shut you down? That's not right."

Dealing with people in extreme circumstances, whether from fire or injury or loss, had taught him a thing or two about human nature, but he was acutely aware that right now he was wading in over his head. All he could do was offer honesty. "I didn't like it."

"I know you didn't. It was awful of me."

"I wouldn't say that. I just didn't like it. I wanted to hear more about what you were thinking, but you have a right not to tell me."

She rose and joined him at the counter, pulling out the cutting board and bread knife, turning the loaf into neatly cut diagonal slices while he spooned the chicken dish into a serving bowl.

"You know," she said as she placed the bread on a plate, "a friend of mine went to see a psychologist years ago, and he told her she needed to learn to set boundaries. And you know what she said to me?"

"What?"

"That I had boundaries so high she envied me. I'm not feeling enviable right now."

"You told me how rootless you were as a child. Is it because of that?"

"My boundaries? Maybe. Maybe not. At this late date it would probably take a shrink several years to figure it out. Doesn't matter anyway. Regardless of what caused it, this is how I am. And the way I am is always on the run."

He put the bowl on the table. "What are you running from, Charity? Seriously. Are there monsters outside, or are they inside?"

She tilted her head, her gaze growing distant as she thought about what he was asking. "I don't know. I've asked myself."

She'd forgotten the bread, so he reached for the plate and put it on the table beside the salad and the chicken. As if coming back to herself, she took the plates and silverware he'd set on the counter earlier and placed them on the table.

"What am I running from?" she repeated as they sat. "Good question. I know what I was afraid of when I was a kid, but I'm not a kid anymore. I'm not so sure I was running back then as much as assuming a self-protective crouch. But I'm an adult now, and I'm running. Honestly, I don't know if I'm afraid of the monsters outside or the ones inside."

He paused as he passed her the bowl of chicken. "I can't imagine that you have any monsters inside of you... unless it's fear."

She nodded slowly, and served herself just as slowly. "I think it *is* fear. Fear of being hurt. It's easier to keep moving than to risk it. Don't let anyone in, don't settle, just hide behind my walls. God, what an image of myself!"

"I doubt you're alone in that."

She gave him a crooked smile. "Are you always so positive?"

"Not always," he admitted. "But you're being awfully hard on yourself. I get the feeling you want to change your life. That could be a great thing. But beating yourself up accomplishes nothing, don't you think?"

"Unless it motivates me to make some changes, it's useless."

"Exactly."

"This Florentine is good," she remarked.

He waited, wondering whether she would dart behind the wall of work-related subjects again or open up more. He hoped she opened up. Discussing the Buell fire would hold for morning. And on that subject he now had some serious doubts raging in his head. He suspected she did, too. For that reason alone he wanted to leave it for morning.

"So you get weekends off?" she asked.

"Not always, but I tried to set it up that way after Lisa left because I wanted the time with Lindy. Now she doesn't need me on weekends anymore, so maybe I should pick up some of the slack I've created and let Ken have more weekends."

"He's like your assistant chief?"

"Like. He doesn't get the title, but I managed to get him a raise as alternate incident commander. He could do better in another town, but so far he claims he's happy with the way things are." And here they were talking business again. Frustrated though he felt, he knew he had to let her take this at her own speed.

"He seems like a great guy. They all seem like great guys."

"We're fortunate. We have a team of friends, not just colleagues."

She nodded, eating slowly. "It must be hard to have them trying to cut your budget every year."

"Not every year. They push, I shove back. Unfortunately, with all the arsons this year, they may be questioning our ability to keep a lid on things. They may think we should be able to solve the arsons, or prevent them somehow. So they'll push some more. They may try to funnel some of our money elsewhere if they think it could do more good, like to the sheriff."

She looked up. "If we had a firefighter arsonist, I wonder if he's thought of that. I mean, if he wanted more dollars in the budget and thought he could get them by having more fires, it could backfire."

"Distinct possibility. Especially if we can't catch him."

"Yeah." She looked down again, ate some more chicken and nibbled at her garlic bread and salad.

Wayne studied her, trying not to stare, but wishing he could read her mind. Would anyone ever know what was truly going on inside this woman? He doubted he'd ever met anyone as self-contained.

"Why are you going to the drill on Monday?" he asked point-blank.

She blinked, looking a bit startled. "I told you, I miss it."

He shook his head. "It's more than that. Are you hoping someone will take another stab at killing you?"

"I'm not suicidal!"

"You were the one who said you ought to hang around because the only way we're likely to get this guy is if he slips up. You said you needed to dangle yourself like bait."

Her answer was dry. "I'm hardly dangling myself

when I'm so completely not alone. In fact, I seem to be highly protected."

"And you're going to stay protected. If you drill in the burn room, I'm going to stay right beside you every step."

"I kinda somehow thought you would. You're a very protective man, Chief."

"And I don't think you know how to take care of yourself very well."

He might as well have thrown gasoline on hot embers. She jumped up from the table, throwing down her napkin. "You can go to hell!"

"Somehow I think that's where you intend to send me when you leave."

But he was talking to her departing back. What had possessed him to throw that gauntlet? But he knew. Wanting filled him like a raging storm, wanting something he knew he could never have. He was banging around, trying to open a door to reach her, and she kept locking him out. Somehow, he'd reached his own point of no return. Frustration had goaded him into stupidity, something he usually never let happen.

He rose, too, and found her dressed, pulling her suitcase and carrying her laptop toward the front door.

"Running again?" he asked quietly.

"What do you care?"

"Just happen to."

"Right."

He reached her in two strides, taking the laptop and suitcase from her. "Call the cops and tell them I'm holding you prisoner, 'cause, sweetie, you ain't going anywhere."

"I will!"

"Sure. Be my guest. They'll probably laugh themselves silly, but I won't let you out that door alone. Wanna leave town? Fine, I'll put you on the plane myself. At least I'll be sure you're safe."

She glared at him, her hazel eyes turning almost green with her anger. He didn't know what exactly was going on here, but he suspected she was feeling threatened by the growing closeness between them. At least he hoped she was. If he was scaring her in some other way, then he deserved to be damned.

"You don't have the right," she insisted hotly.

"Nope. But I'm giving it to myself."

"You are…you are…" She appeared to be winding up to dump a pile of insults on his head, but then with startling suddenness, her shoulders drooped and she seemed to collapse in on herself.

He dropped her laptop on the armchair, letting her bag fall to the floor. Then before she could say or do a thing, he wrapped her in a bear hug so tight he was surprised she didn't squeak. At first she stiffened, and he could feel her impulse to break free. But at last she began to soften, and finally just sagged in his arms.

"Wayne," she whispered.

"I'm here."

"I think I'm losing my mind."

"I think you're waking up." For a fireman, she was a light load, and he picked her right up, one arm behind her shoulders, the other behind her knees. He carried her to the couch and sat with her on his lap. He cradled her head on his shoulder, rubbing her hip soothingly.

Whatever happened, she needed to deal with her demons. He just hoped he could help, even though some passionate demons of his own demanded a hearing.

She didn't cry, but he could feel ripples of tension run through her and then release. Holding her seemed to be all he could do.

"I'm scared," she whispered finally.

"Of what? The killer? Me?"

"Me. Scared of myself."

Once again he had to wait, but the words finally emerged, small and quiet. "Everything good in my life, every single thing, I've managed to break."

Her words startled him. He got that she couldn't put down roots, but what was she leading to here? He waited again, sensing that she'd talk when she was ready. At least she wasn't fighting him.

"I don't just run," she said. "I break. I've broken several good relationships with men. I didn't think about doing it, didn't plan it, but I look back and see what I did wrong. How I pushed it until it snapped. Firefighting. I loved it, Wayne, but as soon as they wanted to hire me, I broke that, too. I just walked away and said something to the chief that made sure he'd never want me back."

"What did you say?"

"I can barely remember now. Something about how I had better things to do. It was enough."

"Okay." He got it. That *would* be enough.

Another shudder passed through her. "Why would anyone put up with me? Of course no one can. I've broken off friendships when I sensed I was getting too close. It would be one thing if I just packed and moved on but I do more than that. I make sure no one will ever call or write. I clear the decks. That's what I do."

"All right."

"All right?" Her voice came out reedy. "That's not all right. It's not normal. I see normal all around me, and I know that's not me. Stay away from me, Wayne. I'm not worth the time of day."

"I can't agree with that." His heart was heavy with pain for her, but he couldn't accept that. "It might be hard, but you can change. Just take one little step at a time."

"Right." She shook her head against his shoulder. "You could be my first experiment. Are you ready for that? Are you ready for what I might do?"

"Been there, done that," he said. "I survived. I wouldn't be dancing for joy, obviously, but I know I can survive, Charity. If you want to try breaking out, try it with someone who understands what's going on inside you. You already told me to go to hell. I didn't let you leave."

At that something that felt almost like a short, silent laugh passed through her. "Right. You're going to keep me prisoner."

"I wouldn't give up without a fight. That's different."

She sighed, and at last he felt true relaxation as her body weighed heavily against him. "Well, I think I got it all out," she said after a few minutes. "Amazing I have to thank an arsonist for making me face myself."

"Sometimes it takes something that big. You know that. Question is, what do you want to do about it? Anything?"

At that moment she pulled back a little. He turned his head and found her looking straight at him. "I know what I want right now. Question is, do you want to take the risk?"

"I'm a born risk taker," he said with perfect truth. On the outside he might look like a settled small-town guy, but then there was the other man, the man who ran toward fire rather than away from it. Right now, she was the blaze he was facing, and the stakes were high. She wouldn't leave him dead, but she could leave him wounded.

She lifted her hand and cupped his cheek. "Brave man," she said.

He didn't think so. She reminded him of a mare that had never learned to trust. Not that he wanted to tame her, but she needed a gentle hand and an awful lot of patience until she could settle without fear. He didn't know if she'd give him the chance to offer her that, but he was damned if he was going to end this without trying to find out.

Of one thing he was certain, though. She had trusted him more than she had probably ever trusted anyone else. It had to be hard to self-examine this way. Well, of course it was. He'd done it during the time after Lisa had left him. Lots of miserable self-evaluation and re-evaluation. Painful and difficult.

All he could do was hold her, surround her in his arms and let her know that he wasn't going to pull away or dismiss her because of her feelings and self-discovery. What else could any mortal do, other than be supportive?

"How do you get through this?" she asked almost to herself.

"One step at a time, like anything else." Cheap psychology, but he didn't know any other answer for her. "Or you can toss it all out and return to life as usual."

"I'm strangely reluctant to do that," she admitted. "It wasn't much of a life. I kept busy because I didn't have a life. Funny how almost losing it makes me want more of it."

He hesitated, then said, "Which I guess brings us back to this whole thing about you dangling yourself out there. Charity..."

She laid a finger over his lips. "Like I said, I don't seem to be doing much dangling, thanks to you. But let's not go there right now."

"Where do you want to go?"

"Straight to bed with you."

The Fourth of July couldn't have any more fireworks than the ones going off in Wayne's head and body. Charity stripped for him again as they stood beside his bed. Her lack of self-consciousness surprised him, as much as he enjoyed watching her reveal all her delightful secrets. No apologies, no hesitation, no sense that she doubted her own attractiveness as a woman.

When she was naked, she lowered herself to his bed and leaned back, everything about her appearing calm, almost casual.

Her lack of hesitation troubled him in some way. Even as he reached for the buttons of his shirt, he paused, bothered. Had she somehow managed to lock herself behind walls so high that she didn't have the doubts most women had about whether a man would find her beautiful? Because she surely was beautiful, comfortable in her nudity in an unexpected way.

Or perhaps she didn't care. Maybe she had learned not to care. Or worse, had she gone into some cave inside herself where nothing could reach her? As if she was offering her body like a sacrifice while the rest of her departed to somewhere safer? Was she even really here with him?

All of a sudden, he felt unsure, wondering if, despite what she said, he was taking advantage of her.

"Wayne?"

He realized he'd been standing still too long. "Are you sure about this?" he asked. Because however much he wanted her, he didn't want her if she had to disappear to some closed-off space within herself.

"I'm sure." Then, amazing him, she smiled and lifted a hand. "Did I put you off?"

"I just want you to be right here, right now, with me."

Her smile faded a little but she continued to hold out her hand to him. "I'm here. I'm more here than I've ever been except in the middle of a fire."

Still feeling a bit unsure, but unable to hold himself back, he stripped quickly. The make-or-break moment, he thought with an almost grim amusement, even as need hammered his entire body. He felt his erection stiffen until the ache became consuming. In a last moment of sanity, he pulled a condom from the drawer and rolled it on.

He knew what she saw. He was in good shape, but being a fireman didn't leave a body unscarred. He waited, watching her gaze trail over his nakedness for the very first time. Lisa had been appalled by some of his scars, had even once asked if he couldn't have them removed somehow.

But Charity didn't do that. Rolling onto her side, she touched his arm, his thigh, causing his heart to beat liked a huge drum.

"Transfer burns?" she asked.

"Yeah." When a fire was hot enough, if the exterior of a turnout uniform heated enough then got compressed against the skin by movement or an obstacle, the heat could pass right through the protective layers. Almost all firefighters got second-degree burns; some got worse. He had a few that were worse.

"I was lucky and never got one."

Before he could answer, she seized his hand and pulled him down. He nearly fell on her, twisting just in time so that he caught most of his weight on his elbow, one leg across hers.

Then he heard the most wonderful sound in the world: Charity laughed. He looked down into her face and saw no more of the distance he had feared. She was definitely here with him in the now. Those sparkling eyes, the smile, the catch in her breathing... Oh, yes, the fire had been lit.

She raised her hands, running them over his shoulders, still smiling. "You're a beautiful man, Wayne Camden. Of course, I knew you would be, but it's more than that gorgeous body of yours. It shines from your eyes."

He didn't know how to answer that, so he gave up all attempts to speak and instead covered her mouth in a deep kiss that tried to spill all his hunger into her. Her arms tightened on his shoulders as she opened her mouth to him, holding him close, pulling him closer still.

When she pulled her mouth from his, it was only to draw a couple of shuddery breaths and murmur, "Feel me. I've never wanted anyone so much."

Nor had he, he realized. He had thought he had known desire in all its forms, but now he discovered a whole new world, one where it conquered him.

He could smell the heat rising from her, a heady, dizzying scent, joined by his own, he was sure. Her skin felt like silk everywhere their bodies met, and as he lowered his head to taste her sweet mouth again, he ran his palm down her side. She squirmed as if delighted by the sensation, and her nails dug into his shoulders. He could feel impatience building in her just as it was building in him. Just as it had been building since the moment he had heard the swish of her stockings as she'd raised her leg in that teasing fashion.

He wanted to move slowly, to savor this precious gift, but passion goaded him almost to the edge of insanity.

When her hips began to rock beneath him, he knew she was ready, as ready as he was.

He slid his hand down between her legs, drawing a groan from her, feeling her arch into his touch, feeling a dampness that told him she was right with him.

His mind whirled away, with one last thought about finesse, then he slid over her and into her as if propelled by irresistible force. At once her hands gripped his hips, pulling closer still as if she wanted all of him inside her.

The universe began to move in time with the pounding of his body, a syncopation as irresistible as the woman beneath him. Time and again they rocked together; the ache growing, building, consuming them.

When he felt her stiffen and cry out in completion, he followed her almost instantly, everything inside him exploding, erupting, filling his head and body with a million fireworks.

Dazzled, he returned slowly to earth, holding Charity in his arms, knowing she now owned her own place in his heart.

"Wow." The quiet murmur escaped her. His body was still heated, slick now with sweat, and so sated he felt as if the strength had been drained from him.

But when she gave him a little push on the shoulder, he managed to pull away from her and fall flat on his back.

"Delilah," he whispered in response.

Delight filled him as a quiet laugh escaped her. "I didn't cut your hair."

"Might as well have." He opened his eyes as much as he could and saw she now rested on her side, smiling at him. She looked sleepy with sated passion, but happy. As happy as he felt.

Her hand came to rest on his chest, and he was sure she could feel the heavy, rapid beat of his heart.

"I demand a rematch," she said.

"Dang, woman, give me a minute to recover."

Her smile grew a bit impish. "Oh, I need it, too. I thought you put out fires. Never occurred to me you caused conflagrations."

He laughed. "Be right back." Drained though he felt, he hurried to his bath to take care of some necessary business, and returned with a warm, damp washcloth. Kneeling beside her, he began to wash her gently, removing any remaining stickiness.

"Heaven," she said, closing her eyes and giving herself up to his ministrations. Her movements beneath his touch were sinuous, almost catlike, and so very sexy. He was sure he enjoyed it every bit as much as she. He took the opportunity to explore her, returning to the bath a couple of times to dampen the cloth again with hot water.

Every line of her was perfect. Neither overendowed nor underendowed, she struck him as elegant right down to the arches of her feet. Even her toes might have been carved by an expert sculptor. Bending, he kissed the inside of each foot, and felt a shiver run through her.

When he finished, he snagged a corner of the covers and pulled them over her. "You must be getting chilled."

"I could never get chilled around you."

A smile filled him as surely as it appeared on his face. At last he slipped beneath the blanket with her, and she came into his arms as naturally as if she had always belonged there. She certainly fit against him as if she did.

Then, trying for another peek into her mind, he spoke. "I noticed you don't seem to be troubled by nudity. Not even a little shy. What were you thinking about when you stripped for me?" Because given the way this woman had of disappearing inside herself, he still wondered if she had been doing that initially.

A small laugh escaped her. "When I was growing up, I spent a lot of time in Europe. Nudity isn't a big deal there."

"Really?" He tried to imagine it. He was used to something very different.

"Really. To give you an example, some women my mother knew got caught in a downpour and darted into a restaurant. They stripped to their underwear and had lunch while their clothes dried over the radiators. It shocked Mom, which was why she mentioned it, but it made perfect sense to me. But I'd already been exposed and I was just ten."

"Cute story."

"Bet I'd get arrested if I tried that here."

"Maybe. After every guy in the vicinity got an eyeful anyway."

She laughed again and stretched against him, reawakening the hunger that never seemed to die around her. She must have felt him hardening, because all of a sudden she tossed the blankets aside and reached for his stiffening erection. "Nice," she murmured. "I like being able to do that to you."

Then she astonished him by kissing the burn scar on his upper arm.

"What?" she asked, apparently feeling him tense.

"Nothing really. Well, Lisa thought those scars were ugly. She asked if I could get them removed."

"Not likely." She bent and kissed him there again, then laid her hand over the scar on his thigh. While he missed her warm grasp around his penis, her touch on his leg eased something deep within him. "Badges of courage," she said. "A lot of courage. I was lucky. I never got burned, but that wouldn't have lasted if I'd stayed. I remember more than one of the guys suddenly running out of a building, stripping his turnout gear at top speed. Then he'd ask someone to look and it was always the same. 'Hot spot. Get to the ambulance.'"

"Yeah. Just part of the job."

She curled closer, once again wrapping her warm hand around his penis, pressing a kiss to his chin. "Up for another round, Chief?"

Was he ever. This time she put the condom on him, the most exquisite torture ever devised. Then she rose above him, straddling his hips, supporting herself on her knees and arms, giving him a full view of all her delights. Her breasts dangled enticingly close, and he lifted his head, sucking one of her dusky pink nipples into his mouth. Then he slid his hand down between them and found her dewy core, parting her petals so he could stroke that exquisitely sensitive nub of nerves. She caught her breath, arching a little, almost pulling free of his mouth on her breast, but not quite.

"Damn, you light my fuse fast," she gasped.

"Me, too," he answered with the last bit of air he seemed to be able to find.

Drawing her nipple deeply into his mouth, he sucked hard and harder, finally nipping gently until she cried out. Her hips bucked against his hand, and he felt his own hips reaching up, trying to meet her. She was driving him nuts, driving everything from his head except a need to find satisfaction within her depths. She rocked above him, teasing him while pleasing herself, her movements telling him where and how much she wanted.

He ached and throbbed, his entire universe centered on her, on the opening so tantalizingly close, on the scents and sounds that enveloped him and swept him away. He wanted this to last forever, and feared it might, all at the same time. He felt as if his whole body might explode at any moment.

Then, at last, she lowered herself, guiding him into her. The sensation felt like a welder's arc, uniting them, fusing them into a single being. Together at last they rocked with near desperation as they climbed higher and higher until, at last, they soared off the top of the mountain and took flight together.

Much later they showered together. He enjoyed every minute of soaping her body and hair, and then when she was slick all over, he used his hand to bring her to another precipice while she gripped desperately at his shoulders. Her cry of pleasure echoed in the room.

She reciprocated, and only the safety bar he'd installed while Lisa was pregnant saved him from cracking his head as he jetted all over Charity. Laughing, they washed again, then toweled every bit as playfully, as if memorizing one another's bodies and their most sensitive points.

She made everything else go away, Wayne realized when at last she donned her robe and he pulled on some sweatpants. Together they headed to the kitchen, where the remains of dinner had to be tossed because they had sat out too long, and he started another pot of coffee while searching out something for them to nibble on. He didn't know if she was hungry, but he was ravenous.

At last he settled on crackers and some white cheddar, and they carried a platter and some napkins into the living room.

Charity had grown silent again, her happiness and laughter seeming to fade away. Time again for reality, he supposed. He just wondered which reality she was pondering.

"Where are your parents?" she asked, surprising him with the unexpected direction.

"They retired to Arizona. We visit back and forth a couple of times a year."

"I'm glad you still have them."

"I'm sorry you don't have yours."

Her face shadowed a bit. "I miss them sometimes, but I'm not sure I ever really fit in their lives. Which is probably an awful thing for me to say."

"Why?" He moved a little closer, holding out the platter until she took a cracker and a slice of cheese and put it on her napkin.

She shrugged one shoulder. "Truth? Sometimes I felt as though I was accidental baggage they had to carry around. Not always, but sometimes. And maybe that's not fair, considering the constant state of motion we were living in."

"I can't offer an opinion."

She smiled faintly. "Of course not. Kids have a way of exaggerating things sometimes. I'm sure that they did the best they knew how. Maybe I just wasn't a good fit for them, or they for me. Certainly I never felt as if I was the object of malice."

"Well, that's good, I suppose." He wondered if this woman even began to conceive of how alone she was. She'd admitted she herself kept it that way, but it still saddened him until he ached. Even after Lisa had left, he'd had plenty of friends, and Linda, to help him over the hump. Charity stood absolutely alone, by choice or disposition.

"Anyway," she said briskly. "I just wondered about your parents. You're the most prototypical family man I've ever met."

"Or allowed yourself to know." He wished the words

unsaid when he saw her wince, but then she seemed to accept the justice of it.

"True. I'm not liking myself much right now."

"And I think I told you to quit beating yourself up. It's not as if you're a criminal. We're all the products of our life experiences. If we can make a change when it's needed, then there's nothing wrong with us at all."

She ate her cracker and cheese, reaching for another. "Great cheese," she remarked, then sighed. "Okay, for now I'll leave it alone. I don't want to ruin this night with you."

"I don't think you possibly could."

For once he seemed to have found the right words. Her smile was warm and genuine. "You make me feel good in so many ways."

He wondered if she'd ever felt that way before about someone, and hoped she had. But asking would be exactly the wrong thing to do. It struck him that never before had he tiptoed so carefully around anyone, yet he seemed to do a lot of that with Charity. Maybe that wasn't fair to her. After all, she'd exposed some pretty raw wounds to him. She was a tough woman. But one thing he entirely agreed with her about: he didn't want to ruin this night.

"So," she asked, startling him, "I suppose with the upcoming budget cuts, you won't be taking on any new firefighters."

He could almost feel his jaw drop, although he hoped it was only a little bit. "Thinking about a job for yourself?" He hated the way his voice sounded rough, almost hoarse, but now he was on tenterhooks awaiting her answer.

She half shrugged again. "Maybe. It keeps crossing my mind. But you wouldn't want me. I'm out of shape and my training is so old it hardly counts. If I want to start again, I guess it would have to be as a volunteer."

He wouldn't want her? So typical of her, he thought. "I take on inexperienced firefighters all the time. The volunteers get trained. The hires go to the academy. You said you'd been to the academy."

"Arson academy. My volunteer training was mostly done by the department I worked with. Took some classes. Not the kind of totally intensive training a big-city career type would take."

"Any EMT experience?"

"Only the basics. Look, I'm not trying to interview with you." She flushed faintly. "I'm just trying on the idea. I used to love it."

"You told me."

She nodded, looking down. "And then I ran. Typical. I should probably stop thinking about doing things that I'll eventually run from."

"Or maybe you won't run. How the hell are you going to find out if you don't try?"

"Good question," she admitted.

He realized something then, but maybe too late to warn himself off. He was getting tangled with this woman in ways far beyond the professional and sexual. From his reaction, he couldn't deny he was hoping she would want to stay here.

But equally, he couldn't imagine that she would. She was a world traveler. She currently lived in a large city. What the hell could Conard County provide to a woman whose tastes leaned toward globe-trotting?

All righty, then. He was being a damned fool. And when she left next week, he'd better be prepared to fool the world, most especially his daughter. If Lindy thought for a minute he was missing Charity, he could already hear her demand to know why he didn't follow and what the hell was holding him here.

Good questions. Thing was, he loved his job, and would feel like a fish out of water anywhere else. Lisa had never gotten that about their years in Glenwood Springs. She'd enjoyed herself, and he'd felt he hadn't fit. Sure, it was another small town, but with a very different feel. They'd made friends, but not even that had made him feel he'd found his place.

His place had always been right here. Insurmountable problem.

They went back to bed together, and made love for most of the night. Lindy might be home tomorrow, and Charity would be leaving, probably on Tuesday.

This was all they had. He resigned himself to it, and focused all his attention on enjoying her.

Chapter 12

Monday morning arrived too quickly for Charity. Her time alone with Wayne had been transporting, and she'd had a good time with Linda after she came home. She was looking forward to the drill today, but she could have used a few more hours in the cocoon of Wayne's arms.

And the case wasn't over yet. She still hadn't found out why those open stall doors bothered Wayne. She knew they bothered her. At this point she still hadn't ordered payment to the Buells. She kept remembering Edna Buell talking about how she had endlessly complained about life on the ranch. Had she driven Fred to set fire to the whole place, with a result far beyond his expectations? He had certainly gone from lacking motivation to having a really big one. He wouldn't make any money on this, but maybe he'd finally been pushed to the point of breaking. He wouldn't be the first person who'd snapped.

On the other hand, Edna could have done it herself. The whole fire was either the sign of a genius arsonist or someone who hadn't realized what might happen. A fool or an Einstein. She couldn't decide which.

But at the same time, she realized that if she denied the man's insurance claim, she needed more than a suspicion. And if she did, she could forget ever coming back to this place. The weekend had left her utterly confused, to the point where she didn't know what mattered most to her anymore. Her job or this town. This fire chief.

Damn, she thought as she accompanied Wayne to the station. They'd both been subdued this morning, and he was taking her to the station to outfit her properly, not just with turnout gear, but with the fire-resistant uniform everyone wore. As for her underwear, she skipped it except for her cotton panties. All her lacy stuff was an invitation for a serious transfer burn. She replaced her bra with a cotton T-shirt.

"We still have to talk about the Buell fire," she said as they headed for the station.

"I know." He was silent for a minute as he turned a corner. "Unless you want to ride on the truck with everyone else, we'll talk on the way to the training field. It's a bit of a drive."

Since they were so close to the station, she let it drop. She'd let it drop all weekend. A little longer wouldn't matter. She had questions she couldn't answer, and she was fairly certain they were questions that would never get answered. One of the realities of her job was that while she could prove with fair certainty that a particular person hadn't caused the burn, she often never knew who had.

She was handed slacks and a shirt in a man's medium. Probably loose on her, but too tight for most of the guys she saw working here. She wondered where they had come from. Only the department badge had been embroidered on the breast, no name and no rank.

While it wouldn't have bothered her to change in the locker room, Wayne's questioning about her easiness with nudity had reminded her that things were different here. Not something she usually had to think about, but she slipped into one of the bathrooms to deal with it.

When she emerged, a bunch of grinning faces greeted her. "All ready?" Ken asked.

"As I can be."

"So are you riding on the truck with us?" Jeff wanted to know.

"I think the chief's taking me. I'm the newbie, remember?"

That got her a round of laughter and back pats. Even Donna joined the laughter as she passed Charity an SCBA, a self-contained breathing apparatus.

"I hunted up one with a slightly smaller face mask," she said. "I had that problem when I was still on the response team. Wanna try it on?"

"Thanks, Donna. I really appreciate it." Without donning the air tank and harness, she put the mask over her face and adjusted it. "Perfect!"

Donna's grin broadened. "Yeah, been that route."

Impulsively, Charity hugged her. "You've been great."

"Well, of course," Donna said, rolling her eyes. "And I'll be out there to defend you against these dumbheads. You know they're not going to leave you alone."

"Hell, no," Randy chortled. "That's half the fun we're going to have today!"

"Let's roll," Ken said, ending the repartee. "We don't have all day."

* * *

The chief's car trailed behind the truck, the fire rescue ambulance and a string of cars belonging to firefighters and volunteers. Enough personnel had been left at the station house to cover any average fires or car accidents, but it still seemed quite an assortment were looking forward to their chance to drill.

"A lot of volunteers," Charity remarked.

"This is the only fire experience a lot of them will get unless we have a range fire. Plenty will take the knowledge home with them to their local areas. You ever seen ranchers and farmers fight a fire? They've got enough heavy equipment as part of their jobs that they practically bury the fires while digging fire breaks."

"And every rancher is fairly well prepared."

"Believe it. Like you said once before."

Silence again. The radio on the dash crackled with empty air. No one was broadcasting anything at the moment.

"We going to be here all day?"

Wayne shook his head. "I'll run you through the first part, then leave them to it. I don't need to be here all day while everyone takes a turn."

And then what? she wondered. "So when are you going to tell me what's bothering you about those stalls?"

"Yeah." He sighed, once more shaking his head a little as if a gnat was bothering him. "It's simple. I'm no rancher myself, but I get that you never leave stall doors open, whether the stall is occupied or not. Unless you have sliding doors, they block the central area, so you want them out of the way. If you've got animals in, then you don't want them getting out. So basically stall doors are opened only to let animals in or out, or to clean."

"That makes perfect sense. So you think Fred did

this? Or knew something?" Even speaking the words made her feel slightly sick.

"Damn!" The word sounded angry. "I hate being suspicious of people I know. Hate it! But those stall doors didn't open themselves. Our arsonist, for now unknown, opened them. Had to. Maybe hoping the animals would run from the barn when the fire started. Apparently they panicked and didn't get out, or the fire blew up so fast they didn't have time to figure out which way to go, but someone thought they might. I emphasize *someone.*"

"I hear you." She gnawed her lip, a habit she had thought broken years ago. "Wayne?"

"Yeah?"

"We have to be honest about this. Painful or not. I'm even wondering about Edna."

"After that little interview? Yeah, me, too. And we're looking at a fire that theoretically shouldn't have happened. No arsonist is that good. How many times have we agreed on that? So I'm looking at this and thinking this fire was never intended to be that bad. Something went wrong, nearly killing that family. When you look at it that way, everybody's suspect, including Fred and Edna Buell."

"So we're right back at the start." All they had learned hadn't helped them one bit. She looked out the window and the bright morning, the greening countryside, and tried to fit any of this into a pigeonhole. It wasn't working in any way that felt right.

"So what are you going to do?" he asked.

"Probably pay the Buells."

He glanced her way. "Why?"

"Because I can't prove they did this." Suddenly she sat up straighter. "I have a thought."

"Yeah?"

"There were other fires, right?"

"Obviously. We talked about it."

"Someone set them. Someone threatened me. I'm investigating the Buell fire."

"So?"

"What if the other fires were a setup for the Buell fire? So that we'd know it wasn't the Buells."

He shook his head again. "I'm not following."

She twisted until her seat belt pressed against her neck. "I don't think either of the Buells had the time, or even the messed-up minds to conceive of staging fires to make the burning of their ranch look like part of a string of arsons. Someone else did that. It's still possible that the Buells took advantage of the earlier arsons. Certainly the timing of putting in the smoke alarms seems a little weird. But it could have been exactly what Fred said it was. His wife got worried and nagged him to do it. Regardless, they're not responsible for the other fires. It seems like a big leap to think they decided to burn their own place. It doesn't fit."

"Maybe not. But it *could* fit." He slapped his hand on the steering wheel. "I want that arsonist. I want him bad."

"You know how likely that is." Another silence. "Anyway, I want to interview the Buells one more time. Right now there is absolutely nothing to prevent me from issuing their check except a vague suspicion for which I have absolutely no proof. Unless something changes when I talk to them again."

"I'll set it up," he said grimly. "For tomorrow."

"Individually."

"Of course."

The parade of vehicles reached the drill site twenty-five minutes later. Everyone was climbing out and starting to suit up. Soon Wayne and Charity joined them, donning the heavy turnout gear. After Charity checked her breathing apparatus, Wayne lifted her air tank for her while she arranged the harness and tightened it. The weight felt familiar, like an old friend. Excitement began to build in her, and she let everything else drift away.

There was only one thing you could allow yourself to think about in a fire, even a drill: doing the job. Her focus became intense.

She and Wayne were scheduled to be among the first to enter the fire building. Everyone went in teams, Ken reminding them once again of the two-in, two-out rule that must never be broken. He even brought up last week's fire, when Wayne had charged in to save the baby and one of the firefighters had immediately followed.

"Always pay attention to who's going into a building. Good move, that someone saw and followed the chief."

Wayne spoke. "I knew someone would follow. You guys are that good."

A few cheers of approval went around.

Ken spoke again. "I know the chief counts on you. But it's my job to be the meanie. Don't ever assume someone will see you going in. Always take your partner."

Teams separated, some going to work on other drills with the trucks and hoses while the first group entered the fire room by twos.

This drill was flashover and smoke. Her heart raced like a galloping stallion as she and Wayne walked toward the building. It was operational now, and flames shot out the upper-story window. Black smoke must be building inside.

When they stepped through the door, visibility dropped almost to zero in the thick smoke. "Go ahead of me." Wayne gestured. She obeyed, knowing he was right behind her. She dropped to her knees to get below the smoke as far as she could. She could feel the super-heated air through her turnout gear. God, she'd forgotten how hot it could get and how fast. Beneath protective layers she could feel her skin tightening.

She crawled forward, knowing it was her job to get out the back entrance. It wasn't as if she didn't know what was coming. Ahead of her she made out the vague outline of concrete stairs. For the flashover exercise she needed to get past them.

She tasted smoke. Why was she tasting smoke? Her mask should be blocking it. Closer to the stairs she crawled, waiting for the moment.

It took her by surprise. She expected the smoke near the ceiling to flash over. Instead, a huge gout of flame came roaring down the stairs toward her. She flattened herself immediately, and felt Wayne grab her legs as the roaring beast raced toward them, searing raging flames like a huge fountain. Then the smoke above ignited, and the heat became almost unbearable.

She felt a prod from Wayne, and began belly crawling forward to the exit.

Her mind whirled with the suddenness and unexpectedness of those flames coming down the stairs. Like real life. Why had she expected any less?

She was panting with effort, and the more she panted the more she realized something was wrong. Her body was demanding air, and she wasn't getting it. She tried to speed up toward the door. Her head had begun to spin. A bump drew her attention to the side and she saw Wayne had crawled up beside her.

"What's wrong?" His voice crackled on the radio.

"Can't breathe." She struggled a few more inches and then the world disappeared.

* * *

"Turn it off," Wayne barked into the radio. "Fire-fighter down."

The flames across the ceiling began to shrink. Ignoring them, he rose from the floor, grabbed Charity's limp body under her arms and dragged her toward the exit. He had only one thought: get her out of there. He couldn't even feel the fear. Training took over. Fear was for later.

In moments two more firemen burst into the building. With the door open, the air began to swiftly clear, and he picked Charity up, gear and all, slinging her over his shoulder.

Ten more steps and they were outside. Two more guys came over to help as he laid her on the grass and ripped her mask off. Horror hit him as he saw soot around her nose and mouth.

"What happened?" Ken asked.

"Look at her. Give her oxygen. And save that whole damn SCBA and mask. Don't let anyone else touch it. Something went wrong."

Ken released the harness and pulled away the SCBA. Then Wayne rolled her on her back.

Someone held out the oxygen mask, and he grabbed it, placing it over her face. Her lips looked gray from the smoke stains, but her cheeks were too red. Carbon monoxide. A fast killer in a fire like that.

"Charity." He called her name. Someone tried to edge in and take over. He refused to budge. "Charity!"

He thought time would never move again. Fury, fear, pain—they all hit him like a racing train. Incoherent prayers ran around inside his head. An eternity seemed to pass before her saw her eyes flutter open.

"Charity."

"What happened?" she asked groggily.

* * *

Wayne rode with her to the hospital in the fire rescue ambulance. The burn building had been shut down for the day. Any other exercises would be limited to other drills. Not that he thought the burn building had anything to do with this. The respirator Charity had worn was firmly wedged against him as he sat at the end of the gurney. Another paramedic had taken over, Jack Hughes, a man who preferred the paramedic part of being a firefighter. A good man; a good paramedic.

Charity's color was improving, the oxygen mask still strapped to her face. "I'm okay," she kept saying.

"We're going to let a doctor verify that," Wayne said tautly. She was not okay. Not when she kept repeating the same protest. At least some of the cherry color had begun to seep from her cheeks.

"She'll be okay, Wayne," Jack said. "You know that."

"Yeah."

The sirens were loud even inside here. The ambulance jolted quite a bit until it reached smoother roads just outside of town.

She'd be okay. He glanced down at the SCBA cradled beside him and wondered what the hell had happened. How had she been breathing smoke instead of air? He'd checked her gear naturally, since she had been his partner in there. All the guys did it for each other. The gauge had said the tank was full of air, the cock had moved correctly, the mask had been seated properly on her head and face. He'd looked.

He stared at that rig beside him, questions pummeling him. Some things were designed simply enough that they shouldn't fail. This was one of them. Simple tank full of simple air, with a simple hose leading into the face mask. A respiration valve. Pressurized. And over the past few months every respirator in the place had been sent out for maintenance checks. Yet he'd read recently of tanks failing because of shoddy maintenance or manufacture. Well, shoddy maintenance wasn't on the list. He'd managed to eke enough out of the budget to make sure of that.

Tampering? The thought chilled him to his very soul. He needed to prove what had happened. But first to get Charity into medical care. She'd be all right, but she needed treatment whether she thought so or not. Her blood chemistry had to be returned to normal. It was so far out of balance she was still at risk. Despite her short exposure there was even a chance of neurological damage.

He had to find out what had happened. He was responsible for every firefighter in his station. If the equipment company had failed somehow, then any one of his other people could be at risk, hence the decision to stop the burn drills today. And if someone had tampered with this breather, then there was going to be hell to pay.

At the hospital, Charity was whisked away from him. Once the doc heard what had happened, treatment began immediately. He stood for a few minutes at loose ends, holding the suspicious SCBA, wondering where to begin.

Donna arrived. "You okay, Chief?"

"Yeah, I guess."

"Want me to take that breather back to the station?"

"No." He wasn't going to let it out of his sight. "I'm going to look at it myself. If that company screwed up…"

She nodded. "You need anything? Coffee? Ken is having someone bring your truck back, by the way. He should be here soon."

"Thanks, Donna. You're a champ. I'm fine."

She left, and he was grateful not to have to talk. Charity lay in the hospital and he was blaming himself. He knew someone had tried to kill her at least once, yet he'd let her go into that building. Why hadn't it occurred to him...

"God." He whispered the word. If it was tampering it had to be one of his own people. No one else had access. No one.

The doctor came out finally. "We'll need to keep her for a few hours, Wayne. You can see her for a minute or two."

"How bad is it?"

Dr. Joe smiled. "Not bad. Toxic fumes, but she still needs stabilizing. We shouldn't have to keep her overnight."

Gratitude settled over Wayne, briefly driving out the anger. Relief felt like a rush of cool spring water. If anything had happened to Charity... Well, he couldn't bear to think about it.

He went into the cubicle and found her sitting up, an IV in her arm. Someone had washed her face, and when she saw him she smiled. "Who hit me over the head?"

"I guess that's part of it." Not caring that someone might see, he bent and kissed her warmly, trying to tell her with his lips of all the concern and caring he felt for her. He took her hand and squeezed it, just filling his eyes with her. "You're beautiful."

She gave a little laugh. "Better yet, I'm alive." She glanced at the SCBA he still carried. "What was wrong with it?"

"That's what I'm going to find out. We had all the breathers checked out and refurbished over the past few months. They all ought to be just fine. Where'd you get yours from?"

"Donna gave it to me because it had a smaller face

mask. She said she'd always found that more comfortable."

"Donna?" He felt shock crash through him. "I'll be back in a couple of hours."

She looked rueful. "And I guess I'll be right here. Business first, Chief. I guess any one of the guys could be at risk."

He dropped another kiss on her and walked out. Inside his head, though, he answered her. Any of his guys could be at risk? He didn't think so.

On his way back to the firehouse he called Gage Dalton to come over. He wanted a witness to what he was about to do, and Donna would not suffice.

There were still guys hanging out around the firehouse, the standby crew while the others drilled. He went into the tool shop at the back and waited for Gage. The sheriff didn't take long. Maybe five minutes.

"What happened?" Gage asked.

Wayne told him. "Got your camera? I'm going to disassemble this breather piece by piece until we find out what was wrong with it. I want official photos."

Gage smiled crookedly. "Afraid the woman is going to sue?"

"No. But if this was tampered with or repaired incorrectly, I want independent, unimpeachable evidence."

Gage's entire demeanor changed. "I'll get my camera."

With Gage taking photos, Wayne started with the gauge on the tank. "It reads full." He didn't believe it. Pulling a pressure gauge off the shelf, he replaced the one on the tank with it. Another ripple of shock passed through him. "Empty."

"Got it. No air in the tank. How the hell did that happen?"

"It shouldn't happen. Not ever. We refill 'em after every fire."

He checked the metal ring on the tank. "This was sent back from the maintenance company just one month ago."

Gage swore.

"You recording me?"

"Hell, yeah," the sheriff said. "Video. Hi def. We've come a long way. Keep going."

"So malfunctioning gauge. That's enough right there." But he kept looking, checking the hose, attaching it to another cylinder, covering it with dish soap to see if it leaked. No problem with the breathing hose.

Then he took the mask and soaped it, too. When he hooked it to a fresh tank, little bubbles formed on the underside and he had his answer.

"Donna," he said. "Donna. She gave Charity this mask, claiming it would fit better."

Later, sitting beside Charity's hospital bed, he held her hand and listened to her finish her phone call. "I'm approving payment for the Buells. The arsonist was caught. And tomorrow morning I'll be sending my resignation. I've had enough of this, Alex. Threats are one thing. Actual attempts on my life are another. Yeah, talk to you later."

She disconnected and put the receiver back on the hook, squeezing Wayne's hand.

"Just like that, you quit?"

"Just like that. So it was Donna."

"All of it. Every last bit of it. She should have kept her mouth shut, because the only thing we had on her was your attempted murder, but she didn't. Apparently she had herself convinced she was helping the department and helping the Buells. The first fires were to keep us busy so the commissioners would be reluctant to reduce our budget. The Buell fire—well, she claims it was to help Edna. You heard Edna's story, so I won't go into it. Anyway, you were right about one thing—it was either an Einstein or a fool. She was a fool. When she pumped that paint thinner into the house walls it never occurred to her that the fumes would reach the attic and flash over. She was expecting a smoldering fire, one that would set off the smoke detectors before anything really burned."

"Dang!"

"In fact, she thought the house had failed to burn, so that's why she hit the barn. *And* she opened the stall doors thinking the animals would run out. Like newborn calves would have the sense, and their mommas would just leave them before it was too late." He shook his head. "She's still arguing that she was trying to help everyone."

"Except me. Why the hell did she go after me?"

"Jealousy," he said. "Partly fear that you might be a better investigator than anyone thought, and partly she just wanted to run you out of town. Because of me. I'm sorry. You told me she had a thing for me, and I didn't see what was right under my nose. I feel stupid."

"I think you just undervalue yourself. Lisa didn't want you. Why would anyone else?" She shook her head a little. "Don't we make a pair."

A nurse came in and drew some more blood from the IV line. "You're getting there, Ms. Atkins."

"I hope so. I'm feeling dangerously close to being a bad patient."

The nurse chuckled on the way out.

Charity squeezed Wayne's hand, hoping he couldn't

read her heart on her face. She didn't know where she was going after this, or if he'd even want her to hang around. It would break her heart to leave, but she couldn't stay in the same town if he didn't want her. Conard City was too small, and it would be painful to keep running into him.

"So what will you do after this?" he asked.

"I just started to think about that."

She watched his face hungrily, hoping for any little sliver of feeling there that would say he wanted her to hang around.

"Still thinking about getting back into firefighting? Even after today?"

Her heart leaped then crashed. That didn't mean anything at all. But she answered truthfully. "Yes. If I'm going to risk my life, then I'm going to risk it doing something important."

He smiled faintly. "I think I suddenly have an opening in my team. I know we're kind of dull compared to a big city, though."

"If you manufacture dull around here, I want some of it." She thought she saw a spark in his gaze. She hoped she hadn't imagined it.

"You applying?" he asked.

"Absolutely."

"Done. You're hired." Then he sat there, and for the first time since she'd met him, he actually looked awkward.

"Wayne?"

He sighed. "I don't have a lot of practice at this. In fact, I'm totally out of practice. But...I want more than another firefighter, Charity. I want *you*. In my life. As my wife. I know it hasn't been long, but we could date for a while..."

"Shut up and kiss me, Chief."

The merest touch of his lips ignited a blaze in her, and as he tightened his grip on her, she raised her arms to cling to him as if he was life itself. And maybe he was.

"Yes," she whispered when at last he let her breathe again. "Oh, yes."

Just then a sarcastic teenage voice interrupted. "Playing with fire, I see."

Wayne straightened as Lindy walked into the room grinning from ear to ear. "Hey, Char, you okay? He's not giving you a hard time, is he?"

"Only the kind I want."

Lindy laughed. "Figured. Guess I should give you two a few more minutes. But I like it, Dad. She looks good with you."

Then the girl skipped out, probably to tell the whole world.

"Playing with fire, huh?" Wayne said a little thickly as he looked down at Charity.

"All the time, Chief. All the time. If you please."

He pleased. And so did she.

Epilogue

It was both fun and funny. After the wedding, Wayne and Charity, in full wedding togs, rode around town seated on the top of one of the fire trucks, lights flashing, horn blaring. People along the streets had turned out in large numbers to wave and smile. A sheriff's car led the procession and a police car followed. A just-married banner stretched across the sides of the truck.

They were headed to the park for a potluck reception, everyone welcome.

It had been fast, but it had been fun. The only argument had been between Linda and Charity. Charity wanted to wear her new uniform. Linda argued that you only got to be a bride once. Hence the white dress and veil.

Squeezing Wayne's hand, she smiled at him, and from time to time they kissed, garnering more cheers.

They'd talked about everything, from eventually having children to how they were going to fit in the honeymoon. The days since her hospital stay had passed in a wonderful blur.

They were almost to the park when Randy Dinkum, riding on the back of the truck, pulled himself up a little. "Chief?"

"Yeah?" Wayne twisted around.

"Train derailment a mile east of town. Ammonia tanks."

Wayne looked at Charity.

"Let's go," she said, ripping the veil from her head.

He leaned forward and hammered on the roof of the truck. "Let's go. Roll!"

They lay down on coiled hoses as the truck sped up. Wayne surrounded her with his arms, smiling into her beaming face.

"I love you," he said over the scream of the siren. "I'm going to love every minute of every day from here on out."

"You sure know how to show a girl a good time," she teased. Then her smile softened. "I love you, too, Chief. You're my roots."

* * * * *

MILLS & BOON®
The Italians Collection!

2 BOOKS FREE!

Irresistibly Hot Italians

You'll soon be dreaming of Italy with this scorching six-book collection. Each book is filled with three seductive stories full of sexy Italian men! Plus, if you order the collection today, you'll receive two books free!

This offer is just too good to miss!

Order your complete collection today at
www.millsandboon.co.uk/italians

0815_ST17

MILLS & BOON®

It Started With...Collection!

1 BOOK FREE!

Be seduced with this passionate four-book collection
from top author Miranda Lee. Each book contains
3-in-1 stories brimming with passion and intensely
sexy heroes. Plus, if you order today, you'll get
one book free!

**Order yours at
www.millsandboon.co.uk/startedwith**

0715_ST15

MILLS & BOON®

The Rising Stars Collection!

1 BOOK FREE!

This fabulous four-book collection features 3-in-1 stories from some of our talented writers who are the stars of the future! Feel the temperature rise this summer with our ultra-sexy and powerful heroes. Don't miss this great offer—buy the collection today to get one book free!

**Order yours at
www.millsandboon.co.uk/risingstars**

0715_ST16

MILLS & BOON®

It's Got to be Perfect

* cover in development

When Ellie Rigby throws her three-carat engagement ring into the gutter, she is certain of only one thing. She has yet to know true love!

Fed up with disastrous internet dates and conflicting advice from her friends, Ellie decides to take matters into her own hands. Starting a dating agency, Ellie becomes an expert in love. Well, that is until a match with one of her clients, charming, infuriating Nick, has her questioning everything she's ever thought about love…

**Order yours today at
www.millsandboon.co.uk**

MILLS & BOON®
INTRIGUE
Romantic Suspense

A SEDUCTIVE COMBINATION OF DANGER AND DESIRE

A sneak peek at next month's titles…

In stores from 21st August 2015:

- **Switchback** – Catherine Anderson *and*
  Suspicions – Cynthia Eden

- **McCullen's Secret Son** – Rita Herron *and*
  Black Canyon Conspiracy – Cindi Myers

- **Texas Prey** – Barb Han *and*
  Agent to the Rescue – Lisa Childs

Romantic Suspense

- **A Wanted Man** – Jennifer Morey
- **Protecting the Colton Bride** – Elle James

Available at WHSmith, Tesco, Asda, Eason, Amazon and Apple

Just can't wait?
Buy our books online a month before they hit the shops!
visit www.millsandboon.co.uk

These books are also available in eBook format!

0815/46